WE DON'T GROW ON TREES

A novel by hwneild

Published by HNL

First published in 2018.
This paperback published 2018.

ISBN: 978-0-9935318-6-6

For Shea

Contents

CHAPTER 1

The Package...

Last night I dreamt I was back at Rooksdown. But it wasn't a dream at all, it was a nightmare. I immediately thanked God for bright moonlit nights; my eyes hadn't opened to total darkness. I rolled onto my side, palpitating, and stared through half-opened curtains at the final flickers of candlelit stars on the horizon being snuffed out, one after the other. As each star was extinguished, it was replaced with a memory.

I wasn't able to pinpoint exactly what month it was when I had first been admitted to Rooksdown. It must have been winter or perhaps it was early spring as it was still dark, and it was cold, and it was wet and it was windy. But what I was sure of was that the weather was dismal to begin with and then it improved over my incarceration. I'm not the best on that sort of thing, such as recalling people's names. I'm not blessed with the gift for instant face-recognition like some people are. Rather, I am one of those individuals who constantly kick themselves remembering someone's name five minutes after they have left the room. The fact is, it was over twenty years ago that I was there, at Rooksdown, and I was in one helluva state at the time. Besides, I'd never wanted to remember my time there. I had always wanted to forget it, to blot the memories out. That was, until the moment I sat up.

I flicked the switch on my bedside lamp to get some clarity on the situation, reached for my laptop, created a new document and began to type. I'm not a natural wordsmith, either; I was really born a number cruncher. It was now, with a suitable time-chasm of distance, utter hindsight and long-arms-length objectivity, that I realised I could even attempt to write about what had happened all those years ago - as I trust you'll appreciate when you read the following pages. I hadn't truly been able to comprehend the magnitude of what had happened to me then, and I still can't quite believe it now. I would have preferred it if I had been able to delete the whole episode entirely, scrubbed those memories clean away. But that's impossible. Writing them down was to be the next best thing: writing as an exorcism. The time had come to get it all out. Maybe then the shame and the embarrassment I had felt - and still do - would finally go away. I'd thought of it as a different me, in a distant time, in another life. If only it had been.

The dream was all my own fault, of course, and I shouldn't have done it. But out of curiosity I had stopped at Privett Park, where Rooksdown Lodge was housed, the previous week. It was the first time I'd been back for two decades. Naturally memories gushed - but why in such a chaotic jumble? There was no order to the recollection of events that had happened there. That was what prompted me to start writing them down: to get the buzzing hive finally out of my head and arranged into some sort of sequence, a single strand. To attempt the completion of a jigsaw of the mess of experiences. The dream didn't surprise me. I believe dreams to be an incredibly complex subconscious method of assimilation, whereby the mind and spirit work to compute the experiences we've had before filing them away, or nightmaring the retrieval of corrupted folders that need to be reprogrammed and stored properly.

I was on my way to catch a cross-Channel ferry from Portsmouth to France and then suffer the ten-hour drive to Geneva, where I now work as part of the team at Cern, on the Hadron Collider Project. I had my terrier with me, and my wife was in Africa visiting family, so being ahead of myself by an hour, as well as wanting to stop and give the dog a run, I had swung off the motorway at Basingstoke to see if Privett Park, where I'd spent some of the most harrowing months of my life when I was in my mid-twenties, was still there. I didn't think it could have possibly been. But it was.

The Victorian institution, where I'd been forced to grow or wither in the mind, looked just the same from a distance, as if it was defiantly slung across the brow of its hill like an executioner's hood. I glimpsed the instantly recognisable laundry chimney-tower piercing the skyline like a great rusty sword held aloft. My heart winced. I dithered but didn't turn back. I should have. Somehow the ancient complex drew me in. It looked as if it was actually still there after all this time, semi-shrouded behind its defensive stockade of vast pine trees. *It can't be*, I said to myself as I neared the entrance. There was a mass of crows swirling around the high boughs in the greyness, as there had always been - hence the name Rooksdown. However, when I nervously drove through the imposing gates under the cloud of birds I discovered to my great relief that the old asylum had now transformed itself into a shiny, new expansive housing estate. *Phew!* T*hank God for that*, I said out loud.

I sighed with relief at discovering that Privett's old institutional wards, offices and their inhabitants had finally been cleared out, consigned to history and replaced with, hopefully, happy homes and happy families. Looking for somewhere to park, I drove around avenues of hutch-style maisonettes and streets of faux terraces, all painted in muted contemporary colours. It was a spectacular improvement. It was delightful. This was development in any language.

I found a bay to put the car in and then headed rapidly across a playground towards the wilder green spaces I could see beyond. Somewhere where the dog could do his do's, unseen. I had forgotten to bring any mess bags. As I walked around the housing estate's perimeter fence, being tugged by Houdini, who was gagging to get at rabbits, I stopped still, amazed. I blinked. There, still standing, tucked behind yet more pine trees, looking exactly as I remembered it, was Rooksdown Lodge itself: the villa-style ward where it had all happened. A sign said that it was now a maternity outreach centre. *How nice is that*? I thought. *A wonderful transformation for the building.* And to my right I recognised, although now much dirtier and covered in moss, a long wooden bench. This was no ordinary bench, this was the bench where so much of my growing up had happened on all those years ago. I couldn't believe it was still there. I walked over and collapsed onto it as the onslaught of twenty-year-old memories tsunami'ed me.

When I had sat up in bed to write the account of events, I had made the firm decision to tell it exactly as it was. All in sequence. I would start at the beginning and work my way through to the end. I could surrealise the story later if I wanted to, to make it more fantastic. But the important part of the therapy for me now was to put the whole episode in order. That was my goal. However, the tale I ended up writing down wasn't just about me. It was also about someone else. And whether I'd turn out to be the hero of my own life, or whether that position would be held by someone else, these pages were going to allow me to find out.

Sitting on that bench, staring at Rooksdown's entrance, I pictured myself as the younger man I'd been then. The first thing I recalled was a seminal one. It wasn't the memory of my own arrival but that of the other person's. And that someone I can only describe a natural leader. He certainly rearranged me. He would have been a knight in any other time, I was sure of it, or even a king, perhaps. *A spirit of the age*? Undoubtedly. I wonder what has become of him…

My name is Jonathan. I was lost on the corridors deep within my birdcage brain, which at that time was crammed full of numbers bursting to get out, all chirping and twittering for space: fluttering random algorithms, figures constantly buzzing and fizzing within the chaotic confines of my mind. I was gibbering at the top of the corridor when the force field surged into the building. My eyes were flapping naively up to the heavens, as they had been for months (I'd been assured it was a side effect of the medication). Whatever, I knew I had been waiting for that moment to arrive. I could clearly see this good-looking, dishevelled black-haired chap, about my age, staggering up towards me under the burden of his extreme isolation, and no doubt, liquid cosh. Empathy poured out of my pathetic entity. Elect... tricity... the un-elected... trick... had arrived. His arrival felt more like our war-beaten Admiral or General had come to visit his ramshackle barracks, his failed troops, for the last time. He even had one arm tucked up in his coat like Napoleon. It was a feeling, a hush, a presence that overwhelmed us inmates; it blew us around the ward like autumn leaves and shook us about, turning us upside down, and transforming the atmosphere in Rooksdown forever, for the better. When I say 'forever' I mean for the duration of my occupation, anyway. It was a wave that preceded him by ten metres or so; some might call it charisma, and it knocked our socks off, blew the cobwebs right out. People say that Buddha had a vibe twenty miles wide; well, this guy had something similar in bucket-loads. Our carers, the nurses, didn't get it; to them it was just another poor nutter - I mean patient - arriving.

I must admit, I had got into a routine of idiotic manipulated game-playing with the staff and my family for far too long. And when that guy in the corridor - his honesty - caught my eye, that was the moment reality engulfed me, and my infantile nonsense became just that. Infantile nonsense. That was the point in time at which I grew up. I turned on a top. I hadn't fully appreciated the seriousness of my predicament until that instant. Not one bit. I'd thought I was the centre of attention. In reality, though, I was a truly bleating lamb trotting his way naively towards mental slaughter. The real deal, the great sufferer trying to control his rage and his pain, half-stumbled, half-strutted up the red carpet, the ramp, that led to the ward proper. He had exposed his balloon of a bleeding heart, which was suspended, on show, for all to see. But it was only us, the patients, who could appreciate it, could see it, could feel it. It was beyond words, but we all looked at one other and then scattered in the knowledge of that which could not be spoken of but which had to be held close and protected. And that protection was to pretend all was normal. The sharer of the secrets of our future happiness, the real psycho-healer had entered our lives. This was the person who knew pain and loss. Like a tramp, a cowboy, a windswept, weather-beaten trooper. It was as if a rogue, a monk, a spy coming in from the cold had joined our overheated, feather-brained world. This was the real deal, the truly insane, the raging soul, the nine over four, the three times five, who'd pitched up in this ground zero of human frailty. God knows what Hal felt back then; he probably felt he was entering a refuge from the apocalypse, poor soul. I just prayed, or gibbered a prayer's equation, that they would let him down gently; that they'd go light on his dose, his medication. Would he cry out, 'Oh God, oh my God why have you let me down?' or would he keep schtum. Heaven only knew what he had done that had led him here, to Rooksdown. Whatever, my heart went out to him; even if he had killed someone I wouldn't have cared. Had he exploded and raged? No doubt about that. My gangly frame buckled right there on the carpet. I was on my knees insanely muttering, praying to give him the strength to take me away from my shabby hell. This man could do what he wanted with me - I just knew this was my hero, my saviour. If he was wicked and evil I really didn't have given a hoot – this is what that individual engendered in me. He could kiss my head, or kick it, any which way; he would cure my madness. He could beat the living daylights out of me and whatever he did would heal me. Even a wink would do the job.

I knew then, at that moment, that this guy was somehow going to change my life forever. Even if I was going to a higher madness, a purer ranting, a thorough craziness, I really didn't care. At that moment, all I knew was I was going to give myself up... submit to him. I didn't realise, there on my knees, that I was in the final phase of my flight from sanity. My life would never be the same again. My trajectory had changed in an instant. I was on the flight home. Would he sink me or allow me to swim out from my hell? That was a question I didn't ask then, and I don't need to ask now - because I know the answer. I followed the dancer. I didn't even see his face; his head was bowed as he was led past me by two policemen. 'Get away, I can't cope with sorting out my problems, please don't do this to me,' a voice jabbered in my birdcage. 'I'm not ready!' I fell to the ground again like a twisted servant before his master, a writhing Gollum pleading for clemency, fluttering my fingers around my ears. 'I love you, I have been waiting for you all my life,' the canary on my other shoulder replied, chirping like a goodun'. I lay inanely before him as he passed. 'Walk on me, walk over me,' I thought. 'Crush my bones and shiatsu my blood to flow.' To me, he was like a fucking Jesus entering Jerusalem on Palm Sunday, for Christ's sake. God knows what I really thought, it's a haze to be sure, and embarrassing to remember; but I had never felt or could never have imagined a human could have this effect on another. I must be mad.

Poor deluded Hal clutched an empty bottle of whiskey, which he had refused to give up, in his free hand, the one that wasn't tucked into his lapel, and he was roughly herded by the two policemen into a small private room off the male dormitory. They were immediately joined by a nurse furiously wheeling a clinking medicine trolley.

'Ah, cocktails at dawn,' Hal said loudly as the door slammed behind them.

Not another sound came from the room. All was hushed within. After only a matter of minutes, the two burly policemen reappeared, awkwardly eased the door shut behind them and sheepishly trudged out of the building the same way they had entered. Hal had taken his welcome mega-dose on the chin, absorbed it like a man. He had bent over and taken the bum-cheek jab without a squeal. That's the way to do it, cowboy: *Get off your horse and drink your milk.*

Hal wasn't seen again until the next day around lunchtime. But all the while the fellow patients kept a surreptitious vigil, taking turns to peep into his room through the fire-wired glass panel on his bedroom door. And when they could see the white sheet rise and fall over his body, they scurried back to their respective corners as mice would when a priest enters his church.

CHAPTER 2

The Set-up…

Rooksdown Lodge was a luxuriously designed red-bricked single-storied villa set within the manicured grounds of a vast mental hospital complex. The ward had been built in the 1960s, in the shape of the letter T. You entered at the base of the central trunk and walked up a very long, steadily inclining corridor until you reached the cross-section. Off the primary thoroughfare were nurses' offices and a dayroom, a meeting room and the doctors' consulting rooms. When you reached the top of this walkway, when it joined the T's central axis, you had a choice of branching left or right. Branching left led to a dining room and then, just past that, a quiet sitting room. At the very end of this passageway were the men's dormitory and toilets, washrooms and two private bedrooms. If you forked right at the top of the main corridor you immediately reached a day room and then a sitting room for visitors. Next there was the mirror layout of the men's sleeping quarters, but this was where the women's dormitory and bathrooms were housed.

At capacity Rooksdown could house thirty patients, equally split between males and females. The average stay was eight weeks. That was the timeframe the NHS aimed to get you well enough to get you home before costs spiralled, beds got blocked and patients became institutionalised. Being highly adaptable creatures we humans adjust to any environment incredibly quickly. And being sociable creatures, many patients, however chaotic, found the company refreshing, having perhaps felt desperately lonely and isolated at home. For a lot of folk, it was a relief to arrive somewhere where they felt they weren't alone, and weren't the only person on the planet having a meltdown. Such a lot of camaraderie and empathy was to be found.

There were six of these ward-style lodges nestled within the hospital grounds. And then there was the main asylum complex itself where, at that time, hundreds of older patients lived their barren lives. Some may have been at Privett Park for their entire adulthood. Some had possibly been admitted as far back as the Second World War. Each patient was there because they continued to display, or had displayed, excessive symptoms of mental instability, which had made them unfit to live within the community at large. There were schizophrenics, obsessive compulsives and others in the throes of mental breakdowns. There were manic depressives, there were depressives; some were flipping on alcoholism, drug problems or insomnia, while others were bulimic or even victims of post-traumatic stress disorders. The whole gamut of severe mental illnesses was jammed in together and represented at Privett Park, all varieties sparking off one another. The criteria for incarceration, whether one was admitted forcibly or voluntarily, was that these individuals were a danger to themselves or others.

The policy of the system, at that time, was that the doctors, the consultants and the nurses never impinged on any patient's individual problems. They never delved into the causes, the cognitive reasons for the admissions. That was for others to deal with, and if so, at a later date. The carers' primary objective was to get the patients well enough and returned to basic sanity as quickly as possible. The official line was only to care for the patient's physical needs. If you ate well, slept normally, kept clean, and were polite and calm you were fine; you were well. And these were the signs that the staff wanted to be assured of before releasing you back into the community. It was simple, not complicated. There was no psychotherapy, no enquiring into any root causes of the patient's trauma. If you could look after yourself and behave respectfully and rationally to yourself and those around you, and you were not deemed in danger of harming yourself or others, you could go home. After all, that is what society expects from anyone, insane or otherwise. There was no therapy, Freudian, Jungian or any other; there was only occupational therapy. In the realms of national health, the doctors saw no reason whatsoever to delve into anyone's psyche, especially those in such a vulnerable state. All the doctors and staff were concerned about was to ensure patients were calm, well-fed, and clean - and most importantly not considered to be a danger to others or themselves. That was the mantra. If you were relatively balanced and in a consistently rational state of mind – you went home. That was always the target. Vitally, the medicinal drugs on offer gave the doctors definite insurance that patients were suitably sedated not to step out of line. People need to be in a secure environment to undertake therapy, not in the chaos of a mental home. If a person wishes to undertake that in their own time, at their own cost, that is the individual's choice, not the State's.

Occupational therapy, however, was a series of activities simply designed to keep patients occupied. To do something within the framework of a routine that was deemed fun and rewarding. For example, on Monday it was Art Therapy in the morning, then drama classes in the afternoon; on Tuesday it was exercises in the morning and woodwork in the afternoon. A range of activities had been thoughtfully arranged to help individuals express themselves creatively and get back to normality in practical ways.

The official routine was that you had to be dressed if you wanted breakfast. This was served between nine and nine thirty. Then there was a bit of free time before one of the activities started at ten thirty, which lasted until midday. Then lunch was between one and one thirty. Then another activity from two thirty until four o'clock, then tea. Patients had more free time until six thirty to seven when supper was served. The rest of the evenings were available for entertaining visitors or just sitting around smoking or watching TV.

I didn't smoke but Hal did, so I generally hung around in the dormitory or watched the box. There was no official bedtime. The routine in Rooksdown was ordered but never militaristic.

The drugs were the harrowing bit. The lesser of two evils, though: either you were not in control of yourself, or you were sedated. The choice was obvious. Call it the liquid cosh if you like. That's fine. Or the taser tablets. Whatever, the unifying effect was that the medication we were given made us all sleep a lot and, frustratingly, the drugs didn't allow any of us to concentrate on anything for any length of time so we were all in a constant state of flux. We'd be able to sit down for five minutes and then we'd have to - and I mean must - move. As much as you wanted to sit still, after a few minutes, the drugs would force you up and impel you to pace about. It was known as the Lithium shuffle. It must have been the medical concoctions that gave patients the anxiety. Like wild creatures caged in a zoo, rocking with frustration. This was due to the rollercoaster nature of one drug being prescribed for certain symptoms, and then another pill needing to be administered to counter the side effects of the original medication, and perhaps another pill or two necessary to negate the secondary medication's side effects. It was a minefield. All these chemicals in the bloodstream added up to a constant tidal surge on thought patterns. This was on top of dealing with any emotional breakdown that had caused admission in the first place. But the root causes of all admissions had to be placed on the back-burner and dealt with at a later date. Just coping with being in that alien environment and accepting the novel drugs in your system were what had to be dealt with immediately. That was the major challenge every patient had to deal with the instant they were admitted and then got on top of straight away, adding to the sink-or-swim scenario we were all faced with.

Prescribing is a science, and an inexact one at that. The consultant's job was to work hard at giving each patient the correct combination of available drugs for their individual symptoms, and in the correct dosage. That was the primary task: to get the medication right. As a result, there was always a period after admission which was a bit of a trial and error phase, like my eyelids fluttering. The medication trolley was the high altar of this process and being medicated was the religion. Medication came first. It was the serious business of the day. Tablets or liquids would be distributed at mealtimes from the trolley in the corridor. Injections, weekly or monthly, were dealt with privately. But the trolley was public.

The clear objective was to get patients' home, whether they knew it or not. This was the over-arching aim. All staff worked tirelessly towards getting patients out of the claustrophobic, chaotic environment - with or without them helping themselves. Freeing up beds underlined the whole mission, for national budgetary reasons apart from anything else. It was to get us out of hospital as soon as was safely possible. Each patient costs the State a great deal of money to treat in hospital. It must have been thousands of pounds per patient per week, and this was in 1996. God only knows what the cost is now…

Those were my first memories of Rooksdown as I sat on that familiar dank bench under the bone-chilling pines. My mind had re-climbed the interior of the tree-limbed building and I was starting to frame the scene so as to put my story into some sort of order. The damp had penetrated my trousers, and I hadn't even realised! I stood up, pinched my pants free, urged Houdini forward and walked towards the entrance of the old mental ward where I cautiously peered through the automatic entrance doors and into the shiny new maternity facility.

CHAPTER 3

Emergence...

None of us saw much of Hal for the few days after he'd first arrived, and then he had started to emerge as if from a chrysalis, but only at odd times and in fits and starts. Very early each morning, for example, at about dawn, from my bed in the dormitory, I could hear him leave his private room. After a few minutes, I'd pull back my covers, stretch, and then peep out of the window above my bedside table to see him walk through the avenue of trees outside, past the bench. Those trees, those wretched conifers, were the coldest and most sterile of timbers. A defensive static mass, devoid of anything lush or billowy. They always sat motionless, shit brown in colour and reeking of fruitless decay. Having killed off any green shoots around the base of their scrappy canopies, dense layers of fallen antiseptic needles shrouded the ground in thick blankets throughout the year, whatever the season. Those lifeless limbs had reduced the path to resemble a barren route to a morgue. Every morning I peered at Hal wrapped up in his big dark overcoat, his head bowed towards the ground. He would fade around the depressing curvature, sending the crows crazy. And then a nurse would appear about ten metres behind him, and fall in his wake.

For the first week he was shadowed by a duty nurse all the time. This was part of the assessment phase, which was part of the conditions of a Section. Being Sectioned, under the Mental Health Act (1983), meant that a patient was, if need be, forcibly detained for his or her own protection. The Act provided the legislation so that people diagnosed with a severe mental disorder could be confined to hospital for a defined period in order to be assessed or treated, against their will if necessary. The vital element of this Act, which was in effect a court order, as you'll discover, I tried to employ and exploit to avoid spending a lengthy spell in an American prison or correctional facility. Individuals, like me at that time, on a Section of this Mental Health Act, were under the control of the State. Therefore, every patient's action that occurred while being Sectioned was the government's responsibility. A person could not be prosecuted for any crime or transgression committed whilst the Section was in force. Anything a patient did would be the fault of the consultants, clinical psychiatrists or nurses. This category of patient was regarded as not being in control of themselves and therefore they were deemed not responsible for their own actions. The government had, in effect, taken control over all accountability.

Half an hour later, Hal and his covering nurse would re-enter the ward. Hal would go into his room for a short while and then come out in a ragged hospital-issued towelling dressing gown and go for a bath. I wasn't totally sure if he was in shock at finding himself in hospital or not but he seemed to be taking it all in his stride and was finding a routine fast. Maybe finding a routine was what was holding him together. The medication he was being given, no doubt in initially high doses, must have been knocking him sideways. He was going through the triple-whammy effect: finding himself in a mental home, keeping a lid on the effects of the novel drugs in his system and having, or recovering from, a nervous breakdown. It must have been ravaging to deal with. Poor guy.

Psychotic depressants aren't pretty drugs at all, there's nothing fluffy about them. I could see it was one of those impressive cases of strength residing in gentleness with Hal. He just seemed to be internalising it all, not freaking out or disturbing anyone else, but we could all feel it. It was as if his head was physically pulsating like a blasting furnace. As if his thoughts and feelings were pounding inside his head like a steelworks, a foundry, working at full throttle. I could see his willpower trying to hammer his chaotic thoughts into some sort of order on the anvil of rational thinking. Remembering that image is bringing a tear to my eye as I type. This was bravery, a battle royale for his reason, the desperate fight of a mental mechanic crusading to conquer craziness. Lunacy had come to him as a refuge from reality. He had retreated into his imagination, which had taken over his conscious being, and now he had to rein it all back in. To become the master of his runaway thoughts again. But those damn emotional horses were loose, the tethers had snapped, and we could see it was taking the will and strength of a master charioteer to harness his wild imagination.

He would then return from the washroom, dressed and clean. His jet-black hair, with its long fringe parted sideways and swept across, was always brushed neatly flat. And, like that, he'd go into breakfast. He always sat at the back of the dining room, self-absorbed yet aware of everything around him. All the while a dedicated nurse would linger. No one knew what he might do. This was all before CCTV.

I recall a very peculiar incident happened on the third morning after Hal was first admitted, where this awful, nasty-looking stranger suddenly appeared at breakfast. He had a long hooked nose and shoulder-length greasy dark hair tied back into a ponytail, and he looked like someone out of the crew in the Pirates of the Caribbean films. He was sitting hunched over his breakfast emitting a foul odour when Hal came in and the two of them froze upon seeing each other. I was sitting off to one side so I'm not sure exactly what was said at that moment but the tension was electrifying. Hal said a few words and then calmly served himself, but as he went to his seat, he stopped again. He stood over this grubby hippy and a few more words were exchanged. It was as far from the warmest of welcomes that two men who obviously knew each other could possibly have. It was bizarre. Like two stars colliding. The tension was intense. I felt it reach fever-pitch. Fully aware, two male nurses immediately closed in to control the situation. I couldn't help but be alerted to intervene myself, as I saw the seated individual clasp his eating knife and brace himself to lunge, but being tall and gangly, and with the face and heart of a baby, all I could do was fart! Thankfully he controlled the situation masterfully and calmly went to his seat at the rear of the dining hall. The tension eased. He sat keenly monitoring this long-shanks fellow, who soon shuffled out and we never saw him again. God only knows what had gone on between the two of them, or who he was, or what he was doing there. I never did get to the bottom of that but in hindsight I think this was the staff testing Hal somehow, assessing him, and he seemed to pass with flying colours. I think that was the moment Hal went down from being a category A to a category B inmate.

A symptom of being mentally unwell is having an overwhelming conviction that everything happening to you is one big coincidence, or you are living through a constant series of them. Everything you do or see or hear is a déjà vu, which is all part of the mental jumble. As if it has all happened before and every detail has a heightened significance. To see Hal handle this peculiar incident so calmly was impressive and no doubt helped his case with the Rooksdown nursing community. They would have been able to note that he had behaved in a controlled and rational manner. This act, in turn, would have steered him towards being allowed more freedoms and, I am sure, led to the nurses backing off and him being able to talk alone with us not long after the encounter. He had earned himself some trust.

Following breakfast Hal would then go into the smoking room, which was the busiest room in the ward, and puff on some cigarettes while looking out through the window. It was like a stuffy waiting-room in a third-world airport: everyone communing with their ancestors. In the mornings, until the pill trolley had done its first round of the day, everyone was a lot livelier. The radio would be on, and people chatted. I would walk past the door across the corridor and sneak a peek in, to keep an eye on my man. I could see him exhaling smoke hard onto the window panes in front of him, the smoke hitting the invisible barrier and exploding out sideways so that from behind him, where I stood, it looked as if his ears were emitting the fumes. All the time one of the nursing staff would be standing nearby, making all the other patients avoid him.

Gradually, though, he began to attend the occupational therapies, the activities on offer, which in turn allowed him more freedoms from the staff. Within a week or so the constant monitoring tailed off slightly and then, occasionally, Hal was soon to be found alone, watching the news in the television room or sitting outside on one of the benches reading a newspaper.

I remember all I wanted, to the exclusion of everything else, was for Hal to get better. Seeing these green shoots of recovery made my heart beat with joy. I even skipped on occasions like the lambs leaping over fresh grass in the fields nearby.

CHAPTER 4

Seeds Are Sown…

The first person Hal gravitated towards was my friend, Matt, a twenty-five-year-old musician with incredibly thick, high-wired bushy brown hair. Matt never went anywhere without his headphones on, which were sunk so deep in his mass of locks that they were virtually invisible. He would often stop, anywhere, and do a jig or a manoeuvre and rock his mop to some beat or another that he was listening to: a rhythm that had momentarily overwhelmed him. He had a happy, fun nature undiminished by a recent attempt to commit suicide. Matt had leapt from a bridge eight months previously. He had jumped, had made the commitment, but had landed on a muddy bank. The sludge had saved his life but he had twisted and mangled one of his legs so badly that he now walked, and was told he always would, with a pronounced limp, making him bob along with an amusing gait, like a funky chicken.

Matt's breakdown had happened because, two years prior to his admission, he had sent some of his music demo tapes to an internationally recognised musician, Walter Lodger, who used to be part of the global sensation Colour Void. The next year Matt was utterly distressed, distraught and enraged to discover that Walt had released a new album which was in fact a professionally produced and engineered version of Matt's original songs and concept.

Matt's demands and then pleas for recognition were completely ignored, resulting in him eventually being thrown out of Walter Lodger's management office in London by a heavy. Being completely devastated by the art theft and not having the money to sue and revert to the courts, he threw himself off the bridge. This trauma released an underlying propensity for depression, which was on the manic scale. Although he was slowly coming to terms with this blatant criminal act and he had realised there was an inkling that at least his ideas had value, he was on the backend of a dangerous high when he met Hal. I dunno, the episode, I think, was exacerbated by his undiminished enthusiasm for weed. He liked talking about and smoking dope at every opportunity: morning, noon and night. I am sure that didn't help.

Coincidentally, I thought I heard Hal say that he had something to do with making one of the videos for the album in question, shot at a coalmine in Wales. I just stood about gormlessly, as usual, feeling awkward as the two of them talked. Matt explained what his concept for the album had been.

'The idea came to me,' he said, 'about a young disabled kid, in a wheelchair, who is a savant, a computer whizz, and he takes over the airwaves by hacking, and manages to broadcast a load of shit out into the world. He hacks into governmental mainframes and satellites and causes chaos.'

'I can do that,' I said.

'Yeah, I bet you can,' said Matt. His head swivelled. 'Can't you tell Jonathan's a mathematical genius, Hal?'

At that point Hal turned to me, and it was the first time that our gazes actually collided. My eyes were oscillating, avoiding contact, but his greeny-blue ones were steady and his gentle earth-coloured orbs were fixed on me. His look, his scan, washed over as if to strip me, to leave me bare. I knew he could do it, and he did. It was like a spell he cast.

'I bet he can - I know he can,' Hal mused dreamily as he studied me.

'I can, I have done. I can hack into anything,' I declared proudly as I pranced a little, excited now.

Then he joked, 'Perhaps Jonathan is the savant you were thinking about, Matt?'

'And I didn't realise it!' Matt replied with a smile.

Out of the corner of my eye I could see that Hal had fallen into a dreamlike state, mulling over the information. And in that mood of mindfulness, information seemed to transfer over to me and I guess that was it, that was when the seed was sown.

It was the start of our threesome and thereafter we would hang around together all the time. I always stood back while Matt and Hal sat talking, or if we were going up to the main hospital for occupational therapy sessions or to the shop, they would walk ahead and I would lope along behind.

One evening, about five days after Hal's admission, his mother arrived at Rooksdown. She was an elegant lady, obviously rather shocked and flustered at first because of what had happened to her son, so she looked awkward when she first entered the ward. Her instinct was to protect, but that had been taken away from her by the State. This soon changed, though, and on her subsequent visits she was always friendly and caring towards us and the staff. She knew Hal was in the correct place.

I believed she worked in a shop so she could only visit in the evenings. There were private visitor rooms off the main corridor and if one of these was free Hal and his mother would go in, having made cups of tea. They wouldn't stay in there for long, though: maybe fifteen minutes. I always loitered around to keep an eye on the situation.

Whenever Mrs Reed passed me she would say in a soft, well-spoken accent, 'Good evening, Jonathan. How are you today?'

And then in a teenage, student-to-teacher voice I would always reply, 'Very well thanks, Mrs Reed,' as I turned and shuffled off, red-cheeked with embarrassment.

I often heard people snigger at my awkwardness but the Reeds never did. They never judged me, and I could see they were firmly planted in a respectful existence: a decent family, gentlefolk.

Hal was obviously ashamed of the position he was in, for sure, and the fifteen minutes with his mother was quite enough for him. I could see him becoming irritable and anxiously holding the door open for her and then ushering her out to her car; they would hug and he would wave as she pulled away. I always rushed to check that she wasn't taking him away from me. She regularly called out in an American accent, obviously amusing herself as she drove off, saying, 'Missing you already'.

I would then dash up to the top of the corridor so Hal wouldn't see me spying, but of course he knew.

He always strode up the corridor in the same manner, his head bowed solemnly.

And so we slipped into a routine. I would go home every weekend as I had been a patient for so long. It was part of the schedule towards being released for good. There was no using computers in the ward, but at home I could. Computing and the Web wasn't in any way part of mainstream culture back then. Not remotely like it is now; hardly anyone even had a mobile phone, for Christ's sake. I was addicted to the world that it had opened up for me. I was made for it. I felt that cyberspace, back then, was mine to inhabit, and mine alone. I am an awkward, socially inept individual, but online and within that universe, made up of numbers, binary and denary, decimals, dots and algorithms, I was king. I could go anywhere or do anything. I had control over everything and anyone that had built the clunky original systems. If there was a chink or fault in any program's construction, I was in like a rat up a drainpipe. Even accessing the very fabric of national institutions and governmental secrets was basic for me. This is what had blown me away: access to all the highest platforms on the earth, at that time. All this information, online confidence, I didn't know what to do with. That's what had made my mind rattle so thoroughly that my thoughts became junk.

I had begun to spend days and days on the computer and hardly slept or ate or even went out. As a result, I had become anaemic, with a horrible white ghostly pallor to begin with, and then, when my mind became a jumble, I turned into some sort of freak who resembled a skinny Lurch in the Addams Family, a young Frankenstein. I had this unconventional power, this unique ability to fly through the Ethernet that I couldn't tell anyone about. I could blast an access code at any firewall, which would echo back to reveal passwords required to force my way into any department, any system I wanted. I was that boy in the sweetshop. I was this odd, gangly creature in reality but online I was a Peter Pan. I could fly right, as light as a feather, and then disappear or reappear at will within a virtual world.

My father had left me and my mother about three years before my hospital admission for his secretary. Surprise, surprise! I hadn't seemed to care very much at all, but to avoid my mother's grief, I simply retreated deeper into this alter-reality as some sort of hideaway from the confusion around me. I was a gifted mathematician anyway, but this mess in my personal life drove me further and further, with absolute determination, into a cyber sanctuary, which fast became a multi-taloned labyrinth. A never-never land.

I was actually crying out for discipline and, perversely, the routine of the hospital suited me just fine back then. Weekends were passed at home and, on the surface of it, I would spend a reasonable amount of time on the computer and then have five days of enforced abstinence in the ward.

But by Sunday afternoon I had generally become obsessed again and it was a real wrench to close my computer down and be taken back to the hospital. Before Hal arrived, I would often gibber and plead, clutching my laptop to my chest, not wanting to be parted from my precious computer. It was chronic behaviour looking back on it; it was if I'd gone off on an online journey, a pathway, and I just had to get to my destination. If I hadn't got there by Sunday afternoon I would be bereft. Somehow, I couldn't just leave it, let it go. And no one then really understood or appreciated my capabilities or what I was up to. I'd show them…

CHAPTER 5

Shoots…

The only impulse that enabled me to switch off my computer – happily, that is - and go back to Rooksdown was my desire to check that Hal was still there and within my orbit. After all, he was my saviour from myself. Bizarrely, because of that desire my mother and my consulting psychiatrist interpreted this change in me as some sort of improvement. To them it was a sign I was getting better.

Returning to the hospital on Sunday evening I would immediately check that Hal was okay. Once that was done, and due to my long weekend of mental exertion, I would go straight to bed on Sunday night, and lie in as long as I could on Monday. I had dropped my early morning vigils of watching Hal ten days after he was admitted. The nurses would come around the ward trying hard to encourage us up for breakfast. If I was forced to I could manage it, and would then go to one of the activities, but more often than not I'd be belligerent and ignore any attempts to get me out of bed at all.

I was locked onto a silly merry-go-round that I didn't know how to get off. I knew that if I went home I wouldn't be able to shut my computer down. The tablets I was taking were winning the battle to slow up my thoughts; I was fighting that headwind too. And utilising staying at a mental hospital as a solution to keep me away from computing… well, it was insane. I was becoming institutionalised, and deserved to be.

But by Monday afternoons I was generally beginning to level out, and although I was having online withdrawal symptoms, it was great to see Hal and Matt talking and laughing about this and that, and to be in the company of people. Listening to the gossip, seeing quirky life in the ward, the random characters and chaos were actually normalisation for me up until Hal arrived and my outlook on life had begun to change so dramatically. My weekdays spent in the ward had become mere distractions from my weekends of nefarious activity. That's what it was like. My weekends were business and the week was for rest and recuperation.

'What did you get up to over the weekend, Jonathan?' Hal asked one Monday.

'I… I… I went to NASA,' I mumbled awkwardly, trying to be clever, to prick his attention. I was really angling for someone to tell my secret to: to unburden.

'Wow! What fun. Lucky you. What was going on there?' he continued.

'They're about to l… l… launch a new mission, Shuttle Endeavour, so they can mend Intelsat, a wonky satellite, but the controllers are worried about the fuselage seals,' I informed him, at a gabble.

'Crikey, the fuselage seals, eh! I hope they sort that glitch out before launch date. When is it, Jonathan?' he asked, perhaps playing along with me.

'Next week, I think… actually it's on the twenty-fourth of March at ten twenty-five Greenwich Mean Time, to be precise. That's right.'

'Okie-dokie. May the rocket crash?'

'The shuttle, yes, it probably will. If not on take-off then definitely on landing.'

'Bloody hell!' he exclaimed, and then tutted. 'Well, well, well, we'll just have to wait and see then, won't we?'

In an attempt to lead him off the scent of knowing all about my secret before I was sure he could keep it, I asked, 'What did you get up to over the weekend, then?' But I could see his eyes had glazed over as he absorbed the inside information I had just shared with him. I guess he was wondering if what I had said was true or if I had just gibbered fantasy nonsense.

'Oh nothing, in fact it was really dull,' he said, coming out of his reverie. 'Matt went home. My mum came up once, and that was about it.'

I had bumped into Matt earlier that morning in the corridor and he'd looked frustrated; he said he had wanted to stay home and play music, which he couldn't do here. He was wiring up a new home studio which he was determined to complete as he had composed some songs that he was going to produce himself.

He was beginning to surf off, to come down and level out from his high by then, and seemed to be fighting to achieve it, wanting to reclaim gentler waves of energy without the crash-landing. I could tell he now wanted to get better, too. The reality, though, against which he had been cushioning himself with mania, was that he was going to be permanently disabled. That fact was hitting home. I was sure he'd been manically busy over the weekend to avoid levelling out completely, as I had been in my house frantic on my keyboard, and that was making him sleep a lot too, in between fits and bursts of his flagging hyper-energy. Nobody in their right mind would ever want to collapse down from outrageous highs to crippling lows. Matt was in a sleeping booth opposite mine. I could see his curtain was closed more often than usual.

His new toy was a handheld video camera which he had started to carry around whenever he emerged from his cell. It was like a new appendage for him and he enjoyed shooting from the hip or whizzing around, zooming in on or out of random objects, like images on the television or an ashtray full of butts. When he did appear, he was still as quirky as ever, but now he rushed around, hobbling, not just halting randomly to shake his head to a bit of a song anymore, but stopping to film things like an ant on his hand, or to crank his head back and shoot the moon. None of this was helping his cause to the nurses and the reporting system. He couldn't help himself, though; his creativity was as overpowering for him as my algorithms were to me.

Hal kept calm; he was the thinker, the observer, the one taking it all in, the controller.

On Tuesday afternoon, he forced Matt and me to go to a

drama workshop. There was a low turnout, but the lady taking the class was a fantastically enthusiastic individual. She was a right thespian, a real lovie. A live-wire character whose energy was infectious. She put the three of us in a group together and got us to enact things like pretending to be frogs, and then she got me to be a tiger, prowling around. It was great, we all loved it and laughed a lot and felt spectacularly better afterwards.

Looking back, I see that none of us was really able to express ourselves cohesively. It was all sparking. That was part of the problem; we were all trying to retrieve our unique voices in life, which had got lost in the maelstrom, having been hijacked by our imaginations. I was in my early twenties, Matt was twenty-five and I think Hal was twenty-seven. The bottling up, suppression, covering over and ignoring of our festering issues, and then them bursting out, at this point in our lives, in our own distinctive forms of madness, resulted in us not knowing quite who we really were any more. This form of therapy was incredibly beneficial to help us to express ourselves and assist in the recapturing of our individuality.

I remember Hal declaring: 'I'm going to write a play. I'm going to write parts in it for you two, and we are going to rehearse it right here.' We were walking back to the ward after that first Drama Therapy workshop. Matt and I looked at him with raised eyebrows. 'I am, guys, I'm going to write my first play here, that's exactly what I am going to do,' he affirmed.

'Well, I suppose it'll give you something to do,' was Matt's response.

'Exactamonto,' Hal concluded.

These classes, and all Occupational Therapies except Gardening, were held up in the hospital, in Privett Park proper. The ground floor seemed to be made up of a miasma of long, arched, whitewashed corridors whose walls were permanently lined with old people. Some stood in soiled pyjamas or filthy nightdresses, others milled about, shuffling on the spot in dressing gowns. Some just hovered around, staring blankly at the opposite wall. The main movements were facial, features contorting into tortured gurns, while their slippered feet shuffled feebly where they stood. We would walk silently past these lost souls, through the pain-ridden tortured passageways with our heads bowed, wondering if this was to be our fate too.

One of the shocks of being in a mental hospital, as a patient, is the level of madness around you, not just inside yourself. You could really do with gentleness and peace to recover but in these institutions, you received the opposite. As we trudged those passageways we could hear the echoes of endless ranting, and often the raging frustrated. The vital unspoken lesson I learnt with Hal on those excursions was the realisation that I had to galvanise myself, to get better as fast as I possibly could, and get out of there. I even thought I could see myself superimposed in some of those patients' faces. It gave me the willies. The atmosphere, again, was one in which I was faced with the starkest of options: do I sink or swim? I was all too aware that I could easily have let myself go and got sucked into being permanently institutionalised or I could have chosen to resolve, to control myself and get back out into society. Those corridors were the ghastliest and most brutal wake-up calls of my reality at that time.

I even felt I could sense the ghosts of all the shell-shocked WW1 men and women who must have died here and who still haunted these corridors; people who had ingested poisonous gasses which disrupted their equilibrium, or bomb-shattered folk who had absorbed explosions that blasted away their reason. I could see the wisps of their spirits lingering still, fluttering through those corridors. Then there were the living WW2 victims who now occupied the spaces that their dead comrades had once done. Men who had returned home after the war to end their days here, shells of the people they once were. They had boldly left their homes with their heads held high, waving to their families, to go and fight the good fight, only to return shattered wrecks. The shambling living and the long dead haunted these corridors, spirits which no amount of disinfectant could remove. We couldn't wait to clang through the electric double-doors and be out in the fresh air again. We would all sigh deeply, look up and rush across the manicured grounds back to the relative comfort and sanity of Rooksdown Lodge - in the first week tailed by Hal's nurse.

Wednesday that second week went rapidly downhill for Hal. He received the first visit from his father, Richard Reed, who arrived in the evening wearing a smart fedora-type hat over a cream- coloured Burberry mac. He was accompanied by someone I assume would be generally perceived as a glamorous lady. She surprised me by her overpowering presence. She was dressed more for Royal Ascot than a visit to her partner's son in hospital. It was her hands that scared me the most; they were more like talons, and the purple nail varnish she wore only seemed to attract the eye to them. Once there your gaze focussed not on her claws but on her gem-encrusted fingers, and the glistening baubles on display: no doubt prizes she had clasped during her many years on the man-hunt. She was a trophy, and she knew it. Her hair was something to behold, too. You instantly knew a big house had been sold to pay for its upkeep over the years. Hal's father seemed to hide behind her and looked particularly awkward about this encounter with his son whom, I discovered later, he had not seen for two years. It was as if Richard Reed had brought the woman along to protect him from facing up to the reality of his neglectful fathering. It was obvious to me that the seeds of Hal's grief and trauma had been sown by this man.

As usual I hovered around. I could tell Hal was stressed by the situation, fazed by the medication and struggling to stay calm. He shuffled around the corridor awkwardly. Richard's partner tried to take control of the situation. Her arms flayed wildly, she placed one of her unrestrained appendages around Hal's shoulder, in a patronising imitation of mothering, and urged them into the visitors' room. His father followed, loping behind them, and closed the door.

It wasn't long before they reappeared and walked the short distance down to the car-park. I had gone outside in advance and had been loitering below, in the jet blackness of the pines' canopy, crunching around blindly on the frosted needles. Mr Reed's car was chauffeur-driven, a dark executive beast.

Hal opened the rear door for madam and, as she got in, I could hear him say clearly, 'Sandra, thank you so much for coming, I really appreciate it.' It was a magnanimous gesture. Impressive.

And then, having closed the door, he turned to his father who immediately clamped his son by two shoulders and looked at him directly, eye-to-eye. It was an arresting sight as they were perfectly spot-lit in a shaft of moonlight.

'Come on, son, buck up. Pull yourself together, man,' I heard Richard say. And then he purposefully released one hand and slapped his son across the face. It wasn't a hard slap, it was more one that you do when you try and wake a drunk. 'I'll come down on my own next week. Look after yourself, my boy,' was what he said as he got into the front seat beside the driver. And then the car purred off, wafting away coolly into the night.

Hal stood still. He was sharply silhouetted in the pool of silver light when he dropped his head. As I spied out on the lonely scene from the dark side of the car-park I could see Hal's male nurse witness the lonely image from the lit doorway. The carer stepped out and put his arm around Hal. 'Come on in, Hal, it's cold out here,' he said. And the two strangers walked slowly into Rooksdown's corridor, the air within still perfumed by Sandra.

I followed Hal but he'd gone straight to his room and I didn't see him again until early the following morning. I made sure I was on alert that morning and was relieved to see him take his regular morning stroll up through the soulless pine trees in the half-light. He was more subdued than normal that day and even Matt couldn't snap him out of his malaise.

'Hey, Hal, check out this new track from Dub Syndicate,' he said, or, 'Have a listen to the new Lee Scratch Perry number – it's wild.' Nothing had any effect. Hal was despondent, depressed, and his mood infectious.

He took another hard knock the next evening when his mother arrived to inform him that his grandmother had died the previous day. Now, this sent him further into his black hole and he was even more distant and removed by the time Matt and I went off for our weekends at home, both of us noticeably concerned about him.

The upshot for us, though, was that this level of concern for someone else's wellbeing was galvanising the two of us into being somehow real human beings. Something about caring for another person's welfare was starting to rearrange our minds in such a way that we both began the chemical process of normalisation. This was the catalyst, another seminal moment in the great chain where we were at last starting to become ordinary people, adults, at last. The moment we forgot about ourselves and stopped being selfish and began to think of others was the point at which we started to not only get better, recover, but also to become men. That was it; it was moments at like that I first began to view the universe and myself, not as chaotic jumbles, but more as complete entities.

CHAPTER 6

Growth…

Something, or should I say someone, had come into the mix at about this time that I had forgotten all about. It's amazing what life delivers when you need it most, when you aren't ploughing ahead blindly under your own steam. I didn't even grasp what was going on back then, or make the connection, but there was a certain person who had been admitted to the ward at the same time as Hal. At first she had kept to herself but then she began to emerge and gravitate towards Hal, and he to her. Her name was Catherine, although she liked to be called Kat.

She was mid-height, blonde, very pretty and oddly, when I think about it now, physically strong. For someone with anorexia she was well built, even muscular. She had got herself into such a state through her obsession with food that eating had transformed into a ritual for her. It completely overrode any awareness about the condition's health risks. For example, at breakfast, she would sit with only an orange on her plate and stare at it in wonder. Then she would peel the skin back very deliberately, all the while gazing at the effervescing tearing, and then, she'd reverently lean forward and sniff the citrus scent. And that would send her into a quiver. When she actually put a segment into her mouth and bite on it, she'd squeal with a restrained orgasmic delight. The acidic burst was obviously so intense and vivid a sensation - or perhaps it was the rush from the sugar or the vitamin C - which enraptured her so much that it would leave her in a trance. That would be enough for her. Perhaps she would have managed two segments but never more. Everything she ingested, however small, seemed to have the most profound effect on her.

She was great fun though, quirky for sure, upbeat, a glass-half-full girl and importantly, she seemed to have responded to Hal's pain over that dark weekend of his; she was right there, on time, just when he needed her most. Sent from heaven above.

I had shut down my computer, I was keen to get back on Sunday to check Hal was okay but obviously I needn't have worried; he was being well distracted.

My mother had reported to the nurses after dropping me off that I seemed to have turned a corner.

I even heard her say, 'We had a lovely weekend; Jonathan seems to be getting back to his old self.' Kerrching! That was going to go down well in my notes for the clinical physiologist to absorb during the week ahead and would surely help towards my release back into the community. I even heard Matt's mother say something similar to the duty nurse.

'Matt, has been much quieter this weekend, Sister; he seems so much calmer.'

So, we all started the week on a brighter, more positive trajectory. Hal wasn't so much happier, he was still subdued, but he seemed to have a glimmer of fascination about him. Something was making his life intriguing, more interesting. And the reason for that was…

Although Hal was obviously still struggling, his depression wasn't quite so contagious anymore. It wasn't radiating out, tainting or adding to our own individual problems. As I said, though, feeling his problems, oddly, helped negate our problems. It was as if the two minuses had equalled a plus. We were all reining ourselves back in, that was the main thing.

I still had all these numbers, equations, formulas and access codes running chaotically around my mind which, now that I was becoming more civilised and more aware of my situation, made me wrestle with my medication. It wasn't entertaining me anymore, the fog, the firewall the medication created; it was frustrating me. I could see intricate numerical patterns above everyone's heads like swirling halos. But then they'd become fuzzy and unclear. I'd have to shake my head and they wouldn't be any clearer; they'd fizzle. Or I would be working out an equation in my mind and before long I would be growling in exasperation; the purity of thought became dirty and frayed. I couldn't carry on like that.

The aim of the drugs I'd been prescribed was to slow down my brain's activity but the issue now was that the medication was clouding my logic. Interfering with my method. Fracking with my concentration and not allowing my mathematical capacity to flow smoothly. As an artist thinks in colours, and a writer in words, a mathematician sees in numerals. Mathematical solutions came to me in forms. Images and pictures turned into numbers, and the fucking drugs were short-wiring, distorting the clarity of my thought patterns, which I needed in order to find solutions. I remember having jabbing waves of fear; sudden jolts surged through me which made me incredibly anxious. I really thought I was going mad and I wasn't going to be able to pull myself out this chasm of insanity. If I was lying on my bed, shocks would go through me like electricity and I would sit bolt upright, gasping for breath, and would then have to walk around for a bit to calm down. It was like natural electro-convulsive therapy, ECT, or like being struck by lightning. In hindsight, perhaps these shocks were simply nature's alarm calls, alerting me to the fact that I was in a very precarious position. Highlighting and repeating the main question, *did I want to sink or swim in life*? That was my immediate, very real and ever-present challenge, as it was for all of us in Rooksdown. We were all in a last-chance saloon, grappling for our sanity. It was fight or flight time.

There followed some lovely bright, warm spring days when the three of us would sit around on one of the various benches outside in the sunshine: Hal smoking, Matt filming or grooving to some tune or another, and me generally standing around, probably, with an equation on my mind. It was here, I recollect, that Matt told us casually that his father had left him and his mother when he was a child, before he could remember. He hadn't seen his father at all in his life but he didn't seem to care one bit. It didn't appear to register with him that he had been neglected and failed by his father, as it did with Hal. Matt had never known his father and therefore he had simply never featured in his life. He seemed content with being the man of his household. He could do what he wanted.

'I don't really think about it,' he said. 'I guess he's out there somewhere but we've never heard from him for as long as I can remember. I don't know if he's dead or alive to be honest, and, frankly, I don't really care.' Tragic.

For me also, my father leaving hadn't bothered me one way or the other. He was an intellectual, a university science professor and would always be at work, away at some conference or another, or shut up in his study when he was at home. We never really did anything as a family anyway. He never disciplined me or showed me any love. He was just like a ghost ship passing in the night, occasionally blasting his foghorn to let us know he was there. And so it hadn't troubled me one way or the other, too, whether he was around or not – or so I thought at the time. The only pain for me was my mother being in bits, which I didn't have a clue how to help with.

For Hal it was different. He was deeply insulted and shamed by what he saw as his father's neglect of duty. It was clear he was angry with his father – furious, even. He couldn't comprehend it.

So here the three of us were, thrown together, coincidentally with a similar scarring but each having a different reaction to it. The revered psychoanalyst, Carl Jung, disagreed by saying: 'There is no such thing as coincidence.' Perhaps it was for a reason life had cast the three of us together at that moment in time? To explore the great mystery of chance.

It was out there, on that bench, on a sunny morning that Hal, questioned by us, talked about his life…

CHAPTER 7

Roots...

He'd been born abroad, somewhere very exotic-sounding but I can't remember exactly where. It was a place at war. His father, Richard Reed, was in the army back then. Hal and his family had travelled extensively throughout his childhood: from war zones, to countries in desperate need of relief from natural disasters, and then on to a nation in the throes of civil unrest. It all sounded exciting to a suburban kid like me but it must have been stressful and confusing for a child; seeing the world at war first-hand, being surrounded by so much human tragedy and finding yourself in the midst of warring nations that were not your own. Because of all the travelling and the instability, his parents had sent Hal to an English boarding school when he was quite young: under ten. He hated it. The weather, the food, the dormitories, only being able to change his pants three times a week; all that.

Then the earthquake in his life happened: his parents' divorce. Suddenly there was no place that was home for him anymore. School certainly wasn't and, as his parents had been constantly on the move, living in a new country every couple of years, home had been wherever his parents were. Now that they had split the bedrock of his tenuous security opened up, crumbled, fell into a fissure in the earth and vanished. He was left foundation-less, and this was the root cause of all his instability - and, I guess, had culminated in his subsequent mental illness, which he was now having to confront.

And then, as an adolescent, he had turned wild by the sound of things, and ended up being thrown out of schools, rebelling and generally rejecting all forms of formal education. I got the impression it was a youth filled with drugs, alcohol, anger and roaring down a highway of self-destruction.

He had stumbled into the film business in his early twenties and managed to get involved with a bunch of people doing location work. Having found the right place to film visually, Hal would then set up the shoot logistically: getting the crew and vehicles to the right place at the right time, getting the right permissions, accommodation if need be, all that sort of thing. This was how he'd come to work on one of Walt Lodger's videos. He had found a suitable coalmine to film in and they'd got a Welsh male choir up there to shoot the orchestral vocals.

As Hal told us this I could see Matt's eyes mist over and he said to us solemnly, out there on the bench in the sunshine, 'That was my idea, too, to have male Welsh voices singing the chorus – *the tide is turning*, right at the end.'

'Yes, that was it,' Hal said. 'I remember it. The choir came out of the wheelhouse dressed as miners, with fake smoke swirling around them, singing *oh, the tide is turning* -

that's right. And at the end of the shoot the thirty-odd blokes in the choir sang a couple of songs to us crew as we stood on a slag heap with the sun setting over the beacons. It was an amazing moment.'

At that bombshell, the telling of Hal's life-story had ended for the moment; Matt started to sob. Just as Hal couldn't comprehend his father's lack of commitment and honour, neither could Matt comprehend Walter Lodger's betrayal and theft. It had been through a family friend that Matt had been introduced to Walter and for him to just blatantly run off with all the ideas for that album had been criminal; the real insult was that Walter could garner public adulation and wealth from Matt's concept with no recriminations. He could sing on stage and broadcast his videos, and the art theft was in no way recognised by the law. The victim was completely unprotected. There was a similar story going around not long after about another singer, Robbie Williams, who had stolen a very beautiful song, 'Angels', from a poor down-and-out busker he'd met in Dublin and was refusing to acknowledge it – though he did end up paying compensation eventually.

Hal put his arm around Matt in a brotherly way and said gently, 'Hey, Matt, look at it this way, you're obviously incredibly talented, otherwise Walter Lodger wouldn't have nicked your idea in the first place.' I shuffled about, stomping awkwardly, and Hal continued. 'Try and take some comfort in that. The truth will out in the end, too, don't worry. I know it's painful, but you're still young and will have lots of success in the future. Stay calm, be strong. Don't let that bastard wreck you.'

'I know, I know. I just can't believe it though,' Matt sobbed, shaking his head.

'We'll find a way to get back at him, just you wait and see,' said Hal.

I couldn't help myself; this seemed to be my cue so I blurted out excitedly, 'I know how to. I'll do it - I'll broadcast it to the world and let everyone know.'

'Thanks, Jon, I know you would,' Matt said through his sods.

Abruptly, a male nurse appeared in our midst, saving me from announcing too much. He had seen Matt in tears, having been loitering around keeping an eye on Hal. He stepped in and determinedly led Matt back inside, probably for an extra dose of medication to calm him down.

That seemed to be the health professional's panacea to every problem in life – chuck a drug at it. If you throw enough chemicals at the problem, something will stick. Bring out the ol' liquid cosh. Knock 'em out danno. Keep the buggers quiet. Besides, they'd argue, drugs are better than straitjackets, more humane. *And we've done away with padded cells*, they'd brag too. Better to be sad than mad these days.

Kat appeared, having sensed the commotion, and wondered what had gone on.

'Oh, nothing. Matt's just upset about something, that's all, but he'll be fine, don't worry yourself,' Hal assured her.

'Crying's good for you,' she declared authoritatively. 'My God, guys, it's just so bright out here, I can't bear it. I'm watching the space shuttle about to take off on telly. Come on in and see it, it's really exciting; it has the first female astronaut on board,' she blithered to our amusement.

Christ! I had forgotten. So the three of us darted inside to the darkened TV lounge: Hal and Kat leading, with me trailing behind, playing the gormless gooseberry. These launches were huge global events back then: headline news.

There were a dozen or so patients sitting around the room on high-backed plastic-covered armchairs, looking at the small flickering screen. The chairs were standard medical issue furniture, easily cleaned after incontinent mishaps and sticky posteriors.

Anyway, I remember standing by the door anxiously rocking from one foot to the other, nervous about what might happen, having been tapping into NASA's systems for months and particularly having intercepted the worrying computerised conversations at the Kennedy Space Centre in Florida the previous weekend saying that the spaceship's outer skin problem hadn't been rectified. The launch team weren't sure the shuttle's panels were flush, aerodynamic enough to withstand the air pressures of take-off or landing.

The launch was attracting quite a lot of additional publicity as it was the first time a woman had gone up to the Space Station, so the team at NASA were under added pressure to go ahead with the launch. But I knew they were nowhere near a hundred percent happy with the joints, the seals, on the outer skin of the fuselage. The rocket's panels were not seamless.

The aircraft took off as scheduled at ten twenty-five but ended, as I had predicted to Hal, in catastrophic failure just thirty-one and a half seconds after launching. The spaceship had exploded and disintegrated before our eyes by the time it had reached the clouds. It vaporised in front of us, live, and we all sucked in air loudly, gasping in shock and awe, aghast at the implications of what we'd witnessed. All seven crew members died instantly. As I surveyed the scene before me, I saw Hal and Kat's hands dive out from their neighbouring chairs and clasp each other tightly.

Subsequently, the investigating commission revealed, many months later, that the fatal accident was caused by an O-ring seal on the rocket's starboard side. There was no mention of the mechanics concerns prior to take-off. If the press had got hold of the intercepts I had been privy to prior launch-time that accident would never have happened.

As the group of viewers stood up and dispersed from the TV room I could see Hal looking intensely at me. He came up to my face and very quietly said, 'You knew this was going to happen, didn't you Jonathan?'

I blithered nonsense, and shuffled off trying to escape, mumbling, 'Ah, me, ah no, I don't know what you are on about.'

I flew off immediately, and rushed to lie down. Though when I did, I couldn't relax and had another series of panic attacks, short circuits. The reality of my capabilities to access secret information was just too much; I didn't know what to do with my talent. I didn't know if I was a criminal or not. I felt this bizarre contradiction: power combined with impotence. The shroud of secrecy was all too intense for me and I knew at that moment for definite that was the reason I was in this mental hospital in the first place. It was no longer a joke. I was addicted to the adrenalin of hacking, that was it, and I remember starting to shake so violently that I actually shook myself to sleep, if that was possible? Matt was snoring on the bed opposite.

I was draped in a modern version of the cloak of invisibility which was utterly unsatisfactory. The power I had over institutional computer systems seemed to make me as anonymous as the weather. I wanted to come out of the cold and stand proud.

When I woke up early in the evening, I felt exhausted, drained and shattered. But instinctively, thinking it was dawn, I peered out of my window and caught a glimpse of Hal walking - not alone, this time, but with a man in a white gabardine raincoat and trilby, going slowly up the deathly avenue of conifers. I froze. The man looked like some sort of grim reaper, a doctor leading Hal to his death-chamber. I panicked, and instinctively got up, slid my feet into their slippers and dashed after Hal as he disappeared around the bend.

When I got outside the crisp spring evening chill cleared my head like a cold shower and I stumbled off dutifully, lurching along like an oversized Gollum, to keep an eye on my Precious. If anything happened to Hal right then I dreaded to think what would happen to me. As I crept up along the treeline I could hear the cackle and babble of rooks or crows, I don't know which, busying around in the canopy, settling down for the night.

I soon approached the pair, and I realised from what I'd seen the previous week that the man with Hal was his father. When I caught up with them they had sat down on a bench silhouetted against the final rays of the most splendid sunset. Dappling shafts of orange light were bursting through the sculptured trees. Creeping a little closer, I could see both the men smoking, blowing plumes into the closing darkness. They were talking quietly, but Hal's was the main voice in the conversation I heard.

His voice occasionally burst out, pleading with his father. 'But Dad, why the hell hadn't you called for nearly two years?'

'I'd been too busy, son, I apologise.'

In spite of his words, Richard Reed's reply seemed to be disingenuous and without emotion.

'But, Dad, you didn't return any of my calls, or send me a card for my birthday or Christmas – nada, not a fucking thing. And now you pitch up here as if you're my knight in shining armour or something. I just don't get it.'

'Well, look, you will one day. I've been busy, okay – that's all I can say. It's officially secret.'

'Yeah, yeah, like fuck it is. That's your excuse for everything, isn't it. I've had your secret shit all my life and I'm just so sick of it - of worrying about you – can you understand that? I've been worrying about you all my flipping life, ever since I can remember.'

Silence. The older man leant down and stubbed his cigarette out underfoot as Hal flicked away his butt, which twirled prettily through the closing darkness and landed with a poof, hissing into a pile of dry needles not far from me.

Of course Hal had been worrying about his father ever since he was a child. His father always being away in war-torn, ravaged regions of the world. Hal not knowing where he was, if he was safe or not. This is the lot of children with parents in the military or, as I was soon to find out with Hal's case, in the security services: MI6. And this lack of communication from his father had compounded the situation. It was cruel and unnecessary.

This was obviously a seminal moment for Hal; he had laid it on the line, brought home to his father for the first time the reality of human emotions, familial ties and bonds that, in this case, had become so torn and tatty through neglect.

'Dad, I'm sorry, there are just no excuses,' Hal continued. 'You could have easily called to say: "Look, don't worry I'll be out of touch for a year or so, whatever." And that would have been fine. But nothing, diddly squat is frankly rude at the very least – isn't it?'

'Mmm, I guess it is. You should try not to be so sensitive though, Hal. It's just by chance I am here in the UK at all. Your mother called and left a message with the office informing me that you weren't well. That's why I can be here for you.' A cough. 'Now, Hal, tell me what happened? I want to know.' Somewhat cleverly, Richard Reed had averted the issue by answering a question with a question.

'Okay, Dad. Look, it's great to see you, it really is, and I'm sorry that you've found me here in a mental home.' Hal took a breath. 'I don't know what happened, I really don't, but I just got this incredible surge of energy about six weeks ago that seemed to go on and on. I couldn't sleep, my mind was racing. I found myself drinking for England. And after a few weeks of that I just spun out and it all ended up in chaos. There were a few incidents, fights and what-not, and I ended up being arrested for being drunk and disorderly and then the cops obviously could see I wasn't right and a doctor was called and they Sectioned me. And here I am; that's about it in a nutshell.'

'Mmm, righty-o, I see. Well, come on now, let's head off.' As they stood up, the old man continued, 'But Hal, this sort of thing is not as uncommon as you may think. It is a form of depression, you'll get over it. Right now, though, you must try and stay calm, rest up and it'll all be fine. Don't worry, give yourself time. And I'm very sorry to hear about your grandmother – she was a wonderful lady. There was a time when I was very close to her. She was so good to you... and to me.'

'Thank you, Dad, I appreciate it.'

And then they walked slowly, side by side, back along the path to the ward as I squirmed around a tree to avoid being seen. Whether I succeeded or not I don't know. I hung around for a while to be sure and it was only when I could see Hal's father's dark sleek car waft up the drive, flicker through the trees and disappear into the darkness that I went back indoors.

Hal had gone straight to his room. Somehow, he seemed to have subdued the ward behind him as he went. Matt had obviously woken up and was alone, sitting glumly watching something on TV, and Kat had vanished to her dormitory. Others milled around in the shadows. It was only when the medication trolley appeared for its evening merry-go-rounds that we thirty or so inhabitants of the ward reappeared like moths and hovered briefly around our supposed nectar source, before fluttering back into the woodwork.

Chapter 8

The Kernel...

The scene at breakfast the following day was pretty much routine: Kat devoured her daily segment of orange like an Evangelical taking communion, Matt's headphones buzzed in the background, Hal had been for his early morning walk and sat looking fresh and clean but a little sad as he ate his cooked breakfast deliberately, never once dropping his impeccable manners. I could see him eyeing Kat, squirming in enraptured delight over her meagre meal. By the look on his face Hal must have truly registered the seriousness of her eating disorder and the effect it must be having on her health. He looked haggard tucking into his bacon and eggs. It was odd because she looked so well, so vibrant and strong, that her problems could never have been detected by a casual observer. For most bulimic or anorexic people, the physical emaciations are shockingly obvious - bandy legs and cancer-like shrivelled complexions - but Kat looked the essence of health and vitality. An enigma. The book inside must have been a very different story to the one that the cover suggested.

If the weather was decent after breakfast, Hal would head straight out and sit on one of the benches and have his post-breakfast smoke there. This particular morning I found him sitting with Kat; Matt was out there, too, but he was buzzing around at the border of the garden with his video camera, frantically trying to film some wildlife, caught up in his own world. I just stood around, shuffling as usual; the morning dose of medication always gave me ants in my pants. It was only when I was sitting over my computer that I conquered all physical or mental barriers. Nothing interfered with that level of concentration. I was super-confident with a keyboard in front of me but real-life company was a different story; I became awkward. Hal and Kat talked, oblivious to me.

'My parents split up - when I was about twelve,' I heard Kat say.

I turned to see her physically deflate. She shrank and crumpled forward until she found rest, propped with her chin on her palms, and her elbows on her knees.

'Mmm, same as me, Kat, same as me,' said Hal.

'My dad went off with someone he'd met at work,' she continued, her mouth labouring under the weight of pressure from her chin. 'And they started a new life together up north. I didn't get on with her at all so the relationship with my dad just sort of, sort of… fizzled out, I suppose.'

At this confession, she put her face fully into her hands and began to sob in hiccups. Hal placed an opened palm on her arched back and rubbed her shoulders gently. He then stroked her hair ever so lightly, repeatedly brushing her locks from around her ears with his fingers to free her wet face from hair. It reminded me of what groups of grooming primates do to soothe or bond with each other.

At that moment a female nurse interrupted and, not quite understanding the situation, tried to interfere. 'Come with me, Katherine,' she said.

Hal held his hand out authoritatively. 'This is all okay. We are fine, please, there's nothing to worry about.'

Kat immediately galvanised herself and looked up at the nurse. 'I'm fine, nurse, really. Thank you.'

With that the nurse went into retreat mode and sort of moon- walked back into the ward.

I could see that these sorts of releases, tears and crying, were very much part of the healing process. To acknowledge the source of pain or grief that has led to any level of mental distress is the point at which you begin to come to terms with the trauma. Tears are often the starting point of being able to recover and move forward in life. A moment of recognition or admission is followed by release: crying as a freeing-up of repressed emotions. Nothing will ever take away the hurt caused, as these events are inerasable, but they can be sublimated. Acceptance allows the sufferer to move forward in life with some sort of grace.

When Kat had calmed down she went on talking, in full flow now, seemingly wanting to expunge her problems whether we wanted to hear them or not. Hal never took his hand from between her shoulder blades, as a healer would over a blocked chakra.

'I remember when I was about fifteen my dad said I was really fat, and I wasn't,' she blubbered. 'I couldn't understand what he meant. I was so angry. That is why my food obsession started. Food was the only thing in my life that I could control. It sounds stupid now.' She actually slapped her own face, then dropped her head again and stared wide-eyed at the grass. Her voice lowered and her lips puckered. 'I guess I was crying out for attention. And my family did finally take notice of me because I made them worry about me. I feel so awful.' She began to sob again. I wasn't used to girls my age crying. God, I had seen my mum doing it enough times though.

But I do remember how incredibly sad I felt back then to acknowledge the self-sacrifices, the pain and suffering people go through for others. What family members can do to each other quite unbeknown. More so children, who are too young to really assimilate their emotions or gauge their actions. They simply react. Children become victims in so many ways themselves, because the love sought by parents, or the fear of the love about to be lost by divorce, makes people spin out in chaotic directions. Children often consider divorce or the breakdown of their parents' relationship as somehow their fault. Or perversely they feel that they can do something about the issue. Somehow children feel it is within their power to hold the family unit together, or at least they must try to. But the problem is that they can take that guilt on board themselves if they don't succeed, and then feel as if they have failed. I knew this anguish must be the seed causes of many eating disorders and mental health problems. I regularly come across adults grimly hanging onto these sorts of childhood hang-ups for dear life. Letting go and growing up often seem the hardest part of adulthood.

It was then I decided that I was going to do something about all this. That was my moment of maximum galvanisation. A light went on. I'd had enough. I leant my head back and stared into the heavenly blue and further, into the celestial white beyond. My internal monologue started quietly enough and then it crescendo'd. *You are going to do something about this, Jonathan. You are going to sort this shit* ***out***. It was the last word that roared skyward.

I could see all of us beating ourselves up over the callous, selfish or pathetic behaviour of our fathers, primarily. Menfolk too weak to love or too scared to assert it. Here we were fighting for our sanity, our health, all over the same thing. I wasn't a doctor then, and I'm not one now, but I did have a clue as to how I could inject a shock right into the heart of that generation. In heavy doses. Give them a therapeutic wake-up call.

The fuse was lit at that very moment. *I, Jonathan Runcorn, am going to do something about all this for my friends*, I bellowed Caesar-like to myself.

There was Kat crying over the pain of an uncaring father. I had seen Hal grief-stricken at the neglect suffered through his father, and Matt running about like a nutter oblivious to the upset he was feeling about the desertion of his father. And here was I gibbering, lost in prime numbers, through the shock of my father's departure.

When Kat's cathartic sobbing stopped, she looked up and gave me one of the most wonderful smiles I had ever received in my life. I can picture it now. It was such a radiant, clean, pure smile which emanated from somewhere that must have been totally refreshing. When she had finished wiping her eyes dry she also revealed to me the most magnificent complexion I had ever seen. A skin-tone I hadn't seen on her before, either: her flushed cheeks made her look like the embodiment of some sort of heavenly pure English rose. A white one with pink tints. She then turned to Hal, quick as you like, kissed him on the cheek, slipped out from under his comforting arm, hopped up lightly and skipped off into the ward.

As we both watched her cat-walk away, totally mesmerised, we were re-joined by a humming Matt who took off an earphone with one hand, whilst with the other he offered us the camera's view-finder. 'I've got some great footage of that Admiral butterfly!' he said. 'The colours are amazing – here, have a look?' He looked at us. No response. 'Is everything alright, guys?'

Matt was the light distraction we needed to change the mood and the three of us then went off quite happily to our first session of the day: Art Therapy.

As we walked into the main hospital, through the harsh bang and clang of the double doors, we braced ourselves for another shocking reality check to remind us we were in a mental home, for real. It was then that Hal told us, 'I've come up with the title for the play I'm going to write; I may even start it today. It's going to be called "The Fourth Monkey".

Like the three brass monkeys: one that hears no evil with his fingers in his ears, another who sees no evil and has his hands over his eyes, and the third one says no evil and has his hands over his mouth. My one will have a fourth monkey in it, though: one that doesn't touch any evil and he will have no arms.'

'Oh no, sir, lay no hands-on evil, no siree, no never,' Matt interrupted with the accent of a mid-western American preacher, flapping his hands wildly.

We negotiated the corridors as quickly as possible and found ourselves in the creative calm of the empty art room: a big light space with two long beaten-up tables in the centre, all covered in splatters of multi-colours. Paint pots, brushes and tubs surrounded the room. Every available square of wall, to outstretched man's height, was covered in pictures of all descriptions - some light and bright with merit, others dark and savage, scrawls of rage.

This was one of the more enjoyable activities for me – and the female therapist was a major part of that attraction. Heather was a homely built, light-coloured Asian who got all our juices flowing with an affectionate soft patois accent. She was definitely the prime equation for me. I did my usual sketches: charcoal boxes or cylinders or triangles shaded into circles. And I remember Hal doing this multi-coloured psychedelic Union Jack that day.

There was never any analysis of our pictures by the professionals. It was a little space to not only pass time gently but to be creative, and we were encouraged to express ourselves. I am sure that if we painted brutality that would definitely be reported.

When we got back to Rooksdown Hal disappeared into his room. I sneaked a glimpse through the square of glass as I passed, and all I could see was him sitting motionless, crouched over a chair beside his bed, writing. He had put a tray on the bed and was using that as a sort of desk. He seemed to be in the same hunched-over position for hours, as if he was praying. He did appear twice that evening: firstly, for supper like an obsessed distracted professor. He ate quickly for him and then disappeared back to his work. Even at speed his table manners coped perfectly. His knife and fork worked overtime, cutting and heaping, piling and scraping in fast-forward mode, like a professional knitter.

Next, he appeared quite late in the evening when his mother arrived for the first time in quite a few days. She seemed tired and drawn. They went into one of the guest reception rooms and came out tearfully, arm in arm, not long after. The death of his beloved grandmother, his mother's mother, was an added trauma for the family: one which Hal frustratingly couldn't assist with, either physically or emotionally. And him being in distracted literary mode didn't help the situation.

He was obviously distraught when he came back inside after seeing his mother off. He positively marched up the corridor raging loudly, 'You fucking bastards,' outside the nurses' office. One of the nurses sheepishly opened the door immediately after he'd passed and peered out after him. From my vantage point I saw Hal disappear along the corridor, go into his room and slam the door. Luckily Rick, our favourite nurse, was on duty and he soon followed, stopping to ask me if I knew what was up.

'I dunno,' I mumbled: my standard response.

In the ward this sort of behaviour was not uncommon at all; people were exploding randomly, regularly. It was part and parcel of life in a place like that and sometimes the poor nurses would have to run out en masse and physically restrain patients, which was incredibly traumatic for all concerned: patient, staff and onlookers. Anyway, I could see Rick furtively knock on Hal's door and pop his face around the door but not enter. Then his head shot back out like a jolting woodpecker's, followed by a pillow and another to boot.

'Fuck off, you wanker.' *Oops, this wasn't going to be good for Hal's parole notes*, I remembered thinking.

I don't know if she heard, or felt, or was told by someone about Hal's outburst but soon Kat appeared at my side in her pyjamas and fluffy pink slippers, holding a teddy bear of some sort.

'What's going on, Jonathan?' she asked.

'I don't know. His mum arrived, they went into a meeting room down there and then they came out sad, and after that she left and he rampaged up to his room - he rampaged up, Kat.'

'Oh dear. I guess it must have something to do with his grandmother.'

'Mmm, maybe.'

'Shall I go and see if he's okay?' she asked hesitantly.

'Up to you.'

We stood in the corridor for a moment silently wobbling, neither of us able to make a decision.

'I think I'll leave him be tonight,' she finally declared. 'Let me know if you think I can help though,' she added, padding back along the corridor to her dormitory.

CHAPTER 9

The Germination…

I had slept lightly and woke early the following morning after hearing Hal's bedroom door closing. I sat up in bed, and blearily wiped and peered out of the condensed window. A few moments later Hal appeared, his shoulders back, looking dead ahead. I was a bit surprised. That wasn't what I'd expected to see at all. As he strode up the lonely avenue, I was convinced he had a more considered pace about him that day, as if he was positive about something. As if he'd woken up and found an inner firmness. Although the constant trailing of him by the staff had died off considerably over the previous week, this morning a dutiful nurse followed him at a safe distance as a wild fox would trail a bear in the wilderness, obviously alerted by his behaviour the previous evening. The nurse would stop and start whenever Hal did.

I discovered that unwell patients in a mental home have to reach a point where they are absolutely intent on getting themselves out of the predicament in which they found themselves. I had had my Tarzan moment the day before. However, being allowed home was not solely achieved through gritted teeth and steely determination. Release was not a situation in which one succeeded by force or pressure. It was a quiet purposefulness which won that battle. A freedom won with patience and time. And, judging by the way Hal walked that morning, it looked as if he had a certain resolve about him. I got the impression he had fully galvanised himself. He had the right balance of toughness and calmness. Alienation from the hospital environment fails, too; inclusion must be embraced. One must foster a good nature, one which deserves the trusting keys that unlock the hearts and minds of all those around you. And it was the whole community in which we found ourselves who, in turn, unanimously and silently, one after the other, approved our ability to be released. It was not just the consultants and nurses but the fellow patients who helped decide. It was the patients who gave the staff the nod.

However, there were many inmates who actually grew to not only like but feel at home with the security, the company and the worry-free existence that the ward system provided. They didn't want to be lonely at home or look after themselves. But the majority of patients desperately wanted their independence back.

On the return leg of his walk I could see Hal now talking and laughing with his carer, a big young lady from Guyana, who, for her size, had the most delicate ankles. She had only just arrived. And I remember feeling jealous of Hal. After all, he had Kat.

It was then back for his bath and I presume shave as he was looking smart and calm again at breakfast. There was beginning to be some improvement in Kat's eating disorder around this time, too, where she was having a yogurt as well as orange juice for breakfast, but it was pitiful to see her struggle to swallow the smooth creaminess. What should have been an easy action somehow made her face contort into grimaces of tortured pain as she forced it down, as if the yogurt were gravel. And like Hal I think she must have begun to realise that the only way for her to get home was to knuckle down and play the game. Submit to the rules, eat humble pie; thoroughly demonstrate that she could be normal and able to fit into the world at large.

Seeing them both rousing themselves to get home helped me affirm the fact that I had to take control of myself too. I couldn't be left here alone. But I really didn't know how I was going to conquer my adrenalin-fuelled addiction to the cracking of coding: the compulsion to hack into supposedly impenetrable computer systems. That was my problem. The forced routine of not being able to access my computer during the week was the only way I was able to stop. To think back now on the state I was in at the time makes me shudder. I was a lost mute, locked into and out of a cyber world, both at the same time. I had no self-control whatsoever.

After breakfast, if the weather was fair, Hal and Kat would go and sit on the bench on the lawn at the front of the villa or, if it was wet, the one at the back under the awful pines which was dry even in the rain. They always sat close, often holding hands, and I felt invasive if I came too near but still I hovered around. I wasn't sure if this was to their amusement or annoyance. I could tell Hal was trying to empower Kat, as he was all of us.

I could hear him pleading with her, with words like: 'Sweetheart, you must get a grip on this eating problem before it really starts to do permanent damage, not just physically but mentally, please.' He would say these sorts of things only when he held her hand or their heads touched. And he'd hesitate at the end of his plea, holding back from saying *for me*. 'Take control of yourself. You've got to stop beating yourself up over problems long gone that are not yours.' He would regularly use the words, 'Stop the rot.' That was a ditty I definitely remember him using.

I found out that the reason for Hal's outburst the previous evening was that he hadn't been given permission by his consultant to go to his grandmother's funeral the following day.

'I feel so ashamed to be here, Kat, so weak and useless. I know everyone at my gran's funeral is going to be shocked to hear I am here,' I heard him say. 'And it will only add to the sorrow.'

'You mustn't beat yourself up about that too, hon,' she replied. 'These things happen. You'll make it up to them, I know you will. And really, Hal, it is better not to upset yourself and get all emotional. Don't you think?'

'I guess so. You're right, but I wanted to pay my last respects as my gran was so good to me throughout my childhood and my mother even told me she left me an awful lot of money in her will.'

As much as I cringed when I heard him call her 'sweetheart' and Kat call him 'hon', I liked them both so much and I was so happy for them. Love is infectious and it was exciting for me to witness them fall in love there, at Rooksdown, the most unique of environments. I was able to see that this was a genuine union and it was somehow magical that they both had found themselves there for each other: quite incredible. I didn't feel any envy towards Kat for taking away Hal's attention from me, either; we had become a sort of team and it was good to have her around, if only to look at.

'Hey, Jonathan,' Hal called out. 'I'm going off to write some more of my play now but let's rehearse a bit later if you feel like it? Kat's going to make us some masks. It should be fun.'

'Yeah, okay,' I said.

That afternoon it was only the four of us at the Drama Therapy session: Hal, Kat, Matt and me. And of course, the teacher. Hal had got Matt to bring along his camera and he had it set up on a tripod. The teacher agreed to allow us to go ahead with rehearsing Hal's play, having approved the handwritten script. She went off to get some photocopies done for us 'actors'. It was subsequently approved that Hal could type it up in the nurses' office later.

The idea was about a family of monkeys struggling for survival in the Garden of Eden during a drought. The only tree offering any sort of shelter was the Tree of Wisdom which bore forbidden fruit. The father monkey had expressly told his family to avoid this lush tree, in a barren landscape, at all costs whilst he was off trying to gather and hunt food. But his children disobeyed him.

I managed to keep a copy of the typed version when we rehearsed it again the following week and I found it when I began to write this story down and go down a mental memory lane. This is the first scene, which we rehearsed that day:

The Fourth Monkey

Scene 1

Ext. A parched Garden of Eden
Darkness - lights fade up - red dawn - background sounds of animal noises and tropical birds squawking and chittering.

ISOBEL Mother (Monkey)

DOROTHY Daughter (Monkey)

DAVID Son (Monkey)

REX Father (Monkey)

The three monkeys scrabble around nervously. There is a loud screech. Suddenly they all freeze - nervous. And then continue scratching the barren earth.

A deep male voice begins.

REX

The winds are blowing, though even the gusts have reversed and behold… the sun has changed from gold to blood, from hot… to burning. Stay away from temptation, my children. Do not go near the fruit tree. Nay, never even touch it.

DOROTHY

What was that, Mom?

ISOBEL

Nothing, dear. Carry on looking.

DOROTHY

I'm starving.

DAVID

Me too, I'm ravenous.

ISOBEL

Don't worry, children, we'll find some food soon. Keep looking.

DOROTHY

What is that tree, Mom?

ISOBEL

Never ever go near that tree, my dear, do you hear me? That is the tree of wisdom. Stay away from it.

DAVID

But it looks so beautiful and full of lovely-looking fruit. And the branches look so safe and fun to play on. I wonder if the fruit make you wise, too? I want to be wise when I grow up - don't I, Mom?

ISOBEL

Of course you do, darling. But growing wise is never going to be that easy. This tree will make you lazy and arrogant, not wise.

DOROTHY

Yes, David, that's the tree Daddy

told us to stay away from. Remember? He said if we eat that fruit our minds will be poisoned forever and we will never be happy - don't you remember, dumbo?

They circle around, scratching in the dirt. They disappear only to end up back under the only fruit tree in the parched forest.

DAVID

Oh, look, we're back here again. I'm so tired. I am going to sit under the branches of this lovely tree.

David sits back against the trunk.

DAVID

Aah, it's so cool and nice under here.

ISOBEL

Now, David, do as Daddy told you, and don't eat any of that fruit. You shouldn't be even touching it.

DAVID

Come on, Dorothy, the grass is so lovely and cool too.

DOROTHY

Ooh yes it is - isn't it? Lush. It feels so luxurious under here, like another world. Come on under, Mom?

ISOBEL (TIRED)

No thank you. I am just fine out here. You shouldn't be under there.

Isobel defiantly sits out in the open, keeping watch under a blazing sun.

David and Dorothy talk to each other in whispers, without their mother hearing. Lights dim on Isobel.

DAVID

Hey, Dorrit, why do you think Daddy told us we mustn't eat from the tree of wisdom? It's the nicest, biggest and juiciest of them all.

DOROTHY

I don't know, David. I really can't see why. And, oh look, there's so much fruit that some has even fallen on the ground. Ouch, my tummy hurts so much. I'm starving.

DAVID

Me too. Ouch...

DOROTHY

And seeing all that food lying around. What a waste.

DAVID

What a waste.

DOROTHY

But we must do what Daddy says.

DAVID

Whatever Daddy says, he knows best.

They lark around and then David scoops up some of the fallen banana-type fruit and waves it in front of his sister.

DAVID

Na, na, na, na-na.

DOROTHY

Oh, don't, David, it looks and smells so nice.

REX (VOICE ONLY)

Oh, my children, be careful.

Distant voice from the silhouetted Isobel echoes out…

ISOBEL

Put that down.

David looks around, spooked.

DAVID

Perhaps we shouldn't. Come on, let's get out of here, Dorrit. Quickly.

DOROTHY

No no, hold on a moment, Davey, please. Just a little longer. Please.

DAVID

Come on, Dorothy - now.

DOROTHY

No, no, stay awhile David - let's play.

She entices him to play. They throw the fruit around. One splats on Dorothy's arm and she wipes it across her mouth. She gets a taste and is enraptured.

DOROTHY

Oh, my word - it is just so delicious. Davey, you must try some. Once at least. Just so you know.

DAVID

No, I can't. Daddy will just be so angry that he will beat me.

DOROTHY

Well, Daddy's not here - and I'm starving. He hits you so he has to be wrong.

DAVID

No, silly, he hits me because he loves me, and I will really deserve it this time.

She lunges across and wipes some of the delicious fruit on her brother's mouth.

DAVID

Oh, my word, Dorothy, don't, don't. But... mmm - it is heavenly. Like nectar.

```
It must be the fruit of the gods. I
never thought anything could ever taste
as nice.
```

That was the start of the play. We all took our roles seriously. It was easy to perform. Hal was the director and Rex, Matt was Dorothy, Kat was Isobel and I was David. Matt loved it, putting on a girl's voice, and all of us were hidden behind our silly paper masks which Kat had quickly drawn out that day. They all fell apart later but I found the superb one she had made for me later out of paper mache along with the manuscript of the play. Hal took his directorial role seriously and directed us with force and determination, which we needed to hold it together: to stop ourselves from cracking up with laughter. He would keep getting us to do the same scene over and over again, imploring us to be more expressive and get into a monkey mindset.

'Picture yourself in Planet of the Apes,' he demanded. 'Get into the role; be a monkey. Arch your back down, swing your arms in front of you. That's it, like that.'

As a result we aped around twitching and grunting. He would occasionally go back to the drama therapist, who mostly sat back, amazed, to discuss some points. She just allowed us to get on with it. Being a tight unit anyway, a functioning troupe, we were able to gel and get into our parts quite easily. If ever we laughed Hal got annoyed.

'Hey, come on, stop that. Take this seriously – please,' he would order, clapping his hands. He should have added 'children' at the end.

The therapist literally said nothing and contributed very little throughout the session but we could all see she was thrilled with herself when we finished for the day. It was probably a first as well as a last for her to see inmates write and act a play with the minimum of input from herself. I was exhausted and had had enough of Hal's drilling but we all felt elated and chattered about our performances, professionally reviewing and discussing them as we walked back to the ward. And then again, after supper, we analysed the finer points of the play, its deeper meaning, as we gathered around and peered into the small screen on Matt's video camera. If ever there was therapy – that was it.

CHAPTER 10

Incubation…

I recall I woke up the following morning, a Friday, feeling instantly so much happier than I had done for a long time and somehow, dare I say it, normal. I felt refreshed. Lighter in the head. I had a hint of it before and therefore could only put down to the drama workshop the day before, where the acting of a role, the taking-on of a persona, had allowed me the opportunity to come out of myself, to break away from myself slightly. Okay, it was acting an animal, a naughty monkey of all things, but the relief of not thinking in numbers for a couple of hours had somehow enabled me to get a glimpse of myself in a lighter way. It was as if I could suddenly survey my problems from above, as opposed to being enmeshed in them. I'd had a break from dwelling on me personally. The change was as good as a rest. It was just the conscious distraction I needed to begin to get a proper grip of myself. To stop struggling with the person I was holding onto so tightly. I'd let go.

I remember lying in bed waiting for Hal to come around the block and I actually began to laugh out loud, recalling myself cavorting about as a primate. Even now I giggle at the memory. In a nutshell, I felt better for being someone or something else. It was therapeutic.

It was a brighter morning than it had been for many days. The sun was rising noticeably earlier, and as I looked out, I saw Hal, now untrailed, pick up a long stick and sweep the ground rhythmically in front of him as he walked up the avenue, like a blind man with his white stick, tap-tapping, making a composition on the ground.

I then flopped back onto my bed overcome with the dread of going home that evening; I knew it was going to be a lonely, exhausting and unhealthy weekend of being glued to my computer, resuming my mathematical journey through the global networks of power. I was definitely keen to go back into the NASA system and see what I could uncover about the failure of the space shuttle the previous week. Through this particular portal I was beginning to access, and so understand, the mechanics of how satellites were being used and controlled. How information was being broadcast up to and through them and then sent back down to earth. Both public information and encrypted security data used the same satellites. The prospect of this complex challenge excited me, and scared me.

I was using my routine in hospital to spend a few days recovering from the weekend's exertions and then a few days preparing myself for the next cyber mission. I felt like an explorer going on expeditions. I was going to places no man had been to before: to an inner space.

Up until around this time, this point, I had been a simple observer of the places I visited, the supposedly restricted areas I hacked into, and that was the underlying cause of my mental problems: the opposing forces of, on the one hand, being incredibly empowered through being able to freely access these institutional palaces of security, combined with having no role to play in them. It left me powerless to point out faults. Juxtaposed. I could do nothing at all with this secret information I had gathered. I had felt incredibly guilty about the deaths of the astronauts, as if I could have somehow stopped the launch by leaking the Cape Canaveral scientists' concerns to the press. And I hadn't, I'd done nothing.

My family knew I was gifted, as did various teachers, but hacking was something I couldn't talk about, or show off about; it was illegal. My father was the sort of academic who was just too caught up in his own work to be able to confide in him. He was unapproachable. It was all about him. There was only one genius in his house – and that was him. I don't think he would have made the time or had any inclination to have helped. I thought he may well have even shopped me in to the law to get rid of the problem and protect his reputation. He, like me, had no practical skills or common sense; we were purely academic. In hindsight, I was just a young man coming to terms with and comprehending my particular gifts. My talent was as yet un-channelled. The goal that I was beginning to wake up to was to have a professional career. Something tangible to which I could apply my skills to. To have a job. To work with likeminded people. That's what was beginning to seep into and enter my consciousness.

No teacher, no parent, no family member or psychiatric consultant gave me what Hal, Matt and Kat were giving me then - which was confidence in myself. That was all I really needed. I had revelled in my oddness for far too long. I'd had enough of wearing my quirkiness as a badge of honour. There had been no one around in my formative years to discourage eccentricity and encourage me to be normal. The result was that I had been left feral with my abilities. I didn't want to be a weirdo any longer.

As I lay in bed that morning, feeling calmer again, I came to the realisation that it was all going to have to come down to me. No one else could help me before I helped myself. I was going to have to jump through my own hoops. Perhaps for the first time in my life, having had fun with other people the previous day and the seminal moment of waking up laughing, I felt like a valid human being at last, not an oddball whom no one could relate to. I decided then that I was going to take my place in society. I was now a liked person. I was a valid member of a community.

But these changes weren't going to happen until I'd had my swansong.

At school people like Hal and Matt would have shunned me, maybe even bullied me, certainly avoided me. But them, there at Rooksdown, liking me, was the spark I needed to light my own candle. And Kat, too, the gorgeous pretty Kat even being seen with a geek like me made me feel good about myself. That was what I needed to give myself the impetus to rise out of the pit of isolation I had descended into. There was a saying from an ancient Indian sage, Gitanjali: 'The deeper you carve your well of sorrow, the more joy it can contain.' This applied to me perfectly then. And looking back now, it was right at that exact time in my adolescence that I was precariously balanced on the fence between cracking up completely and losing my struggle for sanity altogether. Either I was going to be insane for the rest of my life or I was going to conquer my mind. That decision had to be made right then. And I decided that I was going to fight, not run away. I made up my mind, myself, that that weekend would be different. The start of a new me. I was going to face my problems head on. And the joy of it was that it was not a difficult decision to make at all in the end; it was a soft decision, not a hard one. The time had come. I lay in bed feeling comfortable in my own skin for the first time in my adult life. I finally felt I had become a human being.

It's a hard sensation to describe, but when you have felt like an outcast and a freak and been friendless for most of your life, and then you find you're liked by people you respect, the feeling is overwhelming. I was thankful with a tank full.

It was a paradox that it was here, in a mental home, surely one of the most unlikely of places to find sanity, that I managed it. I came to my senses. I found myself, if you like, in the valley of death. I was at the very bottom of the pit and now I could begin the climb out of the nitty-gritty with ease. No more slipping back into the abyss-like sludge. Friendship was what allowed me to rise. And I thank Hal, Matt, Kat and Rooksdown Lodge for giving me that which no one else in my life had been able to achieve before: inclusion. I felt a part of the whole and not separate from it.

When the moment of realisation came it was like a sweet sigh. A relief. A light release from the anguished, clumsy creature I had become through years and years of negative, defensive thinking and behaviour. I was finally submitting to being myself and it felt wonderful.

The medication I was taking was beginning to be reduced around this time, too. As a result I was able to control my eye-fluttering at last, which was a side effect as it turned out, not me blinking at imaginary numerals tumbling out of the sky. Regaining normal facial movements made me at least look normal, and looking normal helped me feel saner. By the time my mother came to pick me up that evening, having taken a lead from Hal, I had cleaned, shaved and washed myself. I was delighted with the effect it had on her, when she saw me waiting for her. The surprise was palpable.

'My word, Jonathan, you look like a new man, my dear,' she said, peering at me. 'I forgot how good-looking you are. It looks like you've had a good week.'

And then in the car, as she drove, she couldn't help asking, 'So love, tell me - what's happened?'

'Oh, nothing much. The reduction in the medication is helping me feel a bit better, that's all. And there's a really nice bunch in the ward. I dunno, maybe it's the weather,' I muttered.

'A combination of things, eh?'

'Yeah, I guess so.'

'Well, it's great to see, my dear. Well done.' She patted my knee. 'Who are the friends you've met?'

'Um, well, there's Matt who you know, he's doing okay, and there's a new couple I'm hanging around with a bit.'

'Oh, that's great, I'm really pleased,' she said, swinging the car into our drive. She seemed genuinely thrilled that I was, at last, making definite progress.

Matt had gone home, too. As I mentioned, weekends out were stepping stones to being released. A gauge as to how you coped with the outside world, and one of these notches which was supposedly helping Hal towards that goal was typing out his play in the nurses' office that weekend. About half of the patients had disappeared home so the ward was much quieter and there was no need for so many staff. I heard when I got back that apparently Hal was showing signs of obsessive behaviour, though, in that he wanted to carry on and on typing, and had to be forced to stop by the duty consultant. Much like me, I guess, twenty miles away, hammering away on my computer keyboard like a man possessed.

Over that important weekend I approached my computing in a more professional manner and made a point of going downstairs regularly and making cups of tea, and seeing if my mum wanted anything, rather than just ignoring everything and everyone. It wasn't just to demonstrate to her that I was getting better and could soon come home permanently; it was actually really useful to step away from the systems I was penetrating, allowing me to think about where I wanted to go and how to get there. It slowed me down. I felt I had made better decisions by removing myself for a few minutes. Being too immersed in the hack, the rushing adrenalin, often made me too hasty; I would end up in cul-de-sacs. So I would have to return to junctions and then, being frustrated with myself, I would take unbalanced forks in the routing, further compounding the situation. My new-found discipline allowed me to be a better judge and make more reasoned decisions. I thought out actions before executing them. The flip side to this was it made me a more effective hacker.

It was the spark of acting in Hal's play which, I can only think, had suddenly altered my perspective. That brief moment in time had shifted the way I viewed the world and myself. It is amazing how one moment, one day, one event, one conversation or one passage in a book can irrevocably alter the way we look at our lives. Small incidents are the catalysts which light the fires of change. It is within the tiniest details that the source of growth often hides: kernels of knowledge, triggered, which allow us to grow. Answers can pop into life like parched flower seeds coming to life in a desert cracked open by one drop of rain. Miss the point at our peril. I now seemed to be properly looking at my life, and beginning to behave in a more mature manner. I was dotting the i's and crossing the t's of existence.

Over that weekend I flew, through the World Wide Web, out to Cape Canaveral in Florida, the home of NASA. It was, at that time, the main base for launching American satellites, space rockets and the shuttle. I had found major faults in many areas of their security coding, right across the program, over the previous weeks and months. The NASA programmers had allowed people like me the ability to not only monitor what they were doing, but to actually affect the performance of particularly un-manned satellites. What fascinated me most was that I could manipulate the transmission of data from the satellites back down to earth. I couldn't alter the trajectory of information, for instance, as the sending and receiving elements were secure, but it was the point where the transfer of data occurred that I could disrupt. On the satellite itself. That was the chink I'd found in their coding armour. A coding weakness meant I could interfere with the satellites' mirror angles, for example, and so momentarily knock them off kilter, creating a split-second lapse of reception back on earth. The receivers would readjust quite quickly, in a matter of seconds, but during that brief timeframe I could insert whatever message I wanted to, which would then replace whatever information should have been transmitted. I discovered that I could actually insert any snippets of broadcast information I wanted to air and so easily layer it over, cut it into, the official information. I could upload anything I wanted: words, music or a video, data or images, and splice this into the stream of information being transmitted down to earth from any number of NASA's satellites. The coding, the programming of all their satellites was pretty much the same back then. So what I could do with one, I could do with them all. I could create merry hell.

I was well aware that if I could do this then so could any enemy of America, or indeed the United Kingdom too.

I would have loved to have told NASA or whoever that the security of their systems was utterly defenceless. If I had done so, though, I would have been arrested, and locked up in an American prison for decades. For doing them a favour! I would have loved to have sung and danced about my own abilities but hacking, after all, is a bit like trespassing. It is no big deal to walk on the grass in a park after midnight when you are not supposed to but when you are caught up in the Queen's bedroom at two o'clock in the morning or found sitting in the Oval Office at the White House on a Monday morning then it is serious, and that is sort of where I was: right in the sinews of power. I was able to invade the impenetrable. I was like a modern crew member from the Starship Enterprise who could be beamed up to or down at will and go where I wanted. Appear and disappear as I wished. That was what scared me. Luckily I didn't drink alcohol then; the anxiety of hangovers would have killed me.

I was determined to inform NASA of the faults I had found in their system, anonymously, and soon, but there was no rush, no rush at all; I was having much too much fun. And, before I did, I was going to teach them a little lesson. I was going to teach everyone a little lesson.

CHAPTER 11

Nurturing…

Back at the ward, over that weekend, Hal and Kat's romance had well and truly blossomed. By the time I got back on Sunday evening it seemed to be officially out in the open, a full-blown love affair. I couldn't believe it.

The consultants and nurses could never sanction that sort of behaviour to go on in the ward, but there was literally nothing they could do about it. It just had to be conducted as discreetly as possible. Hal and Kat weren't the sort of individuals to flaunt themselves, anyway, or even show overt public displays of affection by going around hand-in-hand all the time. They were both private people. But the relationship was getting physical, magnetically speaking; there was nothing that could be done about that. Those forces of nature are too great to be interfered with. As long as they kept a lid on it then it should be okay.

Hal had managed to write and type his complete play over the weekend and Kat had started working on our stylised monkey masks. She had done a paper mache cast of Hal's face, having got her mother to bring wallpaper glue from home.

Everyone told me that it was hysterical to watch. Strips of newspaper, dipped in a wet-paste glue solution, were built up slowly in layers over the facial contours, with only a straw in each nostril to breathe out of. It took a good half an hour to construct the mask and then for it to set hard enough to be prised off. It came out like a death mask. Apparently, half the patients watching wanted one done of themselves. It was quite a leap of faith though. Kat had then cleverly moulded the mask slightly, while it was still pliable, to give it more monkey-type features: widened nostrils, a more rounded chin and a slit of a mouth like a lipped post-box. Hal's mask, being that of Rex, the father, had been given more of an elongated Orangutan look.

When we all got together on Monday morning, out on the bench after breakfast, Hal told me that he and Kat had been allowed to walk across the fields to a pub with one of the nurses the day before. I had missed out on all the fun.

'My God, it was great to be out in the countryside, Jonathan,' he said. 'To see fields and hear birdsong, and just to be out of the confines of here for once. You can't imagine what a release it was.'

'And we saw lambs jumping around,' Kat added excitedly.

'When the sun came out from behind clouds, the fields of yellow rapeseed flowers just seemed to explode into life, like a search light had been switched on; it was spectacular!' Hal enthused, and then he added, 'Did you get out at all?'

'No, I didn't manage to,' I admitted glumly. 'Too busy.'

'Well, silly ol' you,' quipped Matt sarcastically from the background.

'I'm going to ask if we can all go for a walk this week, that's what I am going to do,' Kat declared confidently. 'Being out with nature was just *so* fantastic.'

'How long did it take to get there? To the pub,' Matt asked.

'Only about half an hour, wouldn't you say, Kat?'

'Yeah, about that. We only stayed for one drink. It was sooo nice to get back out into the fields. I think Josie enjoyed it too,' Kat gushed, talking about the nurse that accompanied them.

'I think she said it was only the second time she had been to a pub, ever,' Hal added, grinning. 'Her first time in a country pub. She was like a fish out of water, it was hysterical.'

'She probably enjoyed it more than you guys,' Matt concluded.

'Yes, I bet she did. But she didn't have a clue what to do, whether to sit or stand, how to order, what to order. It was funny.'

Josephine was the big Guyanan nurse with the nice ankles who I fancied. I was sure, coming from Africa, she must have flipped walking through the green lushness of a British spring and then delighted in the conviviality of an English pub. I wished I'd been there. I would have shown her what's what.

'What did you get up to over the weekend, Matt?' Hal asked.

'Oh, nothing much. I mucked about in my new studio. I did mend my synth, though, and then I composed a song.'

'What's it like?' I asked.

'It's quite orchestral, actually, Jon, haunting even.'

'I'd love to hear it too, Matt,' said Hal. 'Do you want to see if I can come up with any lyrics for it?'

'Yeah, definitely, I'll do a copy next weekend,' Matt replied.

Before he could continue I interrupted. 'What about your camera, Matt, did you bring that in this week?'

'Yeah, I did – why?'

'Oh, I just thought you could film us doing Hal's play again, that's all,' I muttered.

'Yeah, why not,' Matt said, brightening up at the prospect of further creativity.

There was a shout from the open back door. 'Hal, phone call,' called out one of the nurses. There were so many nurses coming and going that we hardly ever seemed to see the same ones from one week to the next.

Hal stubbed out his half-smoked 'oily rag' (Cockney Rhyme for a fag, a cigarette) in the grass and disappeared. Matt and I milled furtively around Kat who blurted out, 'Hey guys, Hal told me his gran left him one and a half million pounds in her will.' She was obviously unable to contain herself.

'What!' Matt and I gasped out loud in unison. Both our jaws hit the floor. 'That much.'

Back then, at our age, it was an eye-watering sum. It still is a life-changing amount of money but to us, in our twenties, living at home with our mums, the implications were utterly mind-blowing.

'Don't mention it though, guys. Promise me?' she quickly added. 'Promise me you won't mention it to him, please,' she pleaded, obviously feeling instantly guilty for telling us.

'Yeah, sure,' Matt said casually.

'And you, Jonathan – promise,' she said determinedly.

'I promise.'

And the three of us fell silent, pondering on this vast fortune that our friend had just come into. We looked at each other furtively with broken smiles, not quite knowing what to feel. It wasn't as if he had won the lottery or anything but it felt a bit like it. He had become rich overnight. Hal was now a gentleman. His cigarette hadn't gone out properly, and as it smouldered on the ground, it looked as if a genie could be about to appear out of the whispering plume of smoke. I remember thinking how extraordinary it was that Hal could have had a breakdown, been admitted to a mental home, found his creativity, fallen in love and become rich all in the space of a few weeks. It was just incredible. Again I think another pop went off in my mind at the wonder of life and what is delivered to you by chance, and when, by nature. Although nothing was actually happening in the ward, in the hospital, all this action was taking place beneath the seemingly routine surface. Right when he was at the rock-bottom of the mire of life, Hal had suddenly found a seam of gold. It wasn't just financial wealth he had been given, but love and creativity too. All at the same time. Like all of us, when push was really coming to shove, when we were either going to sink or swim, literally, life had delivered. Life had come revelling at his feet, it had no choice, and it was doing the same for Matt, Kat and me – if we grasped it.

Hal soon reappeared, looking glum.

'What's up, Hal, are you okay?' Kat asked sensitively, all concern, as he sat down next to her.

'Yeah, yeah I'm fine,' he said unconvincingly. And as we all looked at him, waiting for more words, he finally yielded. 'It was nothing really; just my father saying he was going away and he didn't know when he'd be back, that's all.'

'At least he told you this time,' I blurted out. Hal looked at me quizzically.

'Did he say where he was going?' Kat interrupted, drowning out Matt's prophetic words, 'Same old, same old.'

Hal didn't know who to answer but just said, 'No, he didn't, and I didn't ask either. It's normal, don't worry.'

'Ask no questions, get no lies!' Matt burst out with in a squawky female voice, which broke the mood and made us all laugh.

'What does your dad actually do, Hal?' I asked, somewhat randomly a moment or two later.

'MI6,' he declared, making us all go silent again, wondering whether what he said was true or not.

'Bit of a conversation stopper, that, methinks,' said Matt. 'Say no more, mum's the word.'

I could see Kat was now even more intrigued by this guy she was falling for, as were we. She needed assurance. 'Really?' she demanded.

After a slight pause Hal replied glumly, 'Yes really, he's never around much. Hardly at all.'

'And you don't know where he's gone?' she continued.

'No, not exactly, probably Iran or Iraq or maybe the Middle East – I don't know exactly. Wherever there're any problems in the world. We could look at the news and take our pick.'

'Crikey, poor you, what a worry,' Kat empathised.

'No, not really, I'm used to it,' Hal replied, trying to sound convincing.

The conversation I had overheard the week before between Hal and his father had convinced me that there was no real pride for Hal in the work his father did; it was just a constant concern. And as he had said openly to his father, he was perpetually worried about him and had been ever since he was a child. Where was he? What was he doing? Was he safe? All these things. These unanswerable questions constantly rattled around in his mind and must have been, and still were, an eternal brain ache.

Like me with my numbers. They had all become too much. The order had broken down into a jumble. And the absence, the lack of parental guidance, as with me, had made Hal feral too; wayward, I guess, undisciplined with no moral compass. He sat with his head in his hands, not crying, not angry, but somehow internalising the reality of the hand he had been dealt. The ongoing struggle to come to terms with the distressing. And the fact was: nothing had changed. The cards he was holding were still the same. His father was going to an unknown war-zone somewhere on the planet, as usual, on a mission that was obviously secret and dangerous and all his son could do was… worry. Or pray. And maybe he was doing that then; who knows?

'Right, I'm going in to see if I can get permission for us to all go on a little walk right now. Let's show Jon and Matt the lambs, hey Hal?' Kat piped up. She stood up and stroked Hal's hair back firmly to encourage his head to rise, which worked.

'Yes, yes, good idea,' he replied in obeisance. As he gazed at her beautiful face, his features altered and the world was a noticeably better place for him. God knows what he would have done if she hadn't been there to take the force of the blow. But the instant he saw her I could see his perspective snap out of darkness and into light.

She bounced inside, leaving the three of us on the bench. Hal immediately lit another cigarette, sucked deeply and exhaled forcefully up into the sky. I wished I smoked then. It seemed to help somehow; it was expressive and seemed just the right thing to be doing. Forcibly blowing hot air, fuming all the ancestral pain out, into the ether.

'Did you get any visitors over the weekend, Hal?' Matt asked.

'Yeah, an uncle and aunt came up, and my mum, of course. They had stayed down for the funeral.'

'Oh, that was nice,' I piped in pathetically.

'Did it all go off okay? The funeral?' Matt asked.

'Yes, thanks, apparently it did, it's just a shame I couldn't have been there, that's all,' replied Hal soberly, his face dropping into his hands again.

'Yes of course, but you'll make it all up to them,' said Matt in a brotherly way.

'I hope so, mate,' he mumbled.

Kat reappeared, looking stressed and flustered. 'The bastards said no, they are too busy.' She added sarcastically, '*Maybe later*,' clearly repeating the ultimatum the nurses had issued.

'Calm down, Kat, it is Monday after all. I'm sure they are catching up on their notes and whatever,' Hal interjected, immediately trying to recalibrate the situation.

'Grrr, I guess so,' said Kat, admitting defeat. 'They just treat you like a fucking child so that you end up behaving like one, that's all.'

'I know, babe, I know, but why don't you do one of Jon's or Matt's masks instead? That'd be a laugh.'

'Oh, okay, alright, why not - how about it guys?'

Thank God Matt jumped in first with, 'Yeah, I'll do it, I'm up for it.'

And so we watched Matt lie down on the bench, preparing for his face to be mummified. A few of the other patients had come out to gawp at the spectacle, squinting in the daylight. Literally a fair percentage of the patients just sat inside all day long, gormlessly watching the crap daytime TV. Kat had to rub some fat type stuff, or lard or something, on Matt's face, then cover that with a bit of gauze and then layer strips of wet glue-covered newspaper over that. All the time Matt had to control his breathing through the two straws, and sniff air into his lungs through his nose. Kat had to work quickly out in the fast-drying strong spring sunshine. And soon she prised off the finished article and although the features were a bit obscured by the newspaper print it was definitely Matt's face.

She immediately got to work squashing the nose out with her fingers and rounding the chin with the palm of her hand before it set completely. She then dashed inside to cut out the big rounded monkey-mouth in the kitchen.

CHAPTER 12

Sprouts…

All of that week I could see Hal wrestling to pigeonhole, or ignore, the fact that his father had disappeared again. Clearly the loss had brought tension back into his wellbeing, and it had stirred up familiar emotions about not being any kind of priority in his father's life. And he wasn't able to do anything about it. Whenever we watched the news I could see him intently wondering which trouble-zone his father might be in, and it naturally rattled his cage.

I, for one, couldn't fathom why his father had decided to play the international-man-of-mystery card. He could just as easily have informed Hal he was going on holiday or something. Told a little white lie. Said that he'd be back in a few weeks. Why he hadn't, infuriated me. It would have eased his son's nerves, rather than agitating them. Hal had told his father that he worried about him. The guy was obviously trying to impress, or wasn't thinking about anyone else but himself. *He must be a selfish, spoilt individual*, I thought, *and a cold uncaring one at that*. And I didn't like it. It was cruel and it was nasty and what was bugging the shit out of me was that it was completely unnecessary. *Maybe the man wasn't going off on a special mission at all! Perhaps he was really on holiday*, I joked to myself. Maybe he thought that bigging himself up would impress his son, make him proud of him. Make him strong like his daddy or something. All that week just as it played on Hal's mind so it played on mine. It annoyed the hell out of me. Hal was containing his anger, but mine was about to burst.

The following day was a pleasant enough one weather-wise, and after breakfast Kat declared that it was my turn for my mask to be done before the second rehearsal on Thursday. She could tell I wobbled at the prospect.

'Come on, Jonathan,' she urged.

'Um, err, can we do it later? I'm not in the mood right now.'

'Yeah, come on, Jon, get it done, it's easy,' Matt piped up.

'Why don't we all do yours first, Kat? You need to get one done too,' I pronounced, chuffed I'd found a counter-argument.

'Yeah, Kat, that sounds great. We'll all do yours.' Matt sounded chirpy at the prospect of getting creative himself.

'Okay, okay, I'll do mine first but then you've got to do yours straight after – have we got a deal, Jonathan?' She held out a hand.

'Err, yeah, I guess so, okay,' I said, reluctantly shaking.

And so the three of us worked quickly on Kat, trying not to laugh or even giggle. It was a real bonding exercise. It engendered trust and it was the point at which the four of us really cemented our friendship. It was having faith to permit other people to invade your sacred space. To grant permission to others to nearly suffocate you: that was the key. As you lay on your back, as if in an operating theatre, slowly your face was plastered over and your vital senses became shut off. No light to see, no taste to enjoy, and having to keep really calm in order to be able to regulate breath through the straws. It was incredibly hard. You just had to put trust in the hands of others and have faith.

The result of that cathartic exercise was a wrap-around mask of yourself. Going through that weird experience, which would have been worth doing anyway, you actually got a captured reflection of yourself at the end: a solid memory of the sensory deprivation experience.

Again, the after-effect on me was a similar sensation to the one I had post-performing the role in Hal's play, which had allowed me for a brief time to look at myself, and to come out of myself. The act of submission to others in blocking out the world, while a slimy glue encased all access to three of my four senses; seeing, tasting and hearing, truly helped in my recovery. To have enforced focus on my senses made me appreciate them more.

I had felt terribly nervous, as if I was going to be operated on without anaesthetic. But I shouldn't have done, because the reality was that I went through an act of bowing to others, to life, and to submission. When Kat had peeled off my finished mask I had felt elated, giddy even. I had felt a gentle tear, and then a rip, before life was revealed to me again. In all its glory. I couldn't help but feel I was being born again: to my senses, to myself. Like a layer of skin had been removed to reveal a new me. It was like a snake must feel, post-moult. Suddenly I felt refreshed. I think I'd gone through a sort of rebirth. It's hard to explain but I couldn't help it; I pranced around the garden doing the odd skip of joy that I had never done before or since. I felt then that I was going to do it, I was going to pull through, out of the pit of insecurity and deep confusion I had been in. I was going to do it and humour was getting me there. It reaffirmed that I was truly skipping out of madness and into a bright blue order, and it felt so good. I never realised that not taking myself or life too seriously was a major ingredient to feeling happier. Doh!

I don't know what Kat did to my mask but Matt and I, being the play's children, had cuter chimpanzee-style features, while hers and Hal's were older-looking. All four masks had deep red mouths and ornate gold fringes. The monkey features only fully came out when Kat had painted over the newspaper print. Our masks were all still human in essence but were decorated to look more like stylised Indian deities. Very theatrical.

Kat gave us all our masks to keep. I still have mine hanging in my study at home to this day; I was surprised to find out later that the masks closely resembled the Indian god Hanuman, the Hindu monkey god. I researched him sometime later when I had made the connection and was amazed to discover that he was the god of not just physical but mental strength too. The god who represents overcoming obstacles. I don't know if Kat had intended them to look like the revered deity or indeed if Hal had incorporated the symbolism purposely into the play but it was a pleasant coincidence to discover nevertheless.

We were eventually given permission to go for our walk beyond the hospital confines that week, across the main road, into the fields and out into the open countryside beyond. Hal and Kat were right; just to get out amongst nature was incredibly healing and, for me, being a boffin, it was all slightly alien. I never went for walks. Now, having my dog - and he's my third - I have become a nature lover: all a result of that first walk. Everything that happened to me over those three weeks since Hal arrived and took me under his wing has had the most profound effect on my life. All that I was discovering about myself, and about how to live a balanced life, came to me from those few weeks. It was as if I had been emptied by my mental breakdown and was re-filling my entity, my being, with wholesomeness. And I'm sure that Hal, being the most magnanimous, generous of spirits, could never have guessed for one moment that he had been the catalyst for the changes I was undergoing.

Just as he'd said, the rapeseed fields were incredible when the sun came out. Vibrant carpets of canary yellow flowers rolled out and burst into life the moment the sun was in the clear. We shuffled in single file around this magnificent yet unfamiliar landscape that was a mere stone's throw from our depressingly grey hospital, nestled within the gloomy conifers a quarter of a mile away. Again, this simple activity unexpectedly took me out of myself; my senses were utterly entertained by nature. A cacophony of unseen birds chirruped within the length of the hedgerows and the hawthorn blossom, like a ball-gown frill, contrasted amazingly with the expanse of rapeseed. White, flower-laden hedgerows framed yellow fields. At one point, as we walked beside a thick hedge-bordered path, the fallen hawthorn blossom petals formed a pretty rug for us to walk on like a little dusting of freshly laid snow. The blossom smells were heady and rich, and buzzed with insects. Then we reached the field where the lambs were and all of us in turn got giddy.

'Hey, look at that one over there,' Kat squealed, laughing.

'Wow! Check out that leap,' Matt said, gesticulating madly.

'Oh, oh, look at that one - there, there.'

'Where?'

'There, silly.'

'Oh, yeah.'

'Hey, hay, that was a great one.'

All four of us stood at the edge of the field for ten minutes, like little children, waving, pointing frantically and laughing hysterically at these new-born balls of joy. I am sure that any casual observer would have known exactly where we had hailed from.

'Shit, I forgot to bring my camera. I can't believe it!' Matt said, stomping his feet.

After the excitement passed we stood in silence, taking it all in for a moment and just appreciating this pastoral, quintessentially British scene before us. The sights and sounds summed up the beauty of spring perfectly. Pristine pasture with sheep in the foreground, surrounded by fields of tended crops, and stretching into the distance, hedge-enclosed farmland and pockets of woodland rippling towards the horizon. I thought of my actions when Kat had taken the mask-mould off and I had skipped around. Looking at the little fluffy, pure-white bleating lambs made a connection for me: I had, unbeknown to myself, actually skipped around because I had felt like a little lamb myself, full of the joys of spring. That was how I had felt inside: featherbrained, tickled. If there hadn't been other people present at my unmasking I would have really gone for it and would have leapt about much more vigorously, even whinnied and neighed. Up until that point I had always felt a freak to nature; estranged from it and in no way part of it. That was the first time I actually felt part of creation. It was looking at those lambs in a field when I was in my early twenties. I was at one with them, and was connected to the whole. At that moment when the new me was revealed, I felt reborn, as happy as a ruddy lamb. Every spring now, whenever I see young flocks, I recall that moment clearly, when I looked across the fields and felt at peace with nature for the first time. Even with my mathematical mind I could only bow down in awe at the heavenly coding of creation.

On the walk, however, whenever I glanced across at Hal I could see he was still subdued, lost in his thoughts. I even remember Kat saying to him, 'Wakey, wakey, Hal. Are you okay?'

At this he would snap out of his reverie. 'Yeah, yeah, I'm fine.'

I also heard her whisper into his ear as we all concertinaed at a stile gate: *penny for your thoughts.*

I don't know if he was still trying to bottle his anger towards his father but that was how I read his distraction. He seemed to be stunned, in a bit of a daze.

He was a deep thinker, no doubt, and had probably been diagnosed as a manic depressive. I understand manic depression as being the flip side of depression whereby the highly sensitive being, by no means a weak individual, decides they aren't going to allow other people or situations who upset them to get them down. They are going to go up, way up, to escape going down, right down. In fact, they could even go ballistic rather than crumple. Same condition – depression - but opposite end of the spectrum.

I obviously didn't know the facts but I remember fearing Hal would either crack and begin to rage, or collapse into a heap. His face wasn't going red as if he was about to burst, it was more like the phone punch his father had delivered the previous day had somehow bruised his eyes. He looked battered and deflated by the internalised pain he was absorbing. It was as if the depressing news he received had aged him. It hunched him over, stooped him, and made him look exhausted.

I had to constantly remind myself that, after all, we were seriously mentally ill; otherwise we wouldn't have been there in the first place. His sorry mood was probably more evident as it contrasted sharply with the beauty of the countryside around. He put on a good show, though; I could see he was trying, he didn't whinge.

It did make me feel a real anger towards his father, and I resolved that I would repay the goodness Hal was giving me.

I remember staring at Hal out there in the fields and deciding that I would teach his father a lesson. Through the NASA hack and my discovery of satellites' flawed programming, I determined that, over the coming weekend, I was going to establish exactly what satellite systems MI6 were connected to.

In hindsight, it's shocking to appreciate the resourcefulness and boldness of youth. The sheer fearlessness of inexperience. I had no concept of the consequences of all my deep penetration hacking into the most secure systems on the planet. As far as I was concerned I was not really doing anything that wrong. Not only was Hal giving me the confidence to showcase my abilities but, as I saw when looking back, I didn't really have anything to lose. I was at the bottom rung on the ladder of life, after all. There was nowhere further to fall.

CHAPTER 13

Bulbs…

The week dragged. I was dying to get home to my computer. The only element of excitement was continuing to rehearse Hal's play, *The Fourth Monkey*. We all had our freshly painted masks, which helped get us further into our roles.

'Come on, you three, get in character,' Hal demanded, clapping his hands. 'Okay, come on. Listen up. We left off where the two children have eaten the forbidden fruit, against their father's insistence, and you're all on your own now. Do you understand?' He turned, pointed and clicked his fingers. 'Is the camera switched on, Matt?' Matt nodded obediently. Hal clapped his hands again. 'Okay everyone, if we're all ready?' Crouching in our positions we grunted, *yes*. 'Lovely, good luck everyone, quiet now and… action.'

The two children sit back against the Tree of Wisdom's trunk and begin to lick themselves clean of the fruit, constantly getting wonderful taste sensations.

DOROTHY (CALLS OUT)

Mom, Mom - have you found us any food? Me and David are starving. (And then whispers to her brother, *te-hee, not.*)

Their mother still sits out in the baking sun. She wavers, wobbles and collapses just after she has managed to say, in a feeble voice,

ISOBEL

No, darling, I haven't, my dears. Be strong, your father will be home soon.

David and Dorothy hear the thud. They scamper out and pull their mother to the cool of the shady tree.

DOROTHY

There, Mom, that's better. Coming in here will make you feel cooler.

Dorothy wipes some of the moist fruit around her mother's parched mouth, and her mother soon begins to come to.

ISOBEL

Oh, thank you, my children. I don't know what came over me. My word, it is so lovely and cool under here.

DAVID

You are just so weak, Mom. You shouldn't have stayed out in the sun like that for so long. You're not strong enough, don't move. Have some of this…

Her son hands her a fruit which, in her delirium, she takes and eats. And as her children see their mother eat, they do too. Soon Isobel revives.

ISOBEL

That was delicious, children. I feel so much better - where did you find it?

DAVID (THROUGH MOUTHFULS, POINTS)

I picked it fresh from those branches there, Mom.

ISOBEL (THROWS HER FRUIT DOWN IN DISGUST)

Oh, my God, no. Children, what have we done? We have eaten the forbidden fruit. Your father is going to be furious. He'll be so disappointed with us, with me. You know he told us, I mean me, never to eat from this tree. I promised him. Oh no, what have I done…

DOROTHY

But Mom, it was an emergency. You were nearly dying out there and where was Daddy anyway? Leaving us here to starve. What did he expect?

DAVID

Yes, Mom. Dad has just left us here on our own with nothing to eat. It's his fault. This fruit is delicious, there is nothing wrong with it, believe me. And it is so cool and green and lush under this tree.

DOROTHY

Daddy must be mad not allowing us under here.

ISOBEL

No, no, children you don't know what you are doing. Your father is wise and good. He only ever thinks of you and wants what is best for you. Believe me.

Isobel begins to weep and sob as the children ignore her and begin to play on the branches, lark around the tree's trunk, and gorge on the fruit. Isobel musters her strength and tries to drag them out. They resist.

ISOBEL

Come now, children, we must leave here immediately.

DOROTHY

No, Mother, we are not going out into that harsh drought where there is nothing to eat and it is so hot. Let me go, I want to stay here.

DAVID

Come on, Mom, don't be silly. Give me one good reason why we should leave, and I will obey.

ISOBEL

Just because times are hard doesn't mean we should forget what is good and what is bad. This tree is too good; that is the problem. This tree will make you lazy and weak.

Both children roar with laughter and start rolling around. We see a flash of a tiger or a leopard in the background.

DAVID

That doesn't make any sense. Mom, sorry. When we are parched and starving out there how can being cool, with plenty to eat, make us weak?

DOROTHY

Yes, Mom, how can it?

ISOBEL

Because it does, it makes you idle and arrogant.

DOROTHY

Well, I am staying here. You can't force me to go.

DAVID

Me too, Mom, sorry. You can go out and collapse again. But I am staying here where we are safe and well-fed.

Lights dim. One spotlight shines on Isobel, who sits out from under the canopy alone as her two children, under another spot, frolic around, gorging. Isobel sits as still as a monument. We see a further swish of a tiger in the background.

DAVID (SHOUTS OUT)

When will Dad get back from his hunting trip, Mom?

ISOBEL

In his own good time, my dear.

DOROTHY

Who cares, tee, he-he. We're okay without him. Come on, David, let's play and eat some more.

This is what they do. Then, gorged, they fall asleep. The lights fade down again and flare up quickly after a horrific roar and scream comes out from under the Tree of Wisdom's canopy. Dorothy dashes out and cowers with her mother as we see the tiger clutch a stuffed David in its jaws and return with his corpse to the jungle beyond.

DOROTHY

Oh my God, Mommy, the tiger's got David, he's dead, Mommy, he's dead.

ISOBEL

Come here now, away from that dreadful tree. It's okay, darling, it's okay.

That was what we rehearsed time and time again. Hal would sit back with the tutor discussing certain elements and then come up and explain the nuances to each of us; then we would go back over scenes again or continue. I must say it did get exhausting and it reached a point where the three of us admitted we had had enough. We stood in the classroom with our masks on, our arms drooping by our sides.

'No, Hal, that's it. We've really enjoyed it, thanks, but enough's enough,' Kat declared authoritatively, through her muffled disguise, on our behalf.

'Okay, everyone. Well done,' he replied, admitting defeat.

Again, the simple exercise of coming out of myself, being someone else for a short while, gave me an added confidence. It was precisely the right exercise I needed to be a little bolder with my weekend hack around the Earth and its orbit. The improvement in my newfound self-assurance enabled me to actually force myself onto systems with confidence, if that makes any sense. To impose my will upon the programs was something quite new to me. Before that weekend I would sort of pussy-foot around, as a sort of cyber voyeur. But from now on I was determined to fully engage in the action. Because I had a cause. I was on a mission. I would become the puppet-master. Hal's father, the self-styled international-man-of-mystery, was going to be my target. He had nothing on me. I would emerge as the new Spector, the Dr Strangelove, a Captain Nemo. After all, I was the daddy, the dog's bollocks of the new technical revolution. This was my world.

The discovery I did make that weekend was that I could upload a maximum of a fifteen-second segment of footage and jam it into NASA's satellite transmission system before their mainframe would be alerted and shift signals. Then, at the receiving end of the transmission, the actual satellites, which were called Explorers, spinning around the earth, could be temporarily reprogrammed too. I could make the transmitter either stick or flip the relay mechanism for long enough to alter exactly where the piece of footage I inserted would end up. Those early satellites received a variety of information from a variety of sources. Information was then dispatched to designated recipients. The main recipients of data sent by the Explorers, being American military satellites, were all allies of USA. The whole system was controlled by the CIA and therefore communication doors, through this channel, were open to MI6: my target.

In a nutshell, the revelation was I could hack into a NASA computer and insert a clip of footage up to fifteen-seconds long, that would bounce off my adjusted satellite receiver and end up in MI6's Top Secret inbox, apparently sent from CIA. The shock waves would be massive. The reverberations could have been truly apocalyptic. If, for example, I had decided to send an apparent message from Russia, informing Britain that a nuclear weapon was on its way to London, I could have caused a world war. Or I could have caused chaos by sending a jihadist terrorist video clip saying someone was about to explode a massive bomb in the Houses of Parliament.

Thank goodness, however, I did have just the right amount of sense to transmit something that was going to be instantly recognisable as a joke. I see it now as throwing a custard pie at The System. Making them see how flawed they were. Their method of sharing top-secret information was basically fallible, buggable. And any old idiot, like me, could access that technology. The plan I was incubating was to be a slap in the face, a wake-up call. They should have thanked people like me, and they would in time; but back then, just as it still is, hacking into US institutions is a life-sentence crime. (And it's a secret I have always kept quiet about, until now, of course. I wonder if this is the story I wanted to get out of my mind when I began to write the whole episode down as a way of reclaiming and taking control of a powerless childhood.)

Anyway, the following week I thought through my plan in more detail. No one but me would know. This was a play I was writing for myself, my opus, my dark solo concerto before I went legit.

Walking up the inclined hospital corridor after that weekend my mother stopped to inform the nurses that I was back, and to her surprise she found my clinical psychiatrist in the office. Dr. Feltz didn't usually come in on a Sunday.

'Oh Dr Feltz, do you mind if I have a quick word?' said my mother. And then she continued, whispering loudly like a matron, as soon as the fizzing-with-energy mental health professional approached, 'I thought I'd let you know that Jonathan, having been doing so well recently, just stayed on his computer all weekend. I couldn't get him off it.'

'Oh dear, okay, thank you for telling me, I'll make a note of it. But, Mrs Runcorn, I was going through Jonathan's file today, and we mustn't be discouraged. I read that my staff, the nurses, are all delighted with his recent progress. He has started to fully engage with the other patients, and is now attending many of the activities we have on offer, which is a real step forward,' the petite intelligent consultant said reassuringly.

'Humm, okay, that is good to hear,' my mother said. And then she squinted, glancing across at me as if I couldn't hear, and continued, 'Yes, I agree. Jonathan has been doing so well up until now, so much so that I felt he was coming back to being his old self again, but this weekend seemed to be a step backwards.'

'Okay, Mrs Runcorn, I understand. But on the whole, which is how we must look at this, Jonathan's progress is very positive. All highly encouraging news. We mustn't be discouraged.'

'Yes, yes, you're right. And, thank God, that eye-fluttering has stopped too; that was just awful.'

'Yes, that's an unfortunate side effect of the medication he is taking. We reduced it two weeks ago and we were going to cut the dose down again, but we may well hold back on that for the time being. Just so you know, Mrs Runcorn, I want to implement Jonathan leaving hospital and going home in two or three weeks, all being well. How do you feel about that?'

'Oh, my word. That is a surprise,' my mother exclaimed.

'A good one, I hope?'

'Well, yes, yes, of course. If you think he is ready.'

My mother wasn't as surprised as I was, though, to hear those words from my psychiatrist. On hearing that bombshell, but pretending not to, my heart skipped a beat and my bowels fluttered. Although I was standing upwind, as it were, I couldn't help but let lose a simultaneous rip; a double-barrelled burp and fart which fired out of both chambers in unison. I was instantly excited and scared at the prospect of leaving. I was still, selfishly, rather enjoying my routine, the continued attention and cotton-wool ward existence, so that I hadn't really considered going home for good. I was, after all, pretty well institutionalised. There was no way I could look after myself. I didn't have to think about that. Looking after myself hadn't crossed my radar once. Both of them ignored my rude outpourings.

'This is where we are heading. I am sorry, Mrs Runcorn, I really shouldn't be here over a weekend; there was an emergency. I have got to get going now. But, please, speak to one of the nurses when you come in next Friday and we'll take it from there. Is that okay?' my doctor concluded.

'Yes, of course. Absolutely fine. Thank you for your time,' my mother replied, recovering her composure.

On the way to the dormitory with my overnight bag I stopped at the television room entrance. When my eyes had adjusted to the darkness I could see my gang, my happy trio, glued to the box watching a nature documentary: the life of butterflies, I think.

I coughed, though not another botty one, and Hal turned.

'Hey, Jonathan – welcome home! How are ya?' he said.

'Yes, cool thanks. And you?'

'Tickety-boo,' he said, getting up and coming over to me. 'We're all fine but you just missed a hell of a drama. A new bloke's just arrived kicking and screaming. I moved out of my room and I'm in the dormitory with you guys now. He's in the private room. He's quietened down, but it was one hell of a scene.'

'It was scary, Jonathan, awful,' echoed Kat from the cocooned gloom.

'Yeah, man, savage,' said Matt. 'The guy was like a beast, a big bear. It took an army to hold him down. I don't know if I'm going to be able to sleep tonight with that moose on the loose. A proper loon.'

'Yes right, we'll have to set up a rota for sentry duty!' Hal joked.

'Anyhow, what did you get up to this weekend, Jonathan, anything nice?' Kat asked.

'No, nothing really. Just stayed at home. And you guys?'

'Hal and I went out for the day today. His mum came over and we did that walk we did last week but went on to that pub for lunch.'

'Oh, yeah, was it nice?' I asked.

'Yes, it was. It was lovely.'

'What did you have to eat?' Matt asked.

'I had roast chicken, actually. Didn't I, Hal?'

'Yeah, you did. You did very well.'

'Puds?' added Matt.

'That'd be pushing it,' Hal said with a smile. 'But you did do so well, Kat, so well. Well done,' he added for the blushing Kat.

'Hip hip hooray for Kat. Three cheers for the roast,' said Matt. 'Hey guys, I've got some news. Dr Feltz just told me and my mum that hopefully I'll be going home at the end of the week.'

'I don't believe it!' Kat exclaimed. 'That's great news, well done.'

'She just said the same thing to me and my mum too,' I added 'but not this week - maybe next, or the one after.'

'Wow, that's really good news, guys,' said Hal, and then added quickly, 'I'd better finish off the play then and we can do our last rehearsal together at the end of the week, and do a sort of farewell performance.'

'Oh great, can't wait!' said Matt sarcastically, to our amusement.

'And you must film it, Matt,' I said. 'But, sorry guys, I've got to go to bed, I'm exhausted.'

'But it's only eight thirty, man,' Matt exclaimed.

'Good night.'

CHAPTER 14
Seedlings...

Hal kept religiously to his routine. Although my fascination with him had waned slightly through familiarity I still stirred whenever he woke up. Since he now slept in the main dormitory, and in spite of the fact that he couldn't see me, I felt as if I had to fake being asleep until he went out for his morning walk. I'd lie awake with my eyes squeezed shut. The moment he put his shoes on and swished past my curtain, I'd open them again, then sit up in bed and peep out at him. I'd watch him alone and unguarded walking up that avenue of conifers in the cool blue hues of spring's first light.

One morning when I was watching him stroll, stick in hand, he suddenly stopped dead. I jumped onto red alert. But as my eyes scanned, focussed and recalibrated all I could see was a group of four or five deer frozen in motion, partially hidden, just ahead of him. And then I blinked. They had disappeared and cleared the path. It was an incredibly primal image, like a scene I pictured of a solitary Neolithic man, hunting in a virgin forest in the mists of time. There are certain impressions you have of people that become embossed in the mind for some reason, and that was the one indelible mental postcard I hold of Hal: everything still, him, holding out a branch, outlines of deer and the sculptured trees, all shrouded in this ethereal hazy-blue light. That vision was the cardinal one, and there were two other pictures of him that still stuck in my mind. In second place was the silhouette of him in the moon shadow, head bowed, after his father had wafted away after his first visit. The third was still to come.

I couldn't tell Hal I had seen either of those arresting images for fear of disclosing that I had been snooping on him. Those are the lasting images I have of Hal. Not his face so much, but his outline in the magic light of dawn walking up that dreadful, shrouded, lifeless avenue of evergreens. An evergreen is the wrong word for these trees; it should be everbrowns. Trenches of decades' worth of pine needles had left the rutted route lifeless. It was one of those roads that lead nowhere. The turquoise-coloured deer, not red, had merged into the alien chromatic background. Hal never mentioned it to me.

At those thoughts I stood up, turned back from Rooksdown's entrance and strolled up that path myself into the scene I had just remembered, all these years later, with my dog, Nelson, scampering ahead. I'd never dared to do that walk when I was a patient. It was when I walked beneath the conifers that the haunting memories of what we all went through came shuddering back. What had become of everyone?

Rain began to fall. I shivered as if ghosts were on my back. The barbed trees hadn't moved in over twenty years, ominously constant in their stillness. The only difference I could see was twenty plus years' worth of more pine needles piled up. I turned and went back to the bench kicking the mounds of detritus away with my shoe to dispel my frustrated memories and, as I neared, I exposed the concrete base. Whilst aggressively scuffing the needles, my foot rammed into a fat rusty protruding old screw which connected with my big toe awkwardly. A shot of pain seared up my left leg, bringing me sharply back to reality. And looking around, towards the ward, I flopped back down, and homed in on the very window which I had peeped out at Hal from all those years ago.

The nursing attention within the ward had shifted and had become focussed on this Baloo character who had arrived on a whirlwind the previous Sunday evening. A pop-up nurses' station had been arranged outside his bedroom door 24/7. I first encountered him on the Monday morning. He was a huge guy, dumb and with a club foot, who charged around, crashing and thumping wherever he went. He always wore a silver shell-suit. He was like a Shrek on crack-cocaine. He came from a council estate in Portsmouth. We didn't find out what exactly had happened for him to be admitted but the guy was frantic-manic. He said he was a DJ. His presence made the atmosphere on the ward revert to disorder. Our brief few weeks of pleasantness and relative calm had descended into chaos. He was a bull in a china shop. He had not one iota of respect for anyone's space; he invaded it with impunity. He'd barge into whatever we were doing with a crazed look, often dribbling from his non-functioning lips.

He'd blurt interruptions like, 'You lot, listen to this. It's my music, this.' And then, taking off his headphones, he'd shove them at, say Matt, who would listen for a moment, cringe, and then pass them back saying, 'Yeah right, wicked.' And when Baloo – Liam - put the headphones back on Matt would add, 'Not! What a load of shite.'

I mean, it really was bad music. It was disturbing. Generally remixed cartoon songs. Music to make you mad to. We nicknamed him – well, Matt of course thought of it - Baloo, because he would play, over and over again, this shoddy danced-up remix that he said he had done of the 'I want to walk like the animals, talk like the animals' Jungle Book song.

Out on our bench, after breakfast, early in the week Hal had gone off to finish his play. The three of us milled around waiting for nothing. And then from within the smoking room we heard alarming shouting and screaming and banging and crashing coming out of the open window. Matt dashed over and I followed. Kat didn't budge; she sat frozen to her seat. We peeped in and could see Frank, one of the quieter inmates - a big guy, a farm worker - locked in deadly combat with Baloo.

These huge monsters were splaying around the now empty-of- people room; everyone else had rushed out into the corridor and were looking in, from the outside, in shocked silence. Heavy wing-backed chairs seemed to flutter away like paper to the far walls as the two giants wrestled violently like maimed lions, grappling, lashing and smashing their way around the room.

'Who the hell do you think you are? I'll teach you manners,' roared Frank.

At those words they both stood still, confronting each other, heaving away, arms akimbo. It was a brief lull before the bolt, like poised Sumo wrestlers crouched before they lunge. Pre-pounce, Liam seemed to rise on tiptoe to balance out his club foot when Frank's gorilla-huge clenched fist swung skyward, out of the blue, fast, in an upper-cut. It caught Liam squarely under the chin and we heard the brutal impact; it was a deep cracking noise like an axe splitting a log. The whack would have knocked any of our heads clean off but Liam just seemed to absorb it. He stood there, unsteady, shaking his head, dazed and confused. He put a hand to his cheek and rubbed. It was all in slow motion for me, watching from the framed safety of the window. It was like a television or computer screen. It felt so unreal. *Surely it can't go on. He must fall*, I thought. But Liam simply shook his head again, as if to wake himself up, frothing through his blubbering lips, and then he launched himself back at Frank feebly uttering a ferocious, yet pathetic, howl. The moment they fronted up, before the punch, I could see Frank was beginning to feel shocked at what he was about to do. He looked as if he'd had enough and wanted to just get it over with. However, the crazed, dumb Liam didn't know when to call it a day. The nurses had now mustered around the entrance and were yelling for the heavy-weight combatants to stop. Liam began flaying around pathetically one last time but the fight had deteriorated into farce. Frank was just deflecting the lame blows as Liam began to pant loudly and moan, exhausted. The battle of the ward giants had been fought. The law of the jungle had been meted out. Pecking order had been established. Then the nurses pounced on Liam, as Frank stood aside, shaking. Liam put out one last feeble flay, and then collapsed onto the carpet, honking. Two nurses pinned him down while another appeared with a syringe and jabbed it into his arse, straight through his tracksuit. All was silent except for Baloo's violent sobs, and then they half-carried, half-dragged him off to his room. Matt and I looked at each other, wide-eyed. He held a hand up for a high-five. Our palms connected.

'Boom!' he said. 'Time out.'

Frank was a gentle giant and had always been seen lumbering about quietly not saying much to anyone and seemed, well, just simple. I don't know what his problems were but he was depressed. As a nurse held his bleeding hand he began to blubber too. And between the sobs I could hear him say, 'I told him to leave me alone. I did, nurse. And then he ran up to me and stood on my foot; that was it. I am so sorry. I didn't mean to.'

And then Matt leaned through the window, and called out, in support of Frank, 'Yes, nurse, the guy's been freaking everyone out. He's just charging around and right in your face all the time. He's got no respect for anyone. Well done, Frank, you taught him a lesson. Are you okay?'

'Yes, I'll be fine thanks, Matt, cheers mate,' he replied.

'Come on now, Frank, let's get you cleaned up,' the kindly nurse said, leading him off to the washroom like a big remorseful baby.

Matt and I went back to Kat who had her head in her hands. She was crying.

'I just can't cope with this place,' she sobbed. 'I want to go home - now.'

Hal appeared out of thin air and put his arm around her. Matt and I sidled off, leaving him to it. I could hear him say, 'Come on Kat, it's okay. It's over now.'

'No, it's not – it's a nightmare. It's a living nightmare here.'

'Come on now, calm down, Kat,' he said firmly, holding her tight. 'Don't upset yourself.'

'I can't bear it.'

He let her cry but wouldn't let her go. He soothed her with strokes until she calmed. 'Look at me,' he said eventually. 'We've got to get better, and then we'll go home. I know it's upsetting but this is what it's all about, us being here. We *must* get better, so that we never have to come back to a place like this again. Do you understand?'

'Maybe.'

'No, Kat. We're not here for no reason. We have to rise above this, be strong, be gentle and then we'll go home. If you leave now you won't ever get better. We've just got to see this through. Rise above it, please. We've just got to make a real effort to get well again. You must, Kat,' he implored, 'for me.' He had said it.

'Okay.'

'Promise?'

'I promise.'

'Good. Come on now, let's go for a walk and see how those little lambs are doing.'

He got up and held his hand out for her. And putting an arm around her shoulder he led her into the ward to inform the nurses they were going out. There was no asking for permission this time.

Matt and I stood aside to let them pass. Hal raised his eyebrows and smiled at us.

'Wow, that was a funny five minutes,' Matt declared, when they had gone inside.

'Phew, not half. I'm going to go and have a lie-down. That was all a bit too much for me.'

'Hey, come on, Jonathan, let's go up to the shop, I'll buy you a can of drink.'

'No, no way, I can't face going up there; I'm going to lie down. Thanks though. See you in a bit.'

'Wow, what a punch,' Matt muttered, shaking his head, as I walked off. I turned and saw him emulate Frank's upper-cut into the air. 'Kerrpow!'

Before I lay down on my bed I instinctively opened the window blinds and could see Hal and Kat walking up the avenue towards the open countryside, alone, holding a blanket.

I pictured them crossing the road, over the stile and along the public footpath which hugged the rapeseed crop, and Hal saying:

'God, it's amazing. The moment we cross that road into countryside it feels so good. I can feel the crap back there just fall off me. Do you know what I mean?'

'I do,' she'd answer.

Thrushes and blackbirds sang out from their nests in the hawthorn-blossomed hedgerows. I lay back on my pillow and envisaged the two lovers skirt the field.

And then Hal spotted a gap in the thicket, and said, 'Come on, let's go through here.'

'No, I can't.'

'Yes, you can, hold my hand.' She'd taken it.

And he led her carefully through the perfect arch in the hedge into a totally secluded square of grass, to another world entirely, a very private place, which bordered an adjoining field planted with waist-high barley. He laid the blanket out.

'Let's just sit here for a little while, take it all in, and relax,' he said, holding out his hand, invitingly. 'No one can see or hear us.'

Kat sat down slowly and then immediately clammed up. She put her knees to her chin and wrapped her arms around her shins. Hal, sitting close, began to caress her arched back gently, soothing her and working to straighten her. He then rose, took his weight on one hand, lent across and began to tenderly kiss the nape of her neck, brushing her long strawberry blonde hair away with his free hand which gave him uncluttered access to the velvety skin below her ears. He purposely breathed out through his nose so that his exhalation entered her ear, making her shiver with arousal. He rubbed Kat's arm to ease the goose-bumps he'd created.

'Come, lie down,' he whispered.

With no resistance, she lay back. He gazed at her lovingly.

'You're so beautiful, Kat.' He sighed. 'You are pure English honey.'

And they kissed deep and long in the spring-green fields, enveloped by nature; the trauma of the fight ten minutes ago had vaporised into thin air with their loving embrace. She encouraged him forward. Hal's response was immediate; his hand went beneath her top, and was under her bra before she could resist. He began to fondle a firm, ripe bosom, all the while never flinching from the passionate union of their magnetised lips. *He's done this before*, she thought, fleetingly, before submitting wholeheartedly to Hal's, all-consuming touch. He moved closer, putting one leg over hers. She felt his bulge harden on contact with her waist. She softened, completely. And letting out a sigh of submission she reached right back to clasp the cool moist grass behind with both hands as he came up on her and they writhed together in unified arousal, motioning to the urge of creation. He rose to his knees, undid her clasp and roughly pulled her jeans and pants off in one swift action; then he leant forward above her, supporting himself with his hands on either side of her, poised to mount. He kissed Kat gently on the lips; she quivered, flexed her hips and then rose to meet his. Hal entered her with ease and instantly moved deep within her, warm and solid. He filled the empty void she had felt for so long, completely.

'Oh, my God, that feels so good, Kat,' he said.

'Stop,' she murmured. 'Keep still. Don't move a muscle. Let me feel you inside me.' When she sighed a second time and said, 'Mmm, yes… okay,' Hal continued again in earnest, pulling one of her legs up so that he could force himself, and grind harder into her, so that she could feel his penetration, even deeper still.

'Are you on the pill?' he said.

'No.'

He withdrew, yanked hard on himself, released over her breasts and then reinserted and worked forcefully with the dying embers of his lust. Kat came too, shuddering beneath him, over and above the birdsong. And then they collapsed side by side, lying on their backs, hand in hand, satiated, looking up at the blindingly blue sky, and began to laugh.

I remember thinking how therapy was a most peculiar thing, and that vital healing ingredient to be an even more elusive factor. I realised, for example, that sometimes a punch may be a better cure than a kiss; it's a perverse form of love, the opposite of a kiss, but a whack can be love all the same; a tougher form of love. Like shouting may be more appropriate than gentle platitudes. Alarms delivered in no uncertain terms. Healing moments, like poignant words or actions, can appear randomly, to be received or missed when you least expect or plan for them. Liam, Baloo, had been meted out his brutal therapeutic lesson from Frank, and was humbling back in the ward recovering from the shock of his wake-up call, his reality check, as I pictured Kat lying back giggling with joy in the fields half a mile away reaping the rewards of her years of pain.

Kat had been feeling so utterly uncomfortable with herself for so long, and felt so ugly that to even consider, let alone allow, someone – anyone - to touch her body had been inconceivable just two weeks before. She could find nothing but faults in her figure, however enviable it was. The complete lack of nutrients in her system, up until she was admitted to hospital, had made her thought patterns flutter with the fairies and go haywire. She had been admitted to the mental home because of that; she had experienced a quasi-spiritual experience through lack of food, and had been completely spaced out. Just as Hal had done when he was detained, thinking he was some sort of a Lord Nelson character, fighting federal forces against freedom, so Kat had felt as if she had been a Joan of Arc, in combat with the cosmic battles of good against evil. She had become so phobic about her body, and so completely obsessive about cleanliness, that the mere thought of sex was as repellent as it was unimaginable. Yet here she was lying on solid ground, coming back to earth and reality in the most exquisite way.

Many people take close physical intimacy for granted, especially as they get older, but remain on your own for a year or two, feel lonely, truly solitary, and then maybe you will fully appreciate the warmth and comfort that close contact with another human can bring. When you think you will never have it again, when you resign yourself to a life of solitude and then unity with someone else comes, like a bolt from the blue, it feels like a miracle. This is what Kat felt, lying still, naked, with Mother Nature, exposed. This time her experience was genuinely spiritual.

She had felt literally dried up, which is what bulimia does; it changes the internal chemistry to halt periods, and moisture is not forthcoming. Hal had released a blockage in her natural biorhythms. She had experienced a moment, an unexpected monumental event in her life, which she could never forget, and would never want to. This relief from released childhood tensions allowed her to take a giant step closer to feeling complete again. And healing herself. If there was one pivotal, seminal moment where Kat could begin to say to herself that she was getting better – that was it. Making love to Hal, for the first time, was her nadir, the precise point at which her life began to swing back in the other, more positive direction. She had gone as far as she could go before falling into the abyss of physical and mental abnormality. And now, for the time being, she was reprieved, not just by Hal but, at the last minute, by love itself. She was finally reassembling and being put back on the path to being healed by those few minutes of passion. Her biological imbalance was being restored by human emotions, more than a trolley-load of tablets could ever do.

'Kat, I really don't mean to pry, but can you tell me how you got bulimic in the first place,' Hal said, coming up on one elbow, rubbing her tummy gently. 'But, please, don't tell me if you don't want to.'

'It was my dad,' Kat replied immediately, unreservedly.

'Christ! What do mean? Did he abuse you?' He sat bolt upright.

'No, no, nothing like that,' she said, smiling. 'He said I was fat.'

'Yes, you said that before. And?'

'I know it sounds so stupid, Hal. Pathetic even.'

'It does, hon, sorry. Carry on though, tell me more.'

'God, I'm so embarrassed.' She too sat up to pull her jeans back on and continued, 'When I was thirteen, I was going to a party and I asked him how I looked and he said that I looked fat. It may have just been plump, he'd said, or that I'd put on weight. Whatever, it's just eaten into me since then.'

'Poor guy, does he know this?' Hal said. And then just as Kat was about to put her pants on, he leant across, smiling. 'I'll keep those, if you don't mind, for keepsakes.'

'Stop it, you naughty boy. Well, okay, go on then.'

'I'll frame them. No, seriously, that's ridiculous, Kat, I don't believe it,' he said as he stuffed her knickers into his pocket. 'How could something as small as that, a flippant comment your father made, have caused all this pain for you and your family? It's just ridiculous. I don't believe it. It doesn't make any sense. There must be more?'

'No, seriously, that was it. Look, I'm ashamed. Come now, take me back,' she said, standing up, flustered.

Hal stood up, folded the blanket and, before he led her back through the keyhole in the walled hedge, he came close to her and kissed her fully on the lips. 'You are so beautiful, Kat. Don't ever forget it.'

'Oh shut up, you silly boy. Come on, let's go.'

CHAPTER 15

Feeding...

For the remainder of that week, the atmosphere in the ward reverted to some semblance of normality. Not in the everyday sense of the word - after all we were in a mental home - but there was a peculiar order of calm.

Liam reappeared the day after the big fight, sweetly subdued to everyone's huge relief, and victor-Frank conversely seemed much cheerier. As far as I was aware nothing was done about the incident. No punishments were given out to either of them. Liam, having lost the fight and with his subsequent loss of face, began to slow down; he'd lost his mojo and had stopped charging about so much. His engine had run out of steam. He lurched around furtively with a permanently dejected scowl embossed on his face like a hyena. His pride had been publicly popped, and like a deflated, neutered pussy-cat he limped about awkwardly, on the defensive. What was worse for him was better for us. He didn't realise it but losing the fight was the start of his recovery. As a result we all actually began - slowly, mind - to warm to him.

'Imagine if Liam had won the fight,' said Hal.

'Yeah, right,' echoed Matt, 'it would be chaos in here.'

'He'd be like a quasi lord of the jungle.'

'Don't even go there. It would have been a nightmare. It would have been all hail the great God Baloo!'

'We would all have had to jump on him.'

'Good 'ol' Frank, eh?'

'The dragon-slayer.'

'For sure.'

Frank's self-esteem had reversed, gone upwards, and he was now talking to and participating with the other patients. It was as if he'd woken up. It was extraordinary how that one brief incident, which had erupted in spontaneous violence and ended in three minutes, had completely changed both their characters. It was as if a transfer of energy had occurred with their blows.

As Matt and I looked at Frank pushing a fellow patient's wheelchair up the ramp, I whispered to Matt, 'Frank's become Liam and Liam's become Frank!'

It was a bit like Flann O'Brien's theory whereby, through friction, a part of one object becomes part of another and vice versa. And the fight, the exchange of molecules through punches, had clearly reversed both their moods, at the very least. Their thought patterns had been rearranged. One person's had calmed and the other's had excited.

Perhaps though, for Frank, it was actually asserting himself that had changed his perception of himself. Rather than being seen as weak and submissive, for once he had actually stood up for something. And that, as shocking as it was, had woken him up: to himself. Anger and violence were the balmy medicine to have shaken him out of his depression.

I remember actually seeing them meet for the first time since their fight, in the dining room the day after the scrap. The nurses were all on high alert, covering the encounter, but nothing happened. In fact, I saw them glance at one another, a shared look of recognition, which seemed to say, 'We've caused a stir, created a scene. Aren't we great? Ha! Ha!' God knows, life is so weird that they probably ended up as best mates.

It was then that Hal and Kat couldn't keep their hands off each other; it was pathetic! They had crossed a bridge. I got the impression the health professionals were not happy about their love affair becoming so public either.

I even overheard my favourite nurse, Josephine, the black African lady with the cute ankles, saying to Hal one of those days, 'Hal, you must play it a bit… cool, darling, with Kat. She's still in a vulner-able state, she's fragile, you both are. You know that, don't you?'

'Yes, yes, nurse, I know all about that, thanks.'

'No, seriously Hal,' she said, bringing him to. 'If you don't keep it under wraps they'll separ-ate you, d'you understand me? D'you get it?'

'Oh right, I see. That serious, ungh?'

He had finally acknowledged, at last appreciated, that there was a possibility that one or other of them might be moved to a different ward. They could be forcibly placed apart.

'You're not on vacation, you know. Don't forget that.'

'Quite, thanks, nurse. I won't.'

'Remember,' she said, wagging a friendly finger at him. 'This ain't no holiday camp.'

I didn't have to think too much about my grand hack at all that week; all I needed was a copy of the film footage of Hal's play from Matt. Everything was clear in my mind. The plan was to pre-program the whole sequence of the jam onto my laptop over the weekend. I would choose a good fifteen-second segment of the video footage from Hal's play, download it to my computer, and then line it up.

I had been mucking about in NASA's system for long enough to know exactly what I had to do and how to do it. I would rehearse it, run through every step of the way on Friday night and all Saturday, program the algorithms on Sunday, set the coding and the timing delay, and then just let the show roll. Press the Enter button and the interruption would run itself on the record mode I had formulated. I wouldn't even be anywhere near the computer when the lights came up – when, as it were, the show hit the road!

Hal and I were still on Sections. Which, as I mentioned earlier, were in effect restraining orders. This was going to be my get out-of-jail-free card if I needed it. I was going to be back in hospital by the time my little shockwave would be reverberating around the monster-machine that is the US and British intelligence services. On Monday morning, while I would be in bed, tucked up safely on my all-protective Section, the security services would be waking up to the realisation that they had been exposed and had been made fools of. At the time I realised that I might never know whether my little slap and tickle had even succeeded. There would be no way of finding out. I was never going to go into their system again. In fact I had determined that I would never hack again. I was not going to be a criminal who just had to go back to the scene of the crime. I didn't waver at all during that week. I was positive in myself, so completely sure I was doing the right thing.

It wasn't just for Hal, it was for me, too. At last I was going to showcase my talents to the world: to expose myself at the very highest level. I was calm and peaceful in myself, feeling better than I had ever felt, at ease. I remember that even in Art Therapy that week I was able to express myself much more clearly. I drew a complex, interwoven series of pipework, like a section of an oil refinery.

'Wow, that's amazing, Jonathan,' Hal declared, as we all stood around showing off what we had done at the end of the session.

'It's got a Celtic feel to it, really good,' Kat said.

'Yeah, man, like industrial Celtic knot-work,' Matt enthused.

'Mmm, yeah, it is like a modern maze,' Hal mused.

'Makes mine look like a piece of crap,' Matt muttered, holding up his multi-coloured drawing of a pistol. The gun had a pink barrel, a purple handle and a fluorescent green trigger.

'Hey, that's not bad actually. I like it,' I said. 'It's the sort of weapon a clown would use.'

'Yeah, that's what I wanted to say - "Guns are a joke".'

'I can imagine the barrel either flopping down or tying itself up in a knot.'

As the week crescendo'd a feeling of doom loomed. A certain knowledge that imminent change was in the air. This I could only put down to Matt leaving for good on Friday evening.

'Nothing stays the same, however hard we may try to hold onto it,' Hal said philosophically. 'You know, the horror of waking up in a mental home has actually turned out to be a life-enhancing experience for me,' he continued with a tear in his eye, although smiling.

'Me too,' I said.

'And me,' echoed Kat.

'Yeah man, you've got to make the best of it. There's always a silver lining out there somewhere, if you look hard enough,' Matt said.

'Yes, for sure, it doesn't have to always be watertight and lead-lined, does it?' Hal retorted metaphorically, confusing us all.

'For sure, keep the air in and let the juice loose.'

'Vive la difference. Hey, come on, it's time to do the final act of my play – well, my short parable really. It'll only take a minute. Get the masks, will you, Kat?' Hal declared, standing up.

'Oh, and Matt, get your camera, would you?' I added.

We were soon in the Drama Therapy room. It was a classroom, really. The therapist was there when we arrived, and had set up a block of scenery with trees painted on it which we hadn't seen before, and positioned some angle poise lamps to add a bit of atmosphere. We stumbled in, to be greeted as if we were real actors. It was all very professional. Hal handed out our pages of script, in a nice large font this time, which we looked through while he busied himself and rearranged things. Matt set up the camera on its tripod and reminded Hal how it all worked, zoom, etc. I snooped over too, and then we settled down, and Hal positioned us; the lights came on and it was… action again.

All is darkness. Lights fade up. It is the following day. Mother and daughter are cowering together in the open. There is a loud rustle in the undergrowth. We think the big cat is coming back for more. Suddenly Rex appears, looking exhausted.

REX

Oh, my dears, there you are. I've been looking for you everywhere. What are you doing out here in the blazing sun?

ISOBEL

Sit down, my darling; we've got some terrible news.

REX

What is it? Where is David?

ISOBEL

Sit here, sit down.

Rex sits and, from a bag, rolls before them a whole selection of fruits.

DOROTHY

I'm sorry, Daddy, it was my fault. I didn't listen.

ISOBEL

We were all just so weak, Rex, darling. I collapsed, the children were starving, all we had was that wretched tree to survive. Where have you been?

REX

So, the tiger snatched David?

DOROTHY

He saved my life, Father. The tiger was going for me and David stood in between and it got him instead.

ISOBEL

The children just got fat so quickly. The tree bloated them and made them lazy and sluggish, drugged. He couldn't get away.

REX (WEEPING)

I told you so, I told you. Oh dear, my son. I shouldn't have left you. It is my fault. The only thing wise about this tree is that it's wise to stay away from it. It should be called the Tree of Cleverness. It makes you selfish and lazy - not wise. I told you so, I told you.

They all hug one another. Lights fade.

The End.

The moral: 'If something sounds too good to be true, it generally is'.

Hal narrated the moral in a deep baritone voice.

'Hey, is that it?' Matt blurted.

'Yes, that's it,' Hal declared. 'Short but sweet. Well done, everyone.'

'But that only took a minute, come on! I was only just getting into it.'

Perfect, I thought to myself. *It couldn't be better.*

As everyone was chatting and packing up I casually strolled over to the camera and, unnoticed, pressed the Record button, peered into the lens with my mask on and recorded my piece to camera. I then casually ejected the tape and slipped it into my pocket.

Later that day the three of us gathered outside the ward when Matt's mum came to pick him up and, hugging him in turn, we said our farewells. We knew that it was pointless to exchange addresses and phone numbers as some people do on holiday. Temporary friends, thrown together by chance, with whom you promise to stay in touch with and don't. People you randomly meet who you share a wonderful time with but know that, back at home, it won't ever be the same. We just knew that it was going to be best to strike out on our own. None of us would want reminders of our time here. We subconsciously knew that in the light of day this was going to be an experience best forgotten – for all of us.

'Oh, hold on, Matt,' Kat declared emphatically, just as he was about to get in the car. She dashed back into the ward and reappeared moments later with his mask. 'This is for you.'

As we waved him off, my mum pulled up to pick me up.

'Have a good weekend, Jonathan, see you Sunday evening,' Hal said as we drove off.

PART TWO

CHAPTER 16

Deadwood…

'Sir, it's Lynne at the office, sorry to phone so early - we've got a problem.'

'Carry on.'

'It's best you come into HQ as soon as possible. Nothing major, not red. But we've had a rather disturbing transmission.' Lynne hesitated for a moment. 'It's going to cause rather a stir. You're going to want to be prepared.'

'Right, I'll be in in two hours, max.'

'No, sir, it's more important than that. I've booked the chopper, it's on its way; there'll be a car waiting for you in Battersea.'

'Oh Christ, my neighbours aren't going to like that. Anyway, what's the *something*, Lynne? Come on. We're on a secure line.'

'We've received a scrambled message, sir – well, a bizarre transcript - through the emergency channel from the Americans. It arrived two hours ago. Our communication system from the Americans seems to have been compromised, sir. We thought it best for you to be fully briefed before

Langley gets in touch with us. And you know what's going to happen then.'

'Yes, yes of course. Anything public?'

'Not that we know of, sir.'

'Okay, well done. I'd better get ready. See you as soon as poss. Send me a report now, to my phone, and call me immediately if there is any new info. I guess it'll be Burt Schneider from CIA who'll call. It's only two in the morning there. Look, if he does phone, tell him we are onto it and I'll be in touch as soon as I get to the office. Get the team together now – particularly Q. I want a briefing as soon as I arrive.'

'Yes, sir.'

Fifteen minutes later David Manningham, 'C' Director of SIS, MI6, was staring out through the helicopter window as it whipped him over the Thames, gunning towards London. He could see pleasure boats on the water below, ferrying passengers through locks, and motor cruisers passing under traffic-laden bridges. He could see sweeping lawns leading down to the river's bank, fringed in vast billowy willow trees. Millionaires' manicured riverside gardens, one after the other, were laid out below. Quintessential, genteel images of the English Home Counties displayed in perfect order. You could only appreciate this scene from above. On ground level all was fenced, hedged and out of sight. As the craft entered urbanisation proper David Manningham's attention averted from towerblocks to his mobile phone screen. He scrolled and began to read his PA's perplexing report on the first new drama of the week, and shook his head with incredulity.

Thirty-five minutes later he entered the hi-tech boardroom to be greeted by his senior management team.

'Morning, everyone,' he said, sitting down. He ignored all pleasantries. 'First things first. From what I understand we've received a very bizarre video clip through CIA's most secret communication channel showing three characters, with British accents – now don't laugh - wearing monkey masks and acting out some sort of play. Look, stop sniggering everyone, this is serious. Is this correct, Q?'

'Yes, sir. It is, I've seen it. It's a fifteen-second insert that must have been transmitted at precisely midnight in Virginia. All CIA information comes directly to us here at Vauxhall from a NASA-controlled satellite, Challenger. There is no possible interference our end. The compromise…'

'You mean hack?' Manningham interrupted.

'That sounds the most credible explanation, yes, sir.'

'Carry on.'

'The clip of video footage has come to us directly from the NASA satellite, no question about that. There is no relay whatsoever in between our dishes and Challenger. Just thousands of miles of air. Our dishes on this roof receive the information directly from that satellite. The CIA transmit information up to the satellite from their servers in Canaveral, Florida. I assume that whoever has sent this transcribe, which we presume are British nationals, interjected this footage at that point. That is the only accessible point. I can't believe there to be any possible breach-points between Florida and here. These are my primary assumptions.'

'How sure can we be that it wasn't our systems that were at fault?'

'That is one hundred percent, sir.'

'Double-check that for me, and then put it in writing, will you? I want you to categorically assure me that what we are about to see was received directly from the satellite, with no possible interferences from our end. Is that correct?'

'Yes, sir.'

'Okay, good. Let's view this nonsense. Lynne, roll it.'

With that they all turned to a large plasma screen behind their director. After half a minute of darkness the lights reverted to full brightness.

'Jeepers creepers, where is Richard?'

'He's in the field, sir, in Beirut, running the Syrian operation.'

After a moment of silence Manningham said, 'Okay, everyone, give me ten minutes and then we'll get on with the other business of the day.' Before David left the room he turned to everyone present in turn. 'When I come back, Q, I want you to have found out whether there is any way we can trace who did this. Brian? You look into it too. What we can see is that there are three males and one female, white Brits, in their twenties, wouldn't you say? They're in some sort of British-style school room. Get onto it, all of you, and find out where it was recorded and who the hell these individuals are. Lynne – get Burt Schneider on the phone for me, and recall Richard; he's been compromised whatever happens. Has anyone got any immediate opinions on this before I go?'

‘Well, my opinion, for what it’s worth, sir,’ said Rufus, one of the team, ‘is that it sounds like British Muslim extremists, sent through Fatah, sending us a coded warning about Richard Reed in Syria.’

‘Don’t, for Christ sake, get caught up in conspiracy theories at this stage. Keep an open mind. Thank you, ladies and gentlemen.’

A few minutes later, David was on the phone. ‘Burt, it’s David in London. So sorry to have to call you at this time of the night. Are you aware about the compromise that’s occurred this morning with Challenger’s satellite transmission?’

‘Yeah, I got a call an hour ago,’ Burt Schneider said blearily. ‘There was interference with data transfer and you guys received some unsolicited information, but we don’t know what. We are just checking it wasn’t a technical fault, that’s all. Whadda’ you know?’

‘It’s serious, Burt, your satellite and computing systems have been hacked into. We received a cryptic fifteen-second video clip of some kids in monkey masks, naming our main operative in the Middle East on it! I am going to send it through to you now via email. You must shut the satellite down, though, immediately. Your system is flawed at the very least.’

‘Hey, hey, buddy hold on. It’s four o’clock on a friggin’ Monday morning. Kids in monkey masks you say, shut down our satellite, you gotta be out of your mind.’

‘Burt, just see the clip. Get your guys to talk to Q here and in the meantime don’t transmit information through the satellite, that's all. Not to us anyway. I'm sorry, Burt, that's on the record. No more information is to be sent to British Intelligence through that medium.'

'Jesus H. Christ, Dave, gimme ten minutes, and I'll call you back. Has that email been sent?'

Eight minutes later…

'Dave, Burt. We've shut out the satellite. Now, we've gotta find the punks that did this and bust their asses. Who is this Richard Reed the monkey man names – tell me?'

David was taken aback at the ferocity in his American counterpart's voice. 'He's our man running the show in Syria, Burt. You met him here at Vauxhall last year. Dark hair, greying; he briefed you on Syria's history.'

'Yeah, yeah, sure I remember. Is this frickin' jihadeests we're dealing with? My gad, Dave, if those bastards have attacked our system this is a multi billion-dollar problem.'

'It's not just these guys, Burt, whoever they are, but if they can access your system so can the Russians, the Chinese, whoever. Look, let's not panic for now. Perhaps your boys can shore up the data protection system. Q is here in the office. Send over whoever you want from the Embassy on this. Report everything through Lynne at my office and really there isn't much more we can do for now.'

'Except catch those bastards.'

'Yes of course, we're all onto that. Let's speak again later when you get into the office. You'll know more then, and so will we. But, Burt, the point at which the hack happened, and Q here is categorical about this, occurred in Canaveral. So, that's the point which you need to work back from. Only you can do that from your end. Get your best guys onto seeing if that is the case and if you can trace the computer that did it, or at least its location.'

'Okay, okay, so is the scenario we are looking at now that some British kids did this on British soil, through our system?'

'That's correct.'

'I just don't believe it, Dave. That is one of the most sophisticated, secure systems on the friggin' planet.'

'Well, it's happened, Burt.'

'Okay, buddy, speak later, ciao.'

David Manningham recalled his team.

'Do we know any more about this, anyone? Q?' he said, looking around.

'Sir,' replied Q, MI6's number one technician. 'I have double-checked and there's no doubt whatsoever this transcript came from the satellite. No doubt at all. We've traced it and it's impossible that it could have come from anywhere else. Now, the only possible route to tracing the computer that did this can only be done by the Americans. All my team and I here can do is establish the source back to Challenger. It's a dead end from there for us, technically.'

'Okay, Burt Schneider is getting his guys onto it. It's only five a.m. in Virginia, so we'll know more later. All you can do for now is revive the traditional communication pathways. Speak to GCHQ. Brian – any updates?'

'No, not really, sir, we're scrutinising the clip frame by frame, my team are working through it all now, but nowhere has come up as a possible location yet. The voice recognition programme has only been able to tell us that all the voices are English in origin. And it's pin-pointing southern England by the accents.'

'Okay, that's something. Lynne, have you got hold of Richard?'

'No, sir, apparently he is either up in the Bekaa Valley or on the Golan Heights. He's away from HQ in Beirut for another three days, they think. The office there is calling him now and will get him to phone us on his satellite phone as soon as they make contact.'

'Bloody satellites, his voice will probably come in sounding like Mickey Mouse! Put him through to me when he does though, I'll brief him.'

'Yes, sir,' Lynne replied, smiling.

'Okay, what's next?'

CHAPTER 17

Nursery…

'Ouch, OUCH! Someone? Help, HELP…' yelled Josephine, the Guyanese nurse on secondment, from the floor beside my bed. And then moaned, 'Help me, help me.'

Oh, to hell with that, I thought. I scrunched up towards the partition wall to try and get back to sleep, pulling the duvet over my head, but her racket had made that impossible, so I sat up in my pyjamas. I saw that Hal had entered my cubicle and was now crouched down reassuring Josephine that everything was okay. It clearly wasn't. I could see she was clutching her ankle and I must say it did look decidedly distorted. Her foot was bent around ninety degrees. I realised what had attracted me to her ankles in the first place must have been because they were far too delicate to carry her weight. The math was all wrong.

Nurses arrived en masse. Heads peered at me from every angle.

'What's happened?' one said.

Josephine replied, through grimaces. 'He pushed me, and I fell. I was just trying to wake him.'

'I think you'd better get an ambulance, it looks nasty,' said Hal.

As she was in my way I couldn't even get out of bed to go to the loo so, comically, to the casual observer, I just sat up in bed like a bleary-eyed school boy while she moaned and writhed on the ground beneath me. Folk fussed around her until the paramedics arrived and stretchered her off. She became all delirious and really hammed it up, I felt, putting on some sort of fevered act, as if the world was ending: no restraint. Wailing and gnashing of teeth sort of stuff. I even saw her knickers during one particular spasm. They were clinically white, sadly beneath tights though, but it did add to the entertainment.

When she had been stretchered out of the ward a duty doctor arrived as I was trying to get dressed. 'So, what happened, Jonathan? I've got to do a report about this,' he demanded.

'I don't really know. I was asleep and she shook me and I told her to leave me alone, and then she was on the floor. That's all I remember,' I said, buttoning up my shirt.

The next moment Hal came to my recue again. 'I was right opposite when it happened, doctor,' he said. 'I could see the nurse shake him and I thought to myself she shouldn't be doing that. And when Jonathan woke up suddenly, and sat bolt upright, she just shot back and fell. Recoiled, she did. I guess she twisted her ankle. And that was it, Jonathan didn't touch her. I'll swear to that.'

Two days later, when I asked how she was, I was told that she would be leaving hospital that day but that she wouldn't be able to walk on it for six weeks. So, I had brought her work placement in a UK hospital to an abrupt end. *Oops*! I knew, technically, that her ankles were just not up to the job of supporting her body mass. I knew this was going to be a lifelong problem for her, unless she slimmed down a bit or got a pair of callipers.

That was Monday morning. It was a rude awakening. I had got back from my weekend at about five in the afternoon the day before. I had made a particular point of letting the nurses know I was back and I forced a chat with them, to drum the point home, in case they had to recall the event at a later date. I said I was feeling much better and I wanted a reduction in my medication, forcing them to make a note of it. Log it. All that evening too I made myself conspicuous. Joining in with conversations at supper, and I even clumsily kicked a football around outside for a bit; I was a veritable social butterfly! I wanted everyone to be able to recall that on that particular date if it was required that they could all say, *yes, Jonathan Runcorn was in Rooksdown Lodge that evening, for sure, I remember it clearly*.

I had, though, sat up late into that Sunday night alone in my cubicle, feverishly reading a crappy paperback I had picked up in the dayroom. I kept flicking my wrist to look at my watch. I was anxiously counting down to midnight, the take-off time I had programmed into my computer earlier that morning. And when, finally, the two hands met at twelve, the appointed moment had arrived. Click. *Doomsday*. Everything slowed down. I sighed and then eased my head back onto the pillow, slightly catatonic. I closed my eyes and internalised my thoughts. My heart was beating way too fast. I visualised the timer, activating on my laptop in the bag under leaves with a definite click, and then the piece of video footage was released from its starting block, like a horse race when the gates fly open, and it was off, charging. I imagined the footage, compressed, firing down the cables and squeezing its way through fibres and around loops. As the footage accelerated it would scrunch up and tighten further, concertinaing at checkpoints, and then spring forward again down different coloured cables, blasting its way onwards, looping ever faster, this way and that towards its pre-programmed destination and then… ping! I pictured the video clip of our play was suddenly radio waves blasting up to the starlit heavens, shooting above Florida's mangrove swamps as pink and blue beads towards the hundred and thousands of stars, only to reassemble into the outline of a man and then dive into its target and surf off Challenger's satellite's dish, like a snow boarder on a half pike. I could picture the information then fragmenting into a hive of gold and black bumblebees that formed a throng, and then they charged back down to our blue-earth orb from the dark universe. The swarm only began to mutate into faint images as it closed in on Europe. It became clearer over the British Isles, evident over England, and finally came into full-focus cine-film on reaching the bright night-lights of London. The stream of information hit MI6's dish, in my mind, like rain droplets, and formed a pool on its surface which was immediately sucked into and absorbed by the receiver as mercury is going down a plughole. I sat up. That was it, it was over.

I was enraptured. I didn't know and didn't care whether my master stroke had worked or not. In my mind it had. It was one of those moments, like when you look at something so beautiful it takes your breath away. I actually sat up in bed, short of breath, panting for quite a while. My heart was beating way too fast for its own good; it was thumping like a steam engine, so I got up, put on my dressing gown and slippers and walked, ghostlike, to the toilet. Everyone else in the dormitory was asleep.

It was my miracle. It was an earth-shattering moment for me. I had lived the hack in my mind. I had internalised the data's journey. I had programmed into the computer a snippet of a play, and sent it across the world, up to the stars and back down to earth again, and I had lived it in my brain. My brain had created the data's journey and I had willed it to its destination. I felt I had not only launched a bomb which was exploding as I pissed, but it had blown my mind clean apart too. My mind had expanded. Or perhaps it had been trepanned. I felt as if a hole had been bored into my skull which released an intense, geyser-like pressure. As I shook myself I felt as if I had cleared not just certain cobwebs from my brain, but a whole forest of cobwebs. My head was somehow fully rinsed, cleaned out. If you like, I was wide awake. I placed a hand on the cistern to steady myself.

There was no fear at all; I felt empowered, blessed, special, gifted and quite at peace with it all. I walked back to bed as quietly as I could, so as not to disturb anyone, and I could see Hal sleeping peacefully. I also sneaked a glance at the twinkling stars through the blinds before getting back under the cosy duvet. I can't remember what it was that I was reading but I had to force myself to concentrate, I do remember that. I read for quite a while longer before I could get to sleep. I held my cock tight to ground me. As a result, that was why I was not ready to get up for breakfast the following morning, when the accident with Josephine had happened.

The weekend I had just spent at home was nowhere near as strenuous as I'd thought it would be. The coding I required just flowed out of me. I wouldn't say it was one of the easiest things I had done in life but it certainly wasn't the hardest by a long shot. It was one of those activities you do in life where everything fits into place with the minimum of effort or fuss. As if it was meant to be. I had got home on the Friday evening, hung the mask Kat had given me in my room as a sort of talisman to watch over me, and started at the beginning. I used a secondary computer for this exercise and kept my primary one running, streaming a game. If there was any tracing or blaming I could demonstrate that I was only on that particular device, at that time, if need be. It was so straightforward to upload the footage and since I had been used to accessing NASA's system I was able to program in the access codes of where I wanted it to go and when, at what time and date, with consummate ease.

I then relaxed and forced myself to have dinner and chat with my mum. I was being absolutely professional and focussed about what I was doing. Looking back on it, I behaved as if I was cracking a safe: cool and calculated. I had my technical spectacles on at all times. I actually slept quite well that night and on the following day, Saturday, I had worked on the necessary algorithms to direct the clip up to the satellite. On the Saturday night I broke the nut that opened the pathway to access the streaming of my message onto the MI6 trajectory from the satellite, which was a huge relief. It was like grafting two plants together. That's what it was – a graft. Not a hack. I wasn't hacking away at anything, I was grafting, doing a delicate, precision implant. I really hadn't needed to do any more than that. All the links in the chain were already connected. MI6 would receive the information from the satellite. I had no doubt about that. The host trunk route would accept the clone, the freeloader. I knew there was no way MI6 would be able to trace my computer; that would have to be done by the Americans. I had given myself ample time to erase my cyber footprint. There was nothing I could see from the footage that would give me away; however, I knew the solids would hit the fan sooner or later. And after all, that was the whole idea. God only knew if they had the technology to trace me.

As a safeguard, over that weekend, I kept the computer game running and engaged in it on a regular basis. Sunday morning was just going through the coding again, check, check, checking, and then I checked and checked again. Once I was completely happy, which was after lunch, I surprised my mother by informing her that I was going for a walk.

'Oh, okay, my dear,' she said, a bit perplexed. 'Would you like me to come?'

'No, no, Mum. I'm only going around the block. I'll see you in a minute,' I said, slinking around the door.

There was a dense, wooded corridor that separated my housing estate from a main road. It was generally full of rubbish and was there as more of a sound barrier than a strip of green belt. When I could see there was no one around I dived into the undergrowth and felt my way forward through low branches and over tin cans and past a dumped shopping trolley. I scrabbled around until I found a suitable place to bury my bin-liner wrapped computer where no one was likely to tread on it, and interred it lightly under twigs and leaves. I had a small dongle attached to the USB which had enough power to transmit the signal which would release the code. The starting gun was programmed to fire at midnight, GMT. Once the battery life on the computer ran out, in forty-eight hours max, the device would be untraceable. Having buried the video cassette of the play's recording, I scurried back out onto the pavement, brushed myself off and went the long way home, up through the park.

'Johnny, loser – ungh, ungh, ungh,' I remember one of the local lads, who was at my old school, shouting out from the swings, as I skirted the green. I held my arm up with a clenched fist, for some reason, and walked on. I don't know what signal it sent out, something like a Che Guevara, comrade-type freedom fighter's salute perhaps, but I didn't hear another word as I hotfooted home.

'Nurse, sorry to bother you, I'm Joan Runcorn, Jonathan's mother,' I remember my mum saying, poking her head around the door of the nurses' office when we got back to the ward later that afternoon. 'I just wanted to let you know that this was the best weekend I have had with Jonathan.'

'Great, thank you for letting us know. I'll be delighted to add that to his file,' came a male voice from within. *Result*, I thought. Those brownie points and me going to ask for my medication reduction were the perfect notes to have on my record to cover my tracks. 'Oh, actually I see on his file,' the voice continued, 'that there is going to be a meeting on Wednesday afternoon to discuss Jonathan leaving hospital. Can you attend by any chance, Mrs Runcorn?'

'Um, what time is it?'

'Two-thirty, here in the ward. It's important you come, Mrs Runcorn. Dr Feltz was going to phone you about it tomorrow.'

CHAPTER 18

The Graft…

It took until lunchtime for David Manningham to hear back from his American counterpart in Langley, Virginia.

'Dave, Burt.'

'Burt, my friend, how's it going?'

'It's a friggin' nightmare here,' said the drawling middle-aged Texan. 'The system's down. The White House are spitting blood, you can imagine and, Jeez, everyone's scrabbling for someone to blame already! D'you know any more about who these punks are?'

'No, Burt, we don't. Not yet anyway. We have hypotheticals we are working on, but as I said earlier the only way we can trace the computer that this came from is if it's done from your end. Our vocoder analysis has said that the individuals on the video are all the English and white, and that the likelihood is that this was done in South of England, judging by the accents. I have guys going through the footage, frame by frame, in detail. So far, we've seen nothing to pinpoint a precise location. We've had some of your local, technical guys here all morning, looking at our dish on the roof and our receiving equipment.

Q has categorically assured me that the information definitely came from Challenger, no questions. That is where the hack occurred; only you guys can tell us from where.' Manningham squirmed as he swapped the receiver to the other ear. 'Did the White House see the clip, Burt, the monkey play?'

'Yip,' Burt sighed. 'I heard it was like having goddam apple pies thrown in our faces, friggin' humiliatin' I can tell ya.'

'I can imagine, totally humiliating.' David Manningham grimaced with embarrassment. 'On a more positive note, Burt, what I can say with some assurance is that this is the first incident of compromise we've had since the system was set up four years ago. I've got my team going through all recent transcripts to check if there have been any other causes for doubt, anything we've missed, and, thank God, nothing has come up. We've had nothing to alert or concern us up until now. This is the first glitch. I really don't know how long these elements, and others, have been monitoring the transcripts you've been sending, that's the big question. And again, unfortunately, only your guys can answer that.'

'Yeah, yeah, we're on to it. We've got a whole friggin' battalion of boffs on the case. It's pandemonium. What about this Richard Reed?'

'He's out in the field, and hasn't called in yet. But we're pulling him out, just to be sure.'

'Jesus, David, we're going back to the friggin' Stone Age for a while.'

'We'll all be using Morse again!'

'Ha, ha, and Pony Express!'

'Well, talking to one another for a change is one good thing, at the very least! Anyway, if these breaches help make the new technology more secure then we've just got to bite the bullet, and take it on the chin. A learning curve.'

Burt Schneider became serious. 'No, no, David, that's not good enough. The government here want these punks strung up,' he asserted. 'We don't like being made fools of, do you understand me? We want to make an example of these people. Whoever has done this is going to spend a long time in the pen. We've got to put a halt to this sort of shite.'

'Well, whatever, Burt. The fact is that your system of delivering top-secret information can be accessed and interfered with by any old clown by the sound of things – and let's be frank about this, we should want to know if that is the case. I would prefer to know we have a problem, not hide it. Do you hear me, Burt? We are furious this end, too, believe me. Think about it – ask yourself if these punks, as you call them, can interfere with, let alone monitor, our communications, then who the hell else can?'

'Ugh, yeah, okay, Dave, I know. But get this - these guys will be caught. We need to demonstrate that we can at least trace who did this. We've gotta find the perpetrators of this crime wherever they are. We will track them down. They cannot be permitted to run nor hide.'

'Yes, of course, Burt, we are doing, and will do, everything we can to get to the bottom of this, but we must be assured, going forward, that our lines of communication are secured.'

'A hundred percent, Dave. We're shittin' our pants over here wondering who the hell knows what. It's a friggin' nightmare. Has your press got onto it?'

'No, not yet…'

'I'll call you later; the Vice President is on the other line.'

'Okay, Burt, good luck.'

David Manningham stood up from his desk and turned to look out through the green-tinted, floor-to-ceiling windows behind him. He stared across the tide-rushing, murky Thames towards Victoria, wiped his forehead and buckled; he stumbled momentarily. He was absorbing the potential implications of this horrendous breach in security and thoughts flashed through his mind about what and who else in his organisation had been compromised. David had rapid-fire, flashing images of every worst-case scenario possible. What activities he was involved with were known about, and by whom? He was forced to place a hand on the window pane to steady himself. He stared, fixated by the constant stream of anonymous traffic crossing Vauxhall Bridge directly below: *Which other of my agents around the world are exposed and on the verge of being assassinated?* He felt his head pulsating, and it was as if his actual cranium which contained the brain had turned to rubber.

Manningham wiped another glistening drop of moisture, which had formed in ripples on his forehead, through his greying hair as his phone buzzed.

'Sir, I've got Richard on the satellite phone, do you want to speak to him?'

'Yes, yes, put him though,' he sighed, and picked up the receiver. 'Hello, Richard, how are you?'

'Fine, gov,' Richard said loudly. 'Pressing ahead. Bloody shambolic though. Is something up?' In return David's voice went up a notch.

'Yes, I'm afraid there is,' he replied. 'You have got to get out of there and back here to HQ, PDQ. Do you hear me? You've been compromised.'

'Eh!' A brief silence. 'Can you tell me more, sir?'

'No, I'm afraid I can't. We're on code red. Just get back to London as quickly and safely as you can. Do you hear me?'

'Yes, sir.'

'Look after yourself. Your station is aware of your position and we are arranging suitable transport for you from Beirut. Get back to your station immediately.'

'Yes, sir. Roger rog, over and out.'

Manningham didn't put the receiver down but called straight through to his PA.

'Lynne, inform all stations, and I mean all stations globally, that we are on code red and to act accordingly until further notice.'

'Yes, sir.'

'And call a meeting with the brass here in my office in ten minutes. We'd better get on with other business. It'll take our minds off these shenanigans, if nothing else. Oh, and Lynne, be a darling and get me a coffee and a bun, would you?'

'Of course, sir.'

***

Richard Reed ended the call with his superior in London, pushed the aerial into the body of the mobile phone and zipped it into his cream safari waistcoat pocket. He was positioned with a small convoy on the outskirts of a Lebanese Druze village, deep within the Bekkaa Valley, not far from the Roman ruins of Baalbek, high up in the Shouf Mountains. He had been scouting defensive positions near the Syrian border under the guise of the United Nations but was actually planting and establishing moles, informers, all along the mountain ranges. The informants were mostly local officials who required financial incentives and satellite phones. He was four days into his six-day reconnoitre when he stood on a dusty lay-by, looking back down at the azure Mediterranean Sea glistening in the far distance when he received the bombshell phone call from David Manningham. *Act in haste, repent at your leisure*, he said to himself, twice. He stared at a young boy herding his goats in the foreground, their charming bells chiming out through olive grove in which they grazed. This pastoral scene mesmerised him momentarily as he focussed his mind on what he had to do. The air was clear, there was even a glazing of snow on the highest peaks above him, and he could just smell faint wisps of orange blossom on the soft spring breeze. Fruit blossom was the delight and pride of this valley. All was calm and clean and peaceful around him but Richard was now in defensive mode, deploying his intuition to enable the securest exit strategy he could imagine. His unruffled exterior belied his furious paddling, like a calm-looking swan battling against a raging current.

He had often bought Lebanese marmalade up here to bring home as gifts and had planned on doing the same on this trip as well as buying a case or two of fabulous red wine from Musar up the road. *Fuck it*, he said to himself. And then called out, 'Abdullah, come here. Bring the map.'

When his Arabic translator approached they both crouched in the dirt and laid the map out on the ground.

'You and I are going back to Beirut immediately. I am going to send the other two vehicles ahead to Musar,' he whispered.

'Yes, boss.'

'Right, get in the passenger seat and plot the best route back. I'll drive.'

'Yes, boss.'

Richard Reed stood up and went back to the three white vehicles, emblazoned with black UN livery, with small blue flags on each offside wing mirror.

'Number two, here.' When his field assistant approached Richard continued, 'Right, Steve, I've just received a call from the last guy we saw, Bint Ali, who wants to tell me something important, in person. So Abdullah and I will go back and you lead the other vehicle up to Musar. We will meet you at the winery in three hours, is that clear?'

'Yes, sir, but are you sure that's safe?'

'Just do as I say.'

'Yes, sir.'

Richard hopped into his vehicle and, as he waved the other two on, he said, 'Abs, check the pistols, keep them handy,' to the loyal assistant sitting beside him.

He then swung his vehicle round and eased off the lay-by with the minimum of dust.

CHAPTER 19

Root Stock…

I understood my whole chapter at the hospital was coming to an end. It was shutting down. I was ready for it. The days when you're locked up in mental institutions for years and left to rot were long gone. Bums on beds are an expensive business. Getting people home as quickly as possible and then giving them as much out-patient care as need be was the deal. I knew that. And the important factor which had been established, to ensure my maximum compliance of course, was for me to be suitably medicated: to well and truly ensure that any chemical imbalance I had remained totally neutered.

I had been in hospital for six weeks, which was a long time then, and Hal was just starting on his fourth, so he was just coming to the end of his twenty-eight-day Section. Mine had been extended.

That month-long, lunar cycle, makes you begin to forget where you've been and is a crucial point in time in which you are on the cusp of becoming at home in your new environment, which in this scenario was highly undesirable.

In my case I had crossed that bridge and had really become institutionalised. And I'd had enough.

To some patients these were the happiest days of their lives. They met like-minded people for the first time. Madness was entertaining. That's what it had been like for me to begin with. Suffering the frustration of long hours of loneliness at home may have been the fundamental cause of my mental distress in the first place. Idle days on your own are long and hard, and often boring. People sleep too much in these situations or watch too much television or sit on their computers and therefore have an excess of energy stored, bottled up in the system which when released, can erupt in chaotic behaviour. People on their own retreat into their imaginations. It is company that we all need to keep in check. Being alone, on our own, for long periods of time is a challenge and takes discipline to harness. I felt most of us in Rooksdown didn't have that self-discipline, both physical and mental, to manage ourselves properly alone, and therefore, left to our own devices, we were the sort of people who would easily slip back into bad habits which resulted in our ill-health in the first place. In a lot of cases it wasn't rocket-science. It was simply a case of circumstance. There was no need for therapy or long-term medication. It was a matter of breaking the cycle and creating healthy lifestyles.

Hal came up to me as I lay, now dressed, on my made bed. 'Hey, Jonathan,' he said, 'they've called a meeting with me and my mum for Wednesday afternoon about me going home at the end of the week.'

'Me too.'

'Oh, yeah. They're obviously having a collective cull. Do you want to go home, are you ready?'

'Yes, I think I am.'

'They're trying to get shot of us all at the same time.'

'Out with the old and in with the new. Time for us to get out into the real world.'

'What are you going to do, Jonathan?'

'Well, I'm thinking about doing an Applied Mathematics course in September actually,' I replied. I didn't know where that came from.

'That'll be a great start. You know, getting yourself into a routine for a bit, without too much pressure. It will be so good for you.'

'Yes, that's what I am going to do. And you, what will you do? Wow, I was a bit startled. I didn't have a clue where that revelation appeared from.

'Well, what they have just said, as part of my conditions for being released, is that I will have to live with my mum for a bit. Which I am fine with, and then I thought I'll go to London and see if I can stage any of my plays. But no rush.'

I could see him looking at me differently. After all, I wasn't the poor, inferior gibbering deviant that I was yesterday. The internal combustion that had gone on inside of me the night before had given me a new status in the world. I could feel it. I had actually stepped out of the closet of fear and had exposed myself. My coup, if I could call it that, had elevated me to being more of an equal. As he scrutinised me closely, in my new light, sitting on the edge of my bed, I in turn looked directly back at him, unwavering, no more eye-fluttering, and thought about how his father and his MI6 cronies were waking up to the realisation that Hal was in some way involved, if not responsible, for the infringement of their security system. Images of frantic phone calls between suited men in America and suited men in London in real time flashed through my mind as I looked at him. As long as I shut my mouth Hal could just plead innocence. His father, who was my target, was going to look at his son in a whole new light. When the dust inevitably settled Richard Reed would be forced to have respect for his offspring. This was my goal, my thank you to Hal, for giving me the confidence to be myself at last. For his father to look at him eye-to-eye.

'How's Kat?' I asked as I got up from my bed, unable to cope momentarily with the thought that my hack hadn't worked.

'Oh, she's good. I think she's finally realised how serious her own problems are. She's been pleading to go home and she did put in a big effort over the weekend to eat normally-ish.'

'Oh, that's good. Have you told her you're leaving?'

'No, I haven't. I'll tell her later.'

'Will you see her when you leave?'

'I hope so,' he replied. 'I hope it works out. Come on, let's get outside, it's depressing in here.'

And so we padded along the carpeted corridors and slipped out the front door as quickly as possible to avoid any possible mayhem.

'Phew, that's better,' Hal said as soon we hit the fresh air. 'It's so stuffy in there. It must cost a fortune to heat.'

The fresh air was a relief, a big relief. Just being in the great outdoors, breathing fresh air and hearing birds chirping, was exactly what I needed. My work, my obsession with computing, had really removed me from feeling like a living human being at all. I had, up until that point, been scared of nature. It's true. I had felt alien to it. My parents never walked or gardened or did anything much outside. I had been brought up devoid of any connection with nature. I constantly benefit from walking to this day. I solve problems with the rhythm of pace: both mathematical and personal. I have absolute confidence that each footstep I take brings me one step closer to the truth. Walking is a great combination of being able to get lost in thought and having to construct what is in front of you. It is not necessarily walking through a particular problem, solving it; it is walking out problems, too. Your feet know exactly what to do. We were born to walk. Our eyes simply guide the feet, allowing our minds to do the roaming. Something beautiful or new always catches the eye and brings you gently back to earth however often you beat the same path. Nothing is coarse in nature. Appreciating the tiniest of natural events engenders a feeling of wonder. To do the same walk every day of the year will never bore one; there is always something fresh to see and discover.

And so we walked. We crossed the main road onto a rarely used overgrown footpath around the fields. The rapeseed had lost its brilliant yellow flowers and was now a mass of stringy, bean-like plants. We were silent, lost in our thoughts. Looking back, I am surprised that the realisation of what I had done didn't make me any madder, or more paranoid. I not only lacked any anxiety about the consequences of what I had done, or thought I had, I was positively at peace with what I had done. That is, of course, if the hack had actually succeeded. I guess that's the beauty of youth; there's no fear at that age, in your early twenties. The hack was like a trial of manhood to me, a rite of passage. It was something I had to do. If I had just thought about it and done nothing, it might have made me more impotent and less confident. I was now a man of action as opposed to being a theorist. Frontline soldiers are invariably between the ages of eighteen and twenty-four for that very reason – at that age, young men are fearless. We get softer as we get older. And here I was pleasantly ambling around the countryside with my hands outstretched by my side, brushing plants as I walked like a human jet-fighter.

Even then, as I followed Hal - perhaps it was his aura wafting back over me - I determined I would make it up to the powers that be. I had definitely resigned myself to that. If the security services had only employed me, not just to check their system but to have actually built the system in the first place, then what I had done could never have happened. It was their amateurish system that I had exposed, not the other way around. In my mind I had proved my intellectual superiority in no uncertain terms. In hindsight, and with many years of water under the bridge, I am still proud of my achievement. All that I required then, at that point in time, desperately, was confidence in myself, and that act had achieved that goal.

All it took were a few words of encouragement from the right people to give me reassurance that I had a value. Hal had given me personal validation that I was a likable human being and my hack had given my intellect the assurance it needed to give me the confidence to make something of myself. To believe that I could do it, and not just could but had; I had actually done it. No one could ever take that away from me. I had had an effect. I was sure it had worked. I had the utmost belief in the accurateness of my computing abilities. The only thing I lacked was self-discipline.

As I followed Hal along the green lane, one outstretched hand sweeping the foliage as I passed, I smelt nature, heard the chirping around me and felt the warmth of the sun penetrating my skin. I had a seminal feeling of inner peace. I kept sighing. The swirling numbers I couldn't avoid seeing until so recently had vanished. It was as if each exhalation I took was an exorcism of sorts. My madness, my insecurities were evaporating with every breath I took, releasing the years of doubt out into the bright blue order. Every step and breath I took was leading me to a better place.

I had a Forest Gump moment; I could have just kept going. I could have followed Hal forever. I remember thinking I could have just walked and walked, or run and run, and therefore it was tough to hear him turn and say, 'Time to go back now.'

As he looked at me and I at him, squinting in the brightness, we both knew that it was the last place we wanted to go back to. We had had our bellies full of Rooksdown. It was another moment of healing where we knew our time had arrived to leave hospital, to move on. I said nothing. We trudged back to the ward dragging our feet, heads bowed.

And now, all these years later, back at the hospital where it had all happened, I put my dog on his lead and crossed the road and went up that same path. I still had a little time before I had to catch my ferry. All was just the same, except now a dense crop of barley had replaced the rapeseed. That was all that had changed. A mere crop rotation. The fact that the countryside, the land, was just the same crystallised certain memories. In many ways time had stood still. A cloud passed under the sun causing an ominous shadow to sweep over me. I took it as a sign. I didn't walk any further; I turned back.

CHAPTER 20

Specimen…

Richard Reed drove smoothly but aggressively. Although he was in hostile territory, and didn't want to seem in any way desperate and attract attention to himself, he wasn't going to stop for anyone or anything if he could possibly help it. A solitary UN vehicle on these roads was not normal. Peacekeepers travel in convoys. He handled the heavy estate car well. The completion of a number of pursuit driving courses had paid off; he was enjoying himself. He got particularly thrilled from occasional corners, when he could double-declutch on approach and then perfectly execute a smooth rear-end slide with the hint of a squeal and puff a bit of dust as he accelerated away.

After an hour of motoring down mainly pot-holed, narrow mountain roads Richard Reed and Abdullah arrived at the large mountain village of Chemlan. They passed a basic garage on the outskirts. Richard turned around and went back to refuel, purposefully pointing in the opposite direction in which they were heading: a precautionary measure.

'You do the fuel, Abs. Keep it friendly, and say we are going up to Chemlan. Oh, and don't forget to tip the man.' Richard wanted to stay close to his weapons. It was a tribal, lawless area. All warring factions.

When the vehicle had been filled up Richard leant out of the window, waved and called to the attendant, '*Shukraan*, thank you.'

He drove up the road, spun the vehicle around and started back down the way he'd come. As he passed the petrol station he glimpsed the attendant stop outside his booth. *Oh, shit, he's recognised us*, he said under his breath. Although he then saw, in the rear-view mirror, the man shake his head with bemusement, Richard felt impelled to speed on in earnest. He was pretty sure the attendant wouldn't notify anyone that he had seen a rogue UN vehicle heading down the mountain behaving a bit oddly. *But you never know*, he said to himself. *Better safe than sorry*. He now took reckless overtaking chances one after the other, relying not just on his skill but on his guardian angels too. Abdullah scrunched up silently beside him, tight in his seat, flicking his worry beads furiously.

An incident-free hour later the mountains eased into rounded lowland hills, adorned with squat oaks, juniper and the occasional cedar. Between bends in the road and flickering gaps in the trees they glimpsed a vast coastal plain stretched out below, which reached towards a long sandy belt that fringed the sparkling blue Mediterranean Sea. They swung around corners and rose up to higher ground before the car dropped down again. They knew Beirut sat on the far horizon to their right, engulfed in a brown haze of smog one and half hours to the west. All traffic had petered out.

'Sir, we will come to the Druze checkpoint soon,' Abdullah said.

'Yes, I know. It's lunchtime. I hope the buggers are sleeping. Get some cash handy, just in case.'

'Yes, sir.'

Richard slowed for a moment as he reached down under the steering column and released a pistol, a Walther P99. Flicking the safety catch, he stuffed the gun roughly into the back of his trousers. As he sped on he felt cold steel uncomfortably pressing against his backside. Ten minutes later the car dropped to completely level ground. The road was empty and they could see a makeshift barrier ahead. Richard slowed again and came to a halt beside a flimsy sentry booth.

'Marhabaah, hello,' he called out, as a young armed guerrilla appeared lazily from the shade within. 'Mabsoot? Happy?'

'Where have you been?' the sentry replied snootily, sneering defensively at the foreigner on his land.

'We have been assessing medical needs for your villages,' Abdullah replied, pointing back and holding out official papers.

'Open the boot,' the youth demanded. And, having spat on the ground, he called out for his fellow guards to join him.

Richard Reed and Abdullah got out of the car into the oppressive midday heat as two scruffy individuals appeared from the darkness of their shed.

Richard joined the group at the rear of the car but stood back, positioning himself to get a commanding a view of the whole situation. As Abdullah opened the boot he was shoved aside rudely by two of the men who were desperate to rummage. One guard stood aside holding his semi-automatic loosely with one hand. The two intruders quickly opened the first flight case they came to, revealing half a dozen neatly stacked satellite phones.

One of the lads picked one out, held it up and cried out, 'Ah, medical supplies, eh!'

The alerted lad with the machine gun moved in to peer. When their excited talk began to have aggressive overtones to it, Richard instinctively knew this was not going to be a jaw-jaw situation. *There's no way on earth they are going to let us go now*, he thought. The phones were too precious to leave in their hands, and he was in no mood to begin negotiations. He looked to his left and to his right. The road remained empty in both directions. *Right, time to get the hell out of here*, he said to himself. He fake-yawned and casually began to scratch his head with one hand while the other went for his backside. He reached under his gilet and pulled out his warmed-up pistol into the light of day. In one smooth action his gun-arm swept around his body so that both hands united in front of him to meet and clasp the pistol's butt. With his arms outstretched he was straight down on one knee and began firing at the tight cluster of young men. He fired at each in targeted bursts. Head, body, head, body. The moment Abdullah heard the familiar crack, crack, of close-range gunfire he instinctively shut the boot and scrambled into the passenger seat. The boy with the machine gun took the first two bullets from behind. One, two, thud, thud; he went down like a Coldstream Guard fainting on parade. Another three shots slammed into one of the other young men, making him contort violently; the third youth managed to get cover from the car and then dashed towards the hut, out of Richard's line of fire. Richard got to his feet and cautiously moved the few paces towards the vehicle, picking up the dropped phone as he went. He checked that the boot was firmly shut and then rapidly got into the vehicle, started the engine, revved hard with one foot on the accelerator pedal and the other on the brake, and then, when the wheels were spinning wildly, he released the brake and the vehicle shot forward, bursting through the flimsy wooden sentry barrier. It fell away like balsa. Richard darted a glimpse in his rear-view mirror and saw the two corpses lifeless on the ground behind as a great cloud of sand rained down over them.

'It is the Hezbollah sentry up ahead soon, sir. They won't have heard the shots, though,' Abdullah informed his superior when they'd cleared danger.

'I'm not taking any chances this time, my friend.'

Five minutes up the empty-of-traffic-road, they could see a similar setup to what they had just left: a shack and a makeshift pole across the road. Richard slowed; all was still, apart from the faint blur of a lorry in the distance coming out of the heat-haze, approaching the check-point from the opposite direction.

When they were fifty metres from the barrier Richard said, 'Hold tight.' He double-declutched, chucked the vehicle into second gear and slammed the accelerator pedal to the floor. As he did that a solitary, bleary-eyed sentry appeared from a palm-fronded canopy beside the road. Richard's hefty car – again - smashed through the wooden pole. The cracking timber exploded like gunshots. The roll bars withstood the impact as they erupted through the checkpoint, and as splinters flew around them, Richard Reed could see the guard recoil in shock to his right.

The car careered dangerously forward, swerving violently, just avoiding the oncoming lorry. Bullets began to pepper the vehicle. The thud, thud, thud of the impacts seemed innocuous enough, like small stones hitting the bodywork, but when one shell hit the rear glass panel the interior imploded, and shards of glass splintered all around them. They were then flying free, out of range. Richard sped on furiously towards the nearby main road running parallel to the coast, towards Beirut.

Without looking Richard said, 'All okay, Abs?'

There was only a muffled groan in response. Richard looked beside him and could see Abdullah, slumped and turning grey. He immediately pulled over on the first hard-shoulder of the busy main road he came to. With his hazard lights blinking, he ran to the rear grabbed the First Aid box and came around to the passenger door.

'You've been hit,' he said.

'Yes, sir, on my shoulder. I think. I am okay,' Abdullah managed to say feebly, before going catatonic and collapsing into shock. Only his seat belt kept him vaguely erect.

Richard quickly opened the box, took out a syringe and an ampoule of morphine and proficiently injected Abdullah in the arm.

'You'll feel better in a moment, just relax now. I'm going to get you to a hospital very soon. Don't worry, my friend.'

Richard then grabbed some coats and jackets from the back seats and propped his local guide up as best he could. He was then back in the driver's seat and gunning down the highway towards Beirut, one hour in front of them. Richard could see a railway track running alongside the beach and then they passed the pretty little cemetery of British war dead from the Syrian campaign in 1922 he regularly stopped at. He put his foot to the floor.

The traffic began to concertina as they approached the city's outer limits. Richard relaxed slightly now, less concerned about assaults as differing factions controlled the city's suburbs and Beirut had up to a thousand UN vehicles on the roads. There had been no incidents of aid vehicles being attacked within the city limits for months.

He honked and shoved the vehicle forward with everyone else past the heavily guarded airport and then onwards downtown. He was familiar with these main roads and knew exactly where the hospital was.

'Are you okay, Abs?' he asked, regularly.

'Yes, sir. I am fine,' Abdullah would reply dreamily.

'Stay with us. That's an order.'

'Yes, sir.'

An hour and twenty minutes after their last incident, when his loyal guide had been shot, Richard Reed swung into the hospital forecourt and pulled up abruptly where the ambulances arrived; leaving the car door open, he rushed inside. Minutes later he was back, accompanied by two hospital porters and a wheeled stretcher. Having carefully lifted Abdullah onto the framework he impressed on the porters Abdullah's name and then leant forward over his colleague. 'Don't worry, dear friend. You are in hospital now, you will have the best treatment available. I'll see to that.'

'Inshallah, God willing,' Abdullah muttered, before being rushed away.

Richard got back into his dusty, bruised vehicle and injected himself back out into the streaming traffic. He knew the doctors and surgeons would look after Abdullah as well as in any facility in the world. Gunshot wounds were the most common admissions to Lebanese hospitals, and had been for many years. The staff would know exactly what to do. He would put in an official call to get Abdullah the best treatment available as soon as he got back to base.

Fifteen minutes later Richard swung in and halted at a sunken garage door that led into MI6's underground car-park beneath an innocuous block of apartments. He buzzed the entry system, said his code word and eased his car into the cool, dark earth.

CHAPTER 21

Hybrid…

Hal and I crossed the road and approached Rooksdown Lodge. I was determined that this week I would be Captain Sensible. The incident with the nurse twisting her ankle a few hours earlier hadn't started the week off on the right… footing. I was not going to give my consultant or the nurses any other reason whatsoever to keep me here for a moment longer. I had to go. This was going to be my last week at Rooksdown, even if it killed me. I was better, after all; I had recovered from my illness. This wasn't the right place for me any longer. I was on the path to wellbeing and happiness. I was ready for the world.

When Hal and I entered the ward itself Kat was there, waiting for Hal, glowering at the top of the corridor. Her voice had taken on a different character. 'Where have you been? I've been worried about you,' she hissed.

'Excuse me?' Hal replied, slightly taken aback. 'We've just been for a little walk, that's all.'

'Why didn't you ask me to come?'

'You were in your dormitory, hon. We didn't know what you were up to.' He held out a conciliatory hand.

'Oh, right. It's like that, is it?'

'Don't be silly, Kat, come on. Hey look, let's make a cup of coffee and go outside, I've got something I want to tell you.'

'I don't want one.'

Hal took her hand anyway and led her across the way into the kitchen. 'Do you want one, Jonathan?' he called back.

'Ungh, yes, please,' I replied, to Kat's obvious annoyance, as she huffed.

We stood around in the bare, utilitarian kitchen, brutally exposed under the glare of strip lighting, waiting for the kettle to boil, shuffling about awkwardly.

'I'm going to have a herb tea, I'll just go and get a bag from my locker,' Kat declared, and disappeared momentarily.

'I've got the funny feeling she's not going to take the news of you leaving very well,' I said.

'Mmm, I think you're right.'

When we were all brewed up, I held up my mug and said, 'I'll leave you two, I've got something I want to do. I'll see you in a bit.' I sidled off to the smoking room.

Liam had re-emerged from his catalytic chrysalis and was now so heavily sedated that he lurched and stomped about like a drunkard. His club foot combined with his numbness resulted in him being constantly off-balance. When he went to move he'd lean forwards and then thrust off as if he needed some sort of propulsion just to walk. The result was that he'd stagger forward in a rush, thumping the ground hard. We could hear him coming a mile off, thudding down the corridor as if was a runway, with duty nurses padding in his wake. He had, though, calmed down considerably, no doubt being suitably sedated, but he simply didn't have anything to say. He'd look at us menacingly one moment and then helplessly the next. He really didn't have a clue what was going on. He was on auto-pilot.

Bizarrely, though, when I entered the room I discovered he'd buddied up with Frank, his assailant, and they now sat together for hours with the radio on seeing who could be the first to guess the name of aired songs.

'Proclaimers, *Walk Ten Thousand Miles*,' one of them would exclaim, to the opening chords.

'No, Pretenders, *Brass in Pocket*,' the other would cry out.

This would go on and on and then they'd sing along, completely out of tune, if they remembered the lyrics. The fight they had may have been a cover for them wanting to hug and kiss each other, I don't know. It did cross my mind that they might declare themselves to have fallen in love, but the thought of these two monsters embracing was too much even for my imagination.

They were there when I entered the room, doing just that, competing to name the song. I pulled an armchair to the back of the room where I could look out of the window at the bench and sat down. I could see Hal and Kat turning to face each other. Then, I assume, he told her the news that he was expecting to leave at the end of the week. She turned away from him, facing forward, and bowed her head. I think she began to shake. Hal rubbed her sagging shoulders. She turned to him, desperately reached out and clutched his neck with both arms wrapped tightly around him and began exclaiming. He looked uncomfortable. I couldn't take being nosy any longer so I got up and walked out, leaving my mug on the window sill to a chorus of, 'James Brown, *Sex Machine*.'

'No, Bowie and Jagger, *Under Pressure*.'

I went and lay on my bed, but the minute I stretched out a more paranoid imagination kicked in and I immediately got up again. I couldn't cope with it, I had to keep moving. I was hot, very hot. *Phew*, I said to myself, and, when I got outside, *that's better*. Hal and Kat were sitting in silence on the bench.

'Hi,' I called out. 'It's Art Therapy time. Shall we go up?'

'Yeah, great. Come on, Kat, let's go and do some drawing,' Hal replied buoyantly.

'I don't want to.'

'Oh, come on Kat, it'll be good for you. It'll be fun, come on,' he urged, now up on his feet and holding out a hand.

'Don't tell me what'll be good for me, leave me alone,' she replied, getting up. She brushed past me and stamped back into the ward, leaving us both staring awkwardly at her dramatic departure. We got up and left, walking glumly up to the main aching body of the hospital, towards the art room.

'Did you tell her?' I asked

'Yes, I did, she didn't take it well.'

'What did she say?'

After a short silence he replied, 'She said, "I've got nothing but you, now."'

'Coo-wee, that's a bit heavy,' I said, looking around at him. I could see he was chilled, in shock, seemingly reeling at the implications of his new responsibilities, not his privileges.

'Yeah, I told her she just had to get well, play the game here and as soon as she can demonstrate that she is healthy she will go home too, it's simple. Just behave normally and you go,' he said matter-of-factly. 'And I told her that there is no way I am going to be a nurse for her, worrying about her. She can't just get well for me, as I can't for her. I dunno, but I don't want to stay bogged down in her problems, dominating our life.'

'For sure,' I said, lying. I would have swallowed loads of her shit just to get in her knickers. The truth was I was still a virgin. I had heavy petted once, when I was about seventeen, with the daughter of a friend of my mother's from church. I had gottten hard but she wouldn't let me put it in her.

To get well for someone else was always going to be a tricky thing: a potential burden-shift. If Kat got well for the love of Hal then what would happen if their relationship broke down? I assumed, by the look on his face, that was what he was thinking. She might well revert to being ill again and blame him for her illness. Any little argument and the default card would inevitably be laid down. Maybe she was even starting to do this already? Getting better for someone else is shaky ground for a stable recovery. Suddenly I was happy to be on my own. Love is a responsibility, though, I guessed; you have to care about the person you love more than yourself. Their wellbeing is your wellbeing. You have to nurture the recipient of your love through good times and bad. But how far do you go? I guess tough love needs to be part of the equation. Bad habits have to be broken for the benefit of all concerned. You can't let dependency perpetuate and imbed itself too deeply. You have to break the cycle. I certainly wasn't ready for any of that.

It's somehow easier to blame someone else for your problems rather than take responsibility yourself. It's the same for all of us. Particularly at the age we were then - early twenties - our parents were the obvious targets for our problems. But as you get older you just have to shed blame in order to move forward, unencumbered in life. It seemed as if Kat was crying out for a father figure. Someone to guide her through life. "'I've got nothing but you, now.'" Ouch, heavy, man. That was a burden alright.

We clattered on through the swing doors and into the main institution's cold passageways. We wove our way around to the art room as quickly as possible, passing the moaning geriatrics quivering in doorways, lost in their world. What tragedies had befallen them I couldn't guess at, and these individuals were probably unable to remember what the causes for their incarceration were in the first place. Our villa ward, set in the parkland, was institutional, yes, but this, the asylum, was something else entirely: something from the past, and very scary. A gothic nightmare scenario. Only a few weeks previously I'd thought that this could be my fate but that day I knew it would never be.

That week, I focussed harder than ever on my drawing. I needed to forget myself, my surroundings and the shockwaves I had caused the night before for Hal. I couldn't look too far ahead or my brain began to turn to jelly, thinking about the different possible outcomes: the possible effects of what I had done. And the worst of all was none at all.

As a result I drew great 3-D blocks with holes in them. Well, it was more like three mice getting into different pieces of cheese. I enjoyed sketching and colouring in the overlapping smoothness of Cheddar, the holes for Emmental and veins of Stilton. I drew the mice getting from A to B down corridors of colours to the prizes, the cheeses. When we reviewed all the pictures at the end of the class, the group of ten were all most amused and entertained by mine.

Hal was silent and distracted and not surprisingly drew two figures in grey monotone colours. They were ghostlike. Like sculptures on a windswept beach. One of those figures, I remember, was a lot smaller than the other. Perhaps one was in the distance, I wasn't sure. I hated seeing Hal glum, it confused me, and I remember beginning to resent Kat. I thought she was starting to be a drain on him. Sapping his vitality. I know that three is a crowd, but back then I didn't even consider that I might have been the gooseberry in their love affair. She wanted him all to herself; that was obvious to me now. Okay, I was socially inept, I knew that. It had only been Hal's arrival that had stopped my decline into going beyond eccentricity towards madness proper. But even now I'm not good in general company. Anything work-related, I am fine with, but it can't be purely social. I could really have done without Kat making me feel inadequate. Anyway, I asked the art therapist if I could take my two recent pictures away with me as I was going home. And as I rolled up the two similar pictures I had done that week and the last one of the tubing I glimpsed Hal quietly pin his up on the wall.

'God, roll on the end of the week,' he said as we broke back outside.

'Yes, I know. It just seems all so pathetic now. I feel like a child,' I said.

'Yeah, it's like being back at nursery, a primary school, but without any lessons. It's a reversary!'

CHAPTER 22

The Clone…

Richard Reed hastily parked his battered vehicle in the hermetically secure underground car-park. He dashed up to a third-floor apartment via the service staircase and, heaving hard, entered British Intelligence's operations centre in Lebanon and the Levant, including Syria, like a dervish. This residential apartment covered as an office and was permanently manned by two Middle Eastern ladies Richard knew well. They could tell that the man who burst in, clearly in the last stages of an adrenalin-fuelled rush, was exhausted.

'Sit down, sir, let me get you a glass of water,' Fatima, the elder of the two ladies, said calmly, getting up from her desk.

'Thanks, Fatty,' Richard wheezed, collapsing into the chair in front of her. Having caught his breath and guzzled the clear liquid presented to him, he pulled out a satellite phone from one of his khaki safari jacket's pockets, and dialled.

'Number Two, it's me, Number One, are you receiving?'

'Yes, sir, loud and clear,' replied Steve, Richard Reed's lieutenant up in the mountains at Musar.

'Good. Listen clearly - I've had to come back to Beirut.

The girls in the office will fill you in when you get here. Return to HQ immediately, as quickly as you can. Do not, and I repeat do not, go down through Chemlan but go over the top passes and across through The Cedars. Those checkpoints have been covered. Do you hear me?'

'Yes, sir. Return to HQ via The Cedars.'

'Precisely. Good man. Safe journey, over and out,' said Richard, hanging up.

'Sir, please,' Fatima insisted. 'Put on the local dress which I have laid out in the first bedroom on the left, right now, and then go straight downstairs. Darwish is parked outside, waiting for you. He will take you to the St. Georges Club. Go straight to the bathing area. At the end of the jetty you will find a red speed boat with the engine running. It will take you out to a waiting naval vessel in international waters. I believe you are going to Cyprus and then back to England from there.'

Without hesitation Richard obeyed, thinking, *Christ, they're not taking any precautions. It must be serious.* He reappeared moments later wearing a flowing jalabiya complete with a black and white Palestinian headdress, a keffiyeh, with an ornate gold threaded headband.

'Very good, sir, go now, sir, go-go, quickly,' Fatima urged, trying to usher her boss out of the apartment as fast as she could.

'Hold on, Fats, hold on, my dear,' Richard pleaded as she tried to close the door behind him. 'Abdullah has been shot.'

'Oh, God, no!' she exclaimed, stopping and opening the door wide.

'Don't worry; I think he's going to be alright. He is at the AUH on Cairo Street. Make sure he gets the best treatment. Do you hear me? The best treatment. Whatever it costs. Do that now. Promise me? You may have to go down there in person.'

'Yes, of course, sir. Don't worry. I will do that immediately,' she assured.

'And you heard me on the phone. Steve and the crew are coming back from Musar now. They are going the long way. If they are not back in six hours, maybe seven at the very latest, call him. Prime Hamza and his team that they may have to - and I stress, *may* have to - go and search. You can track Steve's convoy's progress through Sat Two. Are you clear?'

'Yes, sir, all clear.'

'Good girl, and now...' He leant forward. 'Give me that kiss you promised.'

'I promised you no such thing,' she retorted. 'But... ' she added, softening, shifting her hijab to one side and offering a cheek, '... you can give me one.' She took Richard's warm embrace with a smile. 'Now, go, go, you silly man, go.' And he went.

Outside Darwish, one of the firm's regular drivers, was waiting in a familiar old Mercedes, smoking a cigarette. As Richard calmly got into the back seat Darwish flicked his butt out of the window and pulled the car smoothly out of its bay and into the residential street. They were soon back in the hubbub of downtown Beirut, honking and jostling with the rest of the traffic. As they edged forward down Hamra Street, Richard passed his favourite bakery where he often bought manoush on a Sunday morning to help his hangover, and then they eased past his much-loved Chinese restaurant, and finally his bar of choice, the KitKat. He loved this ancient city, and had spent many years over the past twenty-five within its noble walls. Some of the best times in his life had been spent here. When he first came to Beirut in the early 1960s it was known as the Paris of the Middle East: the smartest and most cosmopolitan city in this region by far. Now, however, it was a bullet and bomb-ridden shell of the place he had first encountered. Everywhere Richard looked he could see pock-marked buildings, shot out through nearly twenty years of civil war. The chic had become moth-eaten, the charm had faded and the glamour gone. *But still*, he thought, *this city's blood runs with soul.*

His car swung briefly onto the lower Corniche. The vaulted road floated effortlessly above the speckled Mediterranean Sea. It curved and swept Richard down, around and onto St. George's Marina and past St. Georges' Hotel; soon they were pulling up outside the shabby waterside colonial clubhouse. He strolled purposefully through the entrance and along the main musty corridor and breezed out into the sun towards the canopied jetty. There, waiting for him, was his launch purring warmly and frothing in the Bombay Sapphire gin-clear water.

'*Kaifa haluk, Mabsoot*? Hello, how are you?' Richard said, as he untied the mooring rope and hopped aboard.

'*Alhamdulillah*,' replied his pilot, turning towards Richard as his booted feet hit the deck.

The boatman immediately pulled on the throttle and the craft broke out into open water.

'*Ala mahlak*, slow down,' Richard said. The pilot responded immediately and eased the vessel to a more sedate speed. 'That's better, my friend, no panic.'

Richard sat back facing the fast-shrinking Middle Eastern capital, the pearl of the Middle East. He gazed, long and hard, at the Chouf mountains in the distance, and wondered. That was Richard Reed's form of prayer: wonder. For brief moments, like now, he felt entranced. He could do that with people too. He could gaze at them, as opposed to looking or staring, and see right through them, into them, and somehow, in his mind, rearrange them. He now willed his being to penetrate the view. The far peaks were a strange sour green colour under the livid sky and the gulf between the sea and the rough cedar-coated hills on the purple horizon felt eternal. It was as if he surveyed two worlds, one on top of the other. The city with its modern apartment and office blocks, combined with minarets and steeples, was in the foreground and then the unspoilt mountains loomed in the background, on another plane altogether. It had been a long day, and it had started up there. Richard mentally tried to point out to himself, on the distant snow-capped mountain range, exactly where the spot was at which he had received the message to flee from his superior in London only four hours previously. But he couldn't find it. He shook his head.

Lebanon was one of those rare places on Earth where you can, with ease, water ski in the morning and then have a leisurely drive up into the mountains to ski on snow in the afternoon. This wasn't one of those balmy days of pleasure for Richard, though. He was still, just about, energised on adrenalin but he knew that he was exhausted to his core. At nearly sixty years of age he concluded, there and then as the craft bobbed on the waves, that his ability to withstand the sudden stresses of his job was utterly depleted. There is a clear distinction between a pressurised job and a stressful one. His was definitely the latter. He felt drained, mentally exhausted. He had killed two men that day, and a third, his friend, was fighting for his life. He didn't know how he'd get over the shock of this one. He shuddered, and removed his disguise.

The boat was now bouncing hard, out in a choppier sea. Richard turned to face forward and saw a small gun-metal-grey pencil mark scratched onto the horizon. The squiggle slowly formed into the outline of a small naval cruiser. A single shaft of smoke, heading skyward, plumed gently from its centre.

***

At nine o'clock in the morning, three days later, Richard Reed arrived at MI6's offices in London's Vauxhall. He was welcomed warmly by Lynne, David Manningham's PA, and ushered into the slick boardroom.

'Can I get you a coffee, Richard, or something else?' she asked.

'Thanks, my dear, a coffee would be lovely. White with one.'

He sat alone and in silence for the few minutes before Lynne returned with a tray holding two cups and a cafetiere. She placed it in front of him as David Manningham rushed in behind her.

'Richard, great to see you. You obviously made it back safely. Well done, old boy. All okay?' He came up to Richard and they heartily shook hands and patted shoulders.

'Well, I guess so, David, if you can call it that,' Richard replied. 'Anyway, tell me – what the hell is this all about?' he enquired, sitting back down.

David Manningham placed himself beside his old friend, compressed the plunger and poured their coffee.

'Well, now that the dust has settled a tad, and we have come to terms with what occurred, we - and I say we, the Americans and ourselves - are slightly less panicked by what happened on Sunday night, early Monday morning, GMT. Basically, Richard, the supposedly one hundred percent secure satellite communication system between us and CIA got hacked into. And some information was transmitted by the hackers which named you.'

'Oh! Have we found out where it came from?'

'No, we haven't pinpointed exactly where it was and, by the sound of things, the trail has gone a bit cold. We assume it came from the UK, somewhere in southern England, but we have no verification of that. Only the Americans can supply us with that information, if they can – the breach happened through the conduit hub in Florida apparently. That's where the information is sent up to the satellite from. We just received it here but the actual breach happened there. So it's up to Burt Schneider and his team to supply us with that information. Do you remember Burt?'

'The name rings a bell. Was he the big ex-Vietnam General whom you got me to brief on the Middle East a couple of years ago?'

'Yes, exactly, that's him. It was actually last year. Well, anyway, we received this fifteen-second video clip. I mean it seems like some ruddy kids larking around to me, but when it mentioned your name, alarm bells rang and you know what the Yanks are like. It was panic stations; you can only imagine.'

'Mmm, all guns blazing, eh.'

'Exactly, complete mayhem. Obviously, we don't know who the hell else could hack, receive, divert or monitor our communications. That was the main concern, but it seems as if this was an isolated incident, a one-off. It is a major flaw in the technology, and, frankly, fucking embarrassing for all concerned. Disgraceful. Shocking. However, the people that did this must be some bright sparks, that's all I can say.'

'Can I see it, David? This video clip?'

'Yes, I've got it teed up for you,' David Manningham said, as he fumbled with various touch screen buttons. And then, huffing and puffing, he picked up a phone in the centre of the table. 'Lynne, be a darling and get in here and run this wretched hacking footage for Richard, would you?' He turned to Richard. 'Fucking technology. I can't work it out for life of me.'

Soon Lynne was dimming lights behind her and leaving the two men alone in relative darkness. The amateurish fifteen-second clip faded up and ran. Richard Reed could clearly hear what he thought was his son's voice. '"If it sounds too good to be true, it generally is."' The clip ended with someone's face pressed close to the screen, a monkey mask on his head, saying "'Wise up, Richard Reed, or else.'"

Silence.

'Here, shall I play it again, Rich?' asked David Manningham.

'Mmm, okay then. Well, please, yes. Okay, do,' mumbled Richard. He couldn't believe what he was seeing or hearing. *It can't be*, he said to himself.

'Any ideas?' David said at the end of the second screening.

Richard sat in stunned silence. The next two thoughts that came to his mind were: *Thank God it's dark in here*, and, again, *It can't be*! 'David, sorry, play that one more time for me, please,' he said, trying to sound assertive and buy a bit more recovery time.

At the end of the third viewing Richard was in no doubt that it was his son's voice that he had heard. But he couldn't comprehend it. He was getting thoroughly confused. Sitting in the security of darkness David Manningham finally declared, 'So there it is.'

'Clearly,' Richard muttered feebly

'Now you have it.'

'Mmm, I guess so.'

'Well, have you got any ideas, Richard?' David Manningham said, getting up and switching up the lights. 'Christ, are you okay, dear man? You look ashen.'

'No, I'm not, David, I feel bloody awful,' Richard said in a croaky whisper. 'I'm sorry, David, I don't know what's come over me but I've got to go. Please ask Lynne to get me a car… now.'

'Yes, yes, of course, hold on. Take it easy, old boy.'

David Manningham immediately left Richard slumped and reeling in the boardroom.

'Jesus, Lynne, Richard needs a taxi immediately. Get one outside Reception. And help him downstairs, would you, I don't know what on earth's come over him,' David Manningham said to his PA, out of Richard's earshot.

'Yes, of course sir. Did you tell him about Abdullah?'

'No, I didn't have time.'

As he said that Richard Reed appeared the doorway, looking on the verge of being violently sick.

'I'll call you later, David,' he managed to say before tottering out of the office suite; swaying shakily, he headed towards the nearest toilet. Lynne followed, having ordered the car, and waited for him outside the Gents. She could hear him retching within. It took a couple of minutes for him to reappear.

'Have you got me that car, Lynne?' Richard said, relatively composed, having washed his face and smoothed his thinning, fast greying hair.

'Yes, Richard. Let me help you down.'

'No, thanks. That is very sweet, but I'll be fine.'

And he was gone through the double doors. David Manningham stood back in the entrance of his office and saw Richard stumble forward. He raised his eyebrows and shook his head.

CHAPTER 23

The Sapling…

I clearly recall that the final week at Rooksdown was painfully slow going. The atmosphere had completed its transformation from being the sort of one-big-happy-family type vibe when Hal had been admitted to one fused with tension. All of a sudden it felt like we were in a deportation centre. There were no outward signs of the cause of anxiety, but the ward had the sort of feeling that you have when you know you are leaving somewhere, going on a trip, where the bags are packed, the house is in order but you are an hour ahead of yourself and you just want to get going. You end up pacing around, worrying about what you have forgotten. It was that sort of an atmosphere, a sort of strain. We sought sanctuary in our limited routines.

Hal was still the first up, as usual, and did his dawn walks. I instinctively woke up when I heard him dress but when he left the ward I didn't bother to watch him anymore, I just rolled over and went back to sleep. We were drifting apart before the event of saying goodbye had actually occurred. Like a relationship that's run its course. You end up strangers.

I remember the weather being lovely and warm, which contrasted with the gloomy atmosphere inside.

At breakfast Kat had moved on to a bowl of fruit salad, which wasn't a great leap forward; it was still pitiful to watch her struggling with food. She was furtive and conscious of people watching her spoon as she laboriously chewed one of the easiest dishes on the planet to consume. Hal, I could see, tried equally hard to ignore her. Eating being like a religion for her made it hard to avoid staring at her as she was in raptures over basic foodstuffs that we all shovelled down. Pineapple seemed to make her blink as if she were having visions, apple made her fingers twitch as if she were composing a symphony and bananas made her toes curl within her slippers. It was as if she could feel every mouthful she consumed penetrating her whole system, entering her bloodstream and actually affecting her consciousness. It wasn't a taste sensation so much as she seemed to feel the effect of nutrition on her body immediately. It was incredibly peculiar. *Christ, she should be a nun*, I thought, *or a Buddhist monk religiously masticating a tiny bowl of rice in some remote temple or another.*

She had gone off me, though. Big time. I could tell our relationship had soured. I think it had been okay when I hovered about awkwardly. She could cope with that. Me being a freak, a novelty, somebody to have sympathy for. But now that I had acquired my newfound assuredness it was a different matter. And when Matt had been around there were four of us, she was outnumbered by men three to one, but now the odds were a little more in her favour. I was the sore thumb, basically.

Competition for Hal's attention. After breakfast I would sit on the bench in the rear garden in the sunshine with Hal as he smoked, chatting normally – and she didn't like that. She'd sit on the other side of him twitching nervously, constantly crossing and uncrossing her legs.

He talked blithely, ignoring her. 'You know,' he said. 'I've been mulling this story over in my head. It's a play more than a short story. It's about this old guy who falls on hard times and ends up in a council house on an estate. He's posh, well, actually more intellectual. It's a hard environment and he's resented to begin with. But, in time, the locals accept him and he educates their children on the finer things in life, like different cultures, beliefs, the arts and philosophy. He imparts the beauty of language and the benefits a wide vocabulary has in helping to express yourself clearly. He really makes an impact on the kids and their parents for the better and the community begin to respect and, to a degree, revere him. Then an incident happens and it all goes wrong.'

'It sounds like it could be Jonathan in the future,' I recall Kat quipping - to herself. 'Come on, Hal, let's go for a walk, you and me,' she said, snatching his hand, trying to pull him up, smiling invitingly.

'What sort of incident?' I said, trying to ignore her.

'Come on, Hal, let's go,' Kat urged.

'Oh, okay, I'll tell you later, Jonathan,' Hal said, submitting to her goading, getting up and virtually being dragged off by the victorious Kat, who gave me a glancing sneer as she led her reluctant prize away.

I sat back on the bench, closed my eyes and pictured them going off, over the hill and far away. In my mind's eye they'd crossed the main road and were out in the fields. Hal managed to free his hand from Kat's vice-like grip. He slowed down and dawdled.

'Come on,' she pressed, and then added teasingly, 'Don't you want it?'

'No, not really Kat, I don't actually,' he replied. 'Sorry, hon, I'm just not in the mood right now but I'd really like to chat with you.'

'Oh, bore-ring,' she said.

I visualised her reaching that gap in the hedge, where she waited for him to catch up. When he arrived she immediately darted through the foliage and held out a hand for him to take and follow, which he hesitatingly did. On the other side, straight away, she lay down and stretched out enticingly on the field's grassy border. She did look lovely, he must have thought, as he stood over her fit frame, but he didn't say so. No. Instead, he sat down beside her and stared at the dense and healthy new barley crop in front of him, rustling in the gentle breeze.

'Lie back, Hal, it's so nice.'

Reluctantly he inclined back onto one elbow and instinctively began to gently rub her stomach with his free hand. How could he not?

'You know I'm leaving at the end of the week, don't you?' he said.

'Yes, and I am too.'

'Well, that's not for definite, is it?'

'Yes, it is,' she replied.

'Well, I'm just wondering about the future, that's all,' he said, choosing his words carefully. 'And about us.'

'Oh come here, you silly boy. That'll all be fine, you'll see,' she said, taking his hand from her tummy and placing it on her breast. 'Just love me.'

'But Kat, you haven't even asked where I am going or what I am going to do.'

'I don't care,' she said dreamily. 'I just know we're going to be together forever.'

The last words made Hal freeze, instantly sending a chilled message through his fingertips to her heart. It went unheeded. She plucked his limp hand up again and virtually yanked him down towards her waiting lips. He kissed her feebly as she plunged her tongue into his mouth frantically. He tried to reciprocate; to make it genuine.

'What! Don't you want me now?' she said, pulling back at the rejection moments later. 'Now that you've had me, that's it, is it?'

'Don't be stupid, Kat, calm down.'

'Don't call me stupid, you bastard. You're just like every other man.'

'Hey, hey, hey – Kat, please. Stop it,' he said, recoiling in shock. He put a hand on her shoulder to stop her from getting up. 'Stay here, let's talk, take it easy, come on.'

'No, *I will not*, why should I stay with you? You shithead,' she replied, struggling to get up.

It was his turn to hold her hand tightly now.

'SIT DOWN,' he ordered.

Stunned, she obeyed. No one had ever shouted at her before - ever, she realised. It was just what she needed though. Dynamic breath and high frequency vibrations to shock her back to a more reasonable reality.

She sat back down, pulled her knees protectively up to her chin, and scowled like a spoilt child. He gently rubbed her back and shoulders soothingly as they sat in silence; only the faint rumble of a lorry on the road beyond reverberated through the ground, and a busy blackbird squawked at discovering a newfound threat to its nearby nest.

'Sweetheart,' he said. 'I'm worried, that's all. Believe me, I want our relationship to last.'

'No, you don't.'

'Yes – I do,' he said. 'Look, just so you know, I'm going to live with my mother for a while, which is part of the conditions for me leaving. I'm fine with that but it will mean I won't be able to visit you here – you know that, don't you?'

'Mmm, I guess so.'

'And when you go home it will mean…' He hesitated.

'Mean what?' she said, turning her hurt face towards him.

'Well, it means we have got to…'

'What?' she insisted.

'Take it easy, go slowly – that's all we can do.'

'No, no, I can't do it, Hal, I can't,' she said, suddenly pleading and clutching his neck, weeping uncontrollably. *Oh, shit, man, this is scary*, he thought as she cried freely, wetting his collar. He put both arms around her and held her tight.

'It's okay, it's okay,' he whispered.

Kat looked up at him pleadingly when she had calmed somewhat. Her bloodshot, doey eyes demanded affection. She suddenly darted forward and began to try and desperately snog him again. He hesitated for a moment too long. She recoiled back in abject rejection.

'You fucking bastard,' she yelled venomously. 'You don't love me at all – do you? You never have and you never will.'

She jumped up as Hal gawped up at her, stunned. She dashed towards the gap in the hedge and just before she dived through it, she turned back to him, steel-like, and hissed coldly, 'Fuck you.' And she was gone.

I pictured Hal being left bewildered, alone in nature's glorious solitude, embraced only by the sun, the singing birds and the buzzing bees.

I got up off the bench and was hovering around the corridor waiting for Hal to return when I saw Kat rush up in an angelic fury. Like a cherub that hadn't got the cream. A spoilt sight. I stood back against the wall to let her pass.

'You're a fuckwit too,' she said to me, as she thumped by.

Crikey, what happened there, I thought, slightly amused. And then went outside to see where Hal was. I paced around under the wretched pines, kicking their crispy fallen needles into shapes, and then all of ten minutes later I saw Hal appear, slouching towards me. He looked drawn. All he said as he passed was, 'Have you seen her?'

'Yes – she's gone up there.'

'Good,' he said.

I followed behind him and saw him stop at the nurses' office. He knocked, put his head around the door, and as I passed, I could hear him say, 'Can I speak to someone, please?'

And then he went into the office and closed the door behind him. I hung around, of course, waiting for him to reappear.

This was the point at which I clearly remember starting to have serious panic attacks; surges of anxiety started to crash over me like great breaking waves, crushing me. It was similar to getting caught in the undercurrent of a riptide. I would have terrific mental jumbles which would then just flatten out, leaving me winded, like I'd been washed up on the beach, gasping for breath. I was starting to see the potential repercussions of the chaos I may have caused. And again, I was on my own with no one to talk to, no one to tell. No problem shared for me, no problem halved, nothing aired. These sorts of head rushes began to happen when I was alone. I remember desperately needing company to avert the paranoia I was feeling. This unexpected drama with Kat and Hal was the trigger which made me freak out at the thought that, if what I had done had succeeded, then the weight of the British and American establishments, the gathering cavalry, would be massing and soon would descend here, on the ward. The cops, the arrests and the press would all add to Hal's stress, which is the last thing on earth I ever intended or wanted.

I knew that the battery life of my computer, loosely buried in the woods, would have expired days ago, making it untraceable, but all the same the message on the hacked clip was crystal clear. I began to have desperate regrets.

Hal reappeared from the nurses's office twenty minutes later looking a bit better. He rescued me from myself, again, in the corridor.

'Are you okay, Hal?' I asked in a sensible fashion, much to my relief, as I felt so damn crazy inside. We walked out to the front lawn bench for him to smoke.

'Well, I have just told the staff all about me and Kat, for the record. I'm worried about her, Jonathan,' he said, as we sat down and he lit up. 'I shouldn't have let myself get so involved. I thought we were good for each other but now I don't know. I just don't know.'

CHAPTER 24

Withering on the Vine...

Richard Reed had made it down to the car pick-up point outside Reception and stood there unsteadily, not knowing which taxi was his. *It's like fucking Piccadilly Circus down here*, he said to himself as Lynne arrived at his side, and helped him towards the car she had ordered. MI6's office resembled a busy cosmopolitan hotel with a dozen executive cars jostling to get in and out. Lynne told the driver the address as Richard slumped in the back.

'Thanks, my dear,' he said, opening the window. 'Let David know I'll call in tomorrow, I'm absolutely shattered. I'm so sorry, I'll be alright.'

He couldn't believe what he had just seen and heard on the amateurish video clip. He thought his mind was playing tricks on him. Due to that shock he could no longer assimilate any facts. A mental drawbridge was going up. Nothing more was allowed to penetrate the keep. His faculties were shutting down.

As the car swung out around Vauxhall Cross and headed over the Thames, Richard opened both back windows to let cool gusts of air flow in, in the vague hope this would revive him somewhat. It didn't work, so he sank back in the plush black leather in a catatonic state, staring glumly at the back of the driver's. The car soon pulled up at his grace and favour flat in Pimlico, just over the river.

'Can I help you in, sir?' the driver asked, seeing Richard stumble onto the pavement and fumble for his keys.

'Don't be bloody stupid, man,' was Richard's terse response. He groped his way up the few steps to the front door, unlocked it and tumbled into the corridor. Slowly he climbed the two flights of stairs to his safe London bolthole.

Richard had hardly slept at all since he had received the call on his satellite phone up in the Shouf Mountains informing him to repatriate immediately. He staggered into the sterile, characterless apartment, struggling to comprehend that he had been compromised by his son: *his own son*. He was used to dealing with the unexpected but this wasn't remotely on the scale; in fact it was completely off the radar of all probability.

He went straight into the bedroom, closed the curtains and sat on the edge of the bed in darkness with his head in his hands. His mind was reeling. He kicked off his city shoes, undid a few buttons and lay back on the bed fully clothed. He was asleep before his head got anywhere near the pillow.

Eighteen hours later, at five o'clock the following morning, Richard woke up. It was Friday. He drew the heavy curtains open and was greeted by the enduring civility of a whitewashed stucco Regency terraced street. This was what he enjoyed coming back to London, central London, for. It had an unparalleled quality to it that Richard, at his age, was beginning to appreciate more and more. It was sedate and it was civilised. The sight calmed him as he recalled all that had happened that week. He could see a clear blue sky above the buildings and shafts of dawn sunshine breaking through sharply onto the houses opposite. He blinked at the bright pink light refracting back at him and then frantically straightened his hair in a desperate attempt to humanise the haunted reflection he glimpsed looking in at himself on the window pane. He then turned, slipped on his shoes, picked up his keys, grabbed his coat and immediately headed out.

He swung his cream mackintosh on outside as he walked, and inhaled the crisp spring air deeply, wishing to clear his head from his epic sleep. *Phwoar! That feels better*, he said to himself. He exhaled steam-jets out into the capital's still morning as he strode with purpose. He turned onto Ebury Street to be greeted by urban life kicking off in earnest for another busy day. Red double-decked buses moved freely and bin-men whistled as they slung yesterday's detritus into the back of a lorry. Richard walked into the nearest newsagent, which was more of a convenience store, and picked up a broadsheet and then a pint of milk from the fridge.

'Good morning, sir,' a friendly Asian voice said, when he had reached the counter.

'Hello, mate,' Richard replied. 'Just these, oh and a bottle of Jonnie Walker,' he continued, trying to sound casual, pointing at the bottles of spirits on the shelves behind.

Without any questions the man behind the counter put the bottle of whiskey in a paper bag, placed all three items in a plastic bag and took the notes Richard was handing to him.

As he returned the change the shopkeeper said, 'Have a nice day.'

To which Richard replied, 'That's very kind of you, but I've made alternative arrangements!'

The jest seemed to fly right over the newsagent's head. P*erhaps he'll get it when he thinks about it later*, Richard thought. He walked the long way back to the apartment, part training, part enjoyment, through a cobbled mews, unreservedly admiring the aesthetic pleasantness of England. However, he realised he only really appreciated his home country for a period of weeks before its stuffy class structure and the high cost of living ground him down. Very much like the way he only treasured Great Britain's green and pleasant land when he came back from a hellhole. He couldn't live here. He often laughed that the only exercise he got in England was marching to and from cash-point machines. It wouldn't take long before he would be forced to fly back to his only home on the Eastern Cape in South Africa. He could afford to live well there, but not here. MI6 didn't pay a great salary and didn't have a pension scheme, which made him unable to enjoy a decent standard of living in UK. The perks weren't bad but the actual salary was lousy. Also, Richard liked the tension of the third world, which South Africa gave him. He liked danger beyond his doorstep; it gave life an edge and he thrived on being security-conscious. Added to that fact, *of course*, was the weather, he thought as he pulled his coat collar up. He had lived and worked for so long in the tropics that he couldn't bear the long gloomy months of British winters… and summers.

As he tottered over the cobbles thoughts of what he had seen and heard at the office the day before came juddering back. He shook his head in incredulity. He tried to get the words out of his mind. *If it's too good to be true, it probably is.* My own son had compromised me. *The little shit*, he said to himself, rocking his head. He didn't know whether to laugh or cry out loud.

Back at his flat he made fresh coffee and watched the news. The familiar vagaries of the BBC's global viewpoint amused him that morning. But if he had to live for any length of time with Aunty's agenda, with its liberal, left-wing and in his mind, wishy-washy viewpoint being rammed down his throat, it would annoy the hell out of him. Wherever he was in the world he was always running into their self-important journalists; after all, there were over eight thousand of their employees out there in the world, so it was virtually impossible to avoid them. *All of them being paid royally by the tax-paying majority to talk to half-baked minorities*, he said, laughing to himself.

He poured a large tumbler of whiskey, took a long draught and sighed with a growl as the fiery liquid burnt a passage down his throat and exploded into his stomach.

Before he knew it, he had drunk a quarter of the bottle and washed it down with a strong cafetiere of coffee. *I'd better go and have a shower*. It was only seven thirty. *Boozing at this time of the morning, how very African*, he said to himself, and smiled.

The cascading water created negative ion'd purer air to breathe and when he stepped out he felt instantly revived, re-invigorated and… well, horny. He always had the clearest thoughts in the shower.

He was soon back out on Ebury Street and hailing a taxi.

'Chelsea Harbour,' he said, as he tottered into the back of the black cab.

Richard Reed let himself into one of the riverside blocks and went up to the fourth floor. He opened the apartment door quietly with his key and, as he entered, called out, 'Coo-wee! It's only me.'

A fully flustered Sandra appeared half-naked, wrapping a dressing gown around herself. 'Rich? What are you doing here?' she said.

My God, she looks rough in the morning, he thought, *without her war paint on*.

'Who's that, darling?' echoed a male voice from the bedroom.

Both Richard and Sandra froze as a swarthy man, younger than Richard himself, barged his way into the corridor, buttoning up a crumpled shirt.

'Richard, when did you get back? Why didn't you tell me?' Sandra pleaded.

'You,' Richard said as he pointed menacingly at the confused man. 'Get your kit on and fuck right off.'

'Do you know who this guy is, Sandra?' the younger man blustered, trying to assert himself.

'I only pay the rent here, boy - on your fucking horse.'

'Just go, Paul. I'm fine,' Sandra said, coldly and clearly. 'Just go.'

She and Richard stood in icy silence as the man squeezed his way past them; when he reached the safety of the open front door, where he had the opportunity to run if he needed to, he turned and said, 'I'll call you later.'

'What! Leaving without paying?' said Richard.

After the door slammed, Sandra turned to the kitchen. She went to put the kettle on. Richard came up behind her.

'Get here,' he ordered, ushering her into the bedroom.

He knew from years of experience that she had no qualms about being dominated. His feeling on the matter was that whatever couples get up to in their private lives was their business, but Sandra was obviously not preserving her loyalty towards him in public; he couldn't live with that.

He grabbed her, yanked off her towelling gown and pushed her forcefully onto the bed, face down. He much preferred her from behind: never a great sign in a woman. He had to admit she did have a beautiful arse; it was her best feature. *Shame about the boat race, though*, he thought. He knew from experience that Sandra always acquiesced to force. He had been seeing and supporting her for five years. He pulled his hardened member out opened her cheeks, and rammed into her.

'Oh, yes Richard. Oh yes,' she moaned, as he worked hard. 'Harder, harder.'

He pounded viciously and then bellowed as he exploded into her, letting out his week's worth of steam.

'Oh yes, oh yes,' she groaned as if in unified ecstasy: fake or real, it made no difference whatsoever to Richard. He stood back, tucked himself in, did up his flies and turned to leave.

'That's it, Sandra,' he said. 'Don't call me again.'

Enfeebled, in exhaustion, she uttered, 'What do you mean?'

'That's it, we're finished,' he called out.

He was gone, leaving Sandra flayed out and ragged on the bed. He did turn at the front door and shout back, 'I'll pay for next month's rent and that's it. Do you hear me?'

'Richard, come back please, please,' she wailed out to deaf ears. The door slammed shut.

'Where to, sir?' the cabby asked.

'Ebury Street,' Richard said, sitting back.

'And how are we today, sir? Lovely morning.'

'Indeed it is,' he replied, loudly. 'However, I've just found my girlfriend in bed with someone else and my son lost me my job yesterday. Apart from that, though, I'm tickety boo.' His chirp silenced the taxi driver.

The cab cruised up King's Road as boutique shutters were being flung open. Richard could see that the spring brightness was reflected in the fashion and hemlines were rising with the temperatures. The cab went around Sloane Square and up through Belgrave Square; as it turned right into Pimlico, Richard passed two of his favourite pubs. *I'll be back here later, old friends*, he said to himself. When the cab pulled up on Ebury Street and the cabbie handed Richard his change, he said, 'Well, I hope you have a better day of it today, sir.'

'Thank you,' Richard said, leaning into the cab with a tip. 'A joke I rather like at the moment is when someone says, "Have a nice day", a fun answer to give them is, "That's very kind of you but I've made alternative arrangements". Confuses the hell out of them, every time.'

'Ha, ha, very good sir. I'll remember that one. Very good.'

Soon Richard was back in his flat pouring himself another whiskey, this time adding a splash of water. He thought he'd better call into the office before he began to slur.

'Lynne, sweetie, it's Richard. How are we this lovely morning?'

'I'm fine, thank you, and more importantly, how are you? Recovered?'

'Yes thanks. I slept for eighteen solid hours.'

'Good for you. Look, David's in, and I know he wants a word with you. I'll put you through.'

'Thanks, my dear.'

'Thank you, Richard. Hold on, I'm putting you through now.'

'Richard, morning, how are you, old boy?' asked David Manningham.

'Much better, thanks,' Richard replied. 'Any news on who the hell these hackers who made that ridiculous intercept are?'

'No, the Americans are tearing their hair out wanting us to get our hands on whoever did it, as you can imagine. But the problem we have is that because it was done on home soil, we have to either bring in MI5 or the police, or both. And neither we nor the CIA are willing to do that. There's bound to be a leak and then the press will be all over us like a rash. We all want this breach hushed up. It's embarrassing enough.'

'Yes, of course. Quite right.'

'If we let either of those sods know our systems are vulnerable, we'll be opening up a can of worms. So officially, we're holding fire but the CIA ops here in London are working on tracing the culprits themselves, unofficially, through their embassy.'

'I agree. I think it's definitely the right thing to do: avoid bringing in other agencies. Keep me posted, David, would you?'

'Yes, of course. Obviously, it was done by cranks but the implications are bloody horrendous.'

'Absolutely. If these jokers can penetrate our systems, who the hell else can?'

'Exactly. Oh, and Richard, one last thing,' David Manningham said, his tone turning sombre. 'I'm terribly sorry to inform you but sadly Abdullah died.' Silence. 'Richard, are you there?'

'Yes, I am,' Richard replied hesitantly, before composing himself. 'Thank you for telling me, sir. I trust we'll be taking care of his family?'

'Of course we will, I'm looking after it personally. I know how fond of him you were.'

'Thank you. Yes, I was, he was an exceptional man, a credit to the service. And the others, did they make it back to base?'

'Yes, everyone else is fine. Look, I'm sorry, Rich, I've got to get on, it's a busy day. Come in next Tuesday at eleven, would you? We need to debrief this business and see where we all go from here. I will have heard from America by then. In the meantime, no news is good news, eh?'

'Yup, too true. I'll see you then, sir.'

'Take care, Richard, and do something nice this weekend, yes?'

'Will do, sir.'

In one fluid motion Richard hung up, picked up his glass, swallowed the brackish liquid in three long gulps and shuddered violently as he put the glass back down. His shaking hand made the tumbler clink and tinkle on the granite top before it came to rest.

CHAPTER 25

Buds...

Friday finally arrived: D-Day, departure day, the day Hal and I had been waiting for to leave this house party. That was it.

It started normally enough. Hal aroused me, as usual, from my sleep when he went for his morning walk. I thought I'd look at him for one last time. I propped myself up in bed, turned sideways to flip the blinds apart and saw it was another crisp bright morning. He was dawdling, in no rush, seemingly wanting to take it all in for one last time. He would regularly stop and just look around. Clear spring sunlight, tinged with redness, broke into the conifers' lofty branches, creating sharp, well-defined shafts of light which exploded onto the forest floor at his feet, seeming to set the fallen pine needles ablaze. He stood, silhouetted, in these pools of flaming natural floodlights, oblivious to the drama of his presence. That was the third and last image I've held of him. At one point he turned and stood for a long time staring back at the ward, as if at me, and I froze, not wanting him to discover my prying eyes. I couldn't let the blinds move a millimetre or he'd notice. I held my breath. Whether he saw me or not I don't know but as soon as he turned away I released the parted blinds, feeling caught and guilty anyway, and slunk back down, lying with my head on the pillow and leaving him in solitary peace.

I had slept surprisingly well and it was at that moment, lying fully awake in bed staring at the ceiling, listening to ten male patients snoring in random unison around me, that I felt deflated. Utterly empty. I had no proof, no evidence that the efforts of my hack had worked and I was beginning to feel that the hack's effect was actually all just a figment of my imagination. I felt I had not only let myself down, but having seen Hal that morning in a brilliant light, I felt I had failed him too. My elaborate private plan to stir his father into some sort of paternal responsibility had flunked. I had let Hal down badly. He had helped me so much and I had given him nothing back.

As well as that I had wanted to give the powers which govern us that shot of electro-convulsive therapy necessary to humble their attitude of cold invincibility. I had wanted to alert these arrogant beings to a new generation, emerging bruised but not defeated.

It was a three-pronged failure: I had failed myself by not being the master computing genius I thought I was. Secondly, I had let my hero, Hal, down, and the final poke was that I had done diddly squat to affect the inefficiency of the over-confident – the so-called people in the seat of power. I had failed my tribe.

I had expected police to arrive and for there to be a right royal hoo-ha. That's what convinced me that the hack hadn't worked. I had thought that, in the four days that had passed, the services, both British and American Intelligence, would have been able to trace the source of the hack if it had worked. I would have been able to.

It was going to be difficult for me to continue in the shadows for much longer. My problem, my Catch-22, was the secrecy of what I was doing then. It was my hacking, my underground criminal activity, which I dared not tell a soul about, that had actually made me mentally unwell in the first place. That was the reality I was fully aware of as I was about to leave hospital but nobody else was. I couldn't cope with the helpless power I could wield, and yet now that was the only thing in my life that made me feel in any way good about myself. It was *the* problem, my fundamental problem, and that hadn't been addressed at all during my rehabilitation. It was like an addict who manages to hide their problem successfully from everyone. I knew I was an addict but no one else did. It was a dilemma. The big unresolved issue. Would I be able to stop?

I guess my mum and the doctors thought I was just some sort of gamer, someone who was hooked on computer games, a nerd. And here I was about to go home to nothing new. I was a geek, a computer geek. That was what I was born to be. I knew it was virtually impossible for me to keep off them. I was born for computers, or they for me. I had gone so far, so deep into the complexities of systems that I knew how they were built; I knew their strengths and their weaknesses. I was a cyber sculptor, a coding architect.

Like murderers who often return to the scene of their crime, I became excited about going back into the CIA's system later that day and seeing what had happened. But I knew, as clear as the sunlight outside, as I lay in bed holding my willy, that that action would definitely get me caught. If I went back anywhere near the scene of my crime, they would hook onto me. They undoubtedly knew that. Profiled, the chances were I would go back into the system and like all good spy catchers they would be there waiting for me to retrace my footsteps. The designers, CIA's computer boffins, their encoders, would all be looking out for me. They knew, pathologically, that I would be back and they would be there, waiting for me.

Perversely people who are drawn to invisibility, like me, are often hungry for publicity, too. In other words I really did want to shout from the rooftops, *Yes, this is me. I did it, everyone. Aren't I clever?* You can imagine the dichotomy of my problem and why I went mad – can't you? I kept repeating, *You must not go there again, Jonathan, you must not go there again*, over and over, trying to drum it into my skull. *Do not go there again.* Eventually I even had the good sense to get out of bed, get on my knees and pray. I pushed both palms together and defied logic. *Dear Lord, please, please, please help me not to ever go there again. Please, I pray to you for help. Make me strong.*

'Hey, Jonathan, are you alright, mate?' Hal whispered, poking his head through the half-open curtain that I had forgotten to close properly.

'Me? Oh… oh, yes – I'm fine, thanks,' I mumbled, all embarrassed.

He giggled. 'Praying it's all over? Thanking God we're going home?'

'Yes, something like that,' I stammered, getting up and sitting on the side of my bed awkwardly.

'Lovely day out there. Why don't you go for a walk before breakfast and pray out there? That's what I've just done. It's magnificent.'

'Yes, thanks, I might just do that,' I said.

'I'm going to have a bath. I'll see you in a bit.'

I saw him grab his towel and wash bag from his booth and head off to the washroom with a skip to his step.

I remember not really being able to look at him in the eye anymore; my feelings of shame at letting him down overrode all the deep affection I felt for him.

I dressed and, taking Hal's words on board, walked out into the big wide world, all empty, and all on my own. It felt awesome. I no longer felt awkward. At the very moment I stepped outside, my mood changed; it reversed. I sighed with relief that nothing had happened. Now that I was alone with nature, breathing in fresh air, squinting through the clear spring sun's rays and listening to the birds in high states of excitement, I felt relief. This was the first day of the rest of my life. I forgot about my problems. I walked the path Hal had taken, crunching up his route, enveloped in plain and simple earthy magic, and I pledged then that I would walk every day when I was released: an oath I have kept. My feelings of remorse at not being able to be of assistance to Hal's wellbeing had fully diminished by the time I plumped onto the lonely bench at the top of the path. I sat overlooking the old golf course, its overgrown fairway rolling away beneath me into a shroud of early morning mist, and I felt released from the burden of worry I had been feeling for the past few days.

The adrenalin rush I had felt at the beginning of the week from having thought the supposed hack had worked had worn off. Then there was the period, mid-week, of deep anxiety, and now that was all gone too. The weight of responsibility of what I thought I had done had vaporised. I now felt a certain comfort, a peace that comes with not interfering, not getting involved, absolved of any guilt. *Not guilty, Your Honour*. I felt liberated from the situation, and the whole hospital experience. I was leaving with a clean slate, ready to reengage with my life.

I would be on my own again later that day, back in my own world. *Hal doesn't need my help, for crying out loud*. I was the last person he needed help from, for Christ's sake. Helping me to get better had helped himself to get better. As with love, giving is receiving. And, no doubt, he'd got some sort of rewards for seeing me recover at pace with himself too. That was what I hoped, anyway. He would soon forget me as easily as we had forgotten Matt.

None of us had really even mentioned Matt during that week. The only time I remember him coming up in conversation was when we were sitting out on the bench on the Monday morning after the hullaballoo with Josephine, the nurse, when she twisted her ankle. Her beautiful ankle which I had fantasised about holding while I made love with her. I had made naughty imaginary love to her many times that week, holding that ankle which was now twisted and swollen in my broken wet dreams.

'It's odd not having Matt here,' Kat had said.

'Yeah, but lucky him waking up at home on a Monday morning,'

Hal had responded. 'I bet you miss him, don't you Jonathan?'

'I suppose so,' I'd said, still in the throes of elation at

having thought I had cracked my hack.

'I bet he's rolling up a big fat spliff now,' Hal joked.

And that was about it. Oh, apart from a couple of days later when, during a moment's silence, Kat had said, 'I wonder what Matt's doing?

'Mucking about with his camera or making music no doubt, or bouncing around with his headphones on,' Hal had replied.

'Will you stay in touch with him, Jonathan?' Kat had asked. 'Well, I know where he lives, it's not too far from me, but we didn't make any plans to or anything.' And that was about it: out of sight, out of mind. Here today, gone tomorrow.

I got up off the bench with that thought in mind, in no doubt that it would be the same for me. Hal would wake up tomorrow at his mother's house and I would be rapidly forgotten. But for me, I could never forget him. He stood head and shoulders above anyone I'd met before - and, to a degree, since. I would always place him on a pedestal. After all, he had been the one who had saved me from myself. All he had really done was to talk to me as an equal - which no one had done before. After all the years I had been bullied, because he treated me with respect, everyone else had started to do the same. Most importantly though, I'd started to have respect for myself. That was all I'd needed to wake up and be myself. He wasn't my intellectual equal, he wasn't as clever as me, but he had It, that magic. He was, and probably still is, a global radiator. Simply him being present brought out the best in other people.

I felt anxious again as I walked back to the ward, looking at the building that had been my home for long enough to forget any other. I felt scared. Scared of leaving the security of the hospital and the company I was enjoying. The brief but powerful friendships I had were about to vaporise, to disappear. I was sad and unsure how I would cope. I really didn't want to be on my own again, isolated, with only my computing for company. I shuddered at the prospect of facing reality. If I wasn't careful going home was going to be a massively regressive move, not a progressive one.

When I got back inside everyone was having breakfast, except for Kat. Hal was there tucking into a hearty-looking plateful of the full-English.

'Have you seen Kat?' he asked between mouthfuls.

'No, I haven't. I haven't seen her since yesterday when she flew past me.'

'Oh, crikey, I hope she's okay,' he said, as I sat down at the table next to his.

We both finished eating at the same time and took our dirty plates to the counter where a nurse was standing.

'Excuse me, nurse, have you seen Kat this morning?' Hal asked.

'She's refusing to get out of bed, Hal,' he flatly informed us.

'But is she okay?'

'Yes, I think so.'

We both ambled out to a bench on the front lawn.

'What time are you leaving, Jonathan?' he asked, as he lit a ciggy.

'Normal time, this evening. And you?'

'My mum's going to be here about four-ish. That's when my consultant can make it, to sign me out. She has to officially say that I am off my Section, which should really expire tomorrow.'

'I'm probably still on my Section too. The consultant will have to do the same for me, I guess,' I muttered, utterly clueless.

'What plans have you got for when you get home?' he asked.

'None, really.'

'Oh, come on, Jonathan, surely your consultant and your mum have come up with a plan for you. You need to keep busy, focussed, don't you?' he implored.

'Yes, I do. I do, I know.'

'Are you worried about it, about leaving?' he probed.

'Yes, I am,' I admitted. 'I don't really know *what* I am going to do.'

'Why don't you try and find an interim course to get onto straight away, before the main one starts in September?

Something with a bit of a routine, to get you out of the house. You must.'

'I know, Hal.'

'What about a CV. Have you done one of those?'

'No, I haven't.'

'Well, that's a good thing to do. It's the first thing to do, and then maybe try and find a work placement or something, anything.'

'That's a good idea. An internship or something?'

'Exactly. What I'm going to do is have some leaflets printed and do some gardening work local to my mum. I've got to be there for three months as part of my release programme. So I'm going to get my hands in the soil and my fingers on the keyboard.'

'Do you need to do that, Hal? I heard you've inherited a lot of money. Is that right?'

'Yes, it is but I probably won't get that for months and months. I want to get my hands dirty. Anyway, who told you about that?'

'I overheard.'

CHAPTER 26

Transplant...

Richard Reed staggered and crumpled into a large armchair in his apartment. The impact of the phone call he had just made to his office had curdled with his stunningly cold performance in disposing of his girlfriend an hour earlier, and the fact that his son had something to do with all these events made his facial features collapse to seminal lows.

Never before had his personal life impinged on his professional one to such a degree. Never had he been so not in control of events. He had been fanatical about keeping the two sides of his life as far apart as he possibly could. Ever since the trauma of his divorce he'd pledged to never let them converge again. And now they had car-crashed. His private life, however shabby, had collided, head-on, with his work. His mouth fell into an upended horseshoe, drooping like a clown's. His eyes glazed, unblinking, and he had a job to keep his neck erect enough to support his lolling and thumping head.

Richard began to rock and shake uncontrollably in his seat. The alcohol reduced his resistance and helped release his pent-up emotions. He began to sob violently. Liquid poured from his eyes, flowing down his cheeks and into the channels created by his collapsed mouth, which created the perfect crevasses for his tears to cascade off his chin and onto his shirt front.

He never cried, and he prided himself on that. This was the first time he had shed tears since he had opened a letter as an eighteen-year-old to read that he had been refused entry into the RAF as he was colour blind. He had always wanted to be a pilot. That was over forty years ago. He had not wept for forty years.

He now released the decades' worth of suppressed emotions all over himself. Certain doctors say it is important to relieve the tear ducts regularly as this is where toxins in the body are stored and it is vital to expel these poisons from our systems. If that was the case, Richard had forty years' worth of toxic stockpiles built up behind his eyes.

Richard shook and cried, shook and cried, and eventually began to wipe away the tears but the moment had not yet passed and he continued to struggle to contain himself; the tears just kept coming. He gasped for air through choking sobs.

After a long ten minutes he galvanised himself to stand up; he was worrying himself. He had to support himself on the back of the armchair as he stood, wobbling, his legs seeming determined to fail him. Now really concerned, he put back his head and roared a defiant low rumble up to the gods above; clenching his teeth, he began to growl, imploring life to contain him and not let him fall any further into the abyss:

not to lose any more control. Enough was enough. He looked forward resolutely, swayed slightly and then tottered feebly towards the bedroom as carefully as he could. Once again he collapsed onto the bed and promptly fell asleep, exhausted, drenched in his own tears.

Richard came back to the world two hours later, not knowing what to do. He felt utterly uncomfortable with himself. He pulled off his sodden shirt, sneezed, let it drop to the ground and then went into the bathroom. He looked at himself in the mirror. His sun-soaked complexion couldn't disguise the haggard, haunted man who stared back at him.

He had been living the life he wanted to: utterly selfish, full of subterfuge and danger. He had managed to swerve and avoid dealing with any personal development in any shape or form. It had always been strictly business. But now, the intricacies of his emotional reality were beginning to unravel and come home to roost – he knew that, and he just couldn't cope. The stresses associated with confronting the truth, having avoided it for so long, began to haunt Richard's handsome face. New lines were being etched into his beaten brow that morning.

Richard Reed's main adage in life had always been to stay calm at all times. Keeping control of his emotions and senses was paramount to his existence. *The second you begin to fear something, you've lost*, he'd say. *Whatever you fear immediately has a way of creeping in and catching you. Nothing in nature attacks a bold, steady person; it only runs down the weak and frightened ones.* He knew that where there was less fear there was less danger.

To say he had now lost his composure was an understatement. Richard was shell-shocked, if you like. He had been mugged by reality. Now he was scared, not of death or physical danger, but of losing his sanity, his rationality in the face of the truth. His cage was well and truly rattled.

The news that Abdullah had died was the final straw which had broken the camel's back. It was one piece of news too many. He was getting to grips with his son having hacked into the company's system. He was even impressed with it, and slightly amused. He would protect his flesh and blood above anything. He had taken it as a sign that his son was recovering, and was on the mend. That's how he had read it, up until then. Now, his son was the cause of a loyal friend's death.

He'd enjoyed the thrill of the ride down the mountain, and his escape from Beirut. He didn't care about the two young lads he'd shot, he didn't care about dumping his girlfriend. Secretly, he'd actually enjoyed it all. It'd made him feel young again and full of vigour. But Abdullah dying was one bridge too far.

It was his son's inability to stay in control of himself which had so disappointed Richard when he had heard the shocking news that he had been admitted to a mental home. His son hadn't been able to hold himself together and be a man. And that was weakness. Hal had fallen apart emotionally, and that was unacceptable. It was all too chaotic. There was no control to it. There was no plan, no order. And yet now here he was, unable to manage his own life and mentally struggling to cope with his plateful. As Richard knew his son was pulling himself together, he himself was in obvious danger of falling apart.

He washed with cold water, splashing his face with a dozen handfuls, forcing himself to go through the rituals of freshening up like a robot. He sneezed again as he walked through the bedroom to grab a clean shirt. This brief headwind seemed to help him revive momentarily and he felt unexpectedly clear-headed. The notion that perhaps crying was actually good for you flashed across his mind. But he brushed that pathetic thought aside as he did up his shirt, standing at the same window as he had done earlier.

He loved standing there, unnoticed, above the street and his entrance, soldierly and on duty. Not spying or peeping, but just looking at the hugely diverse range of people passing below. It always amazed him. He stared at an old couple chatting with their shopping baskets, just like his mother used to. And there was a man in a white van, double-parked on the other side of the road. Stop, check. *Oh shit*, Richard thought, *they're watching me.* And as he stood back behind the curtain he recalled that it was his son who had compromised him. He shook his head. There was nothing to be outwardly concerned about. He was getting paranoid. *Calm down.*

That little fucker, he said vehemently. Now he was furious with his son: instantly in a rage. It was all going too fast for him; he didn't know what to do next. He began to scrabble for someone to blame for his state of mind. He turned instinctively towards the bottle. That's what his generation did. He poured himself a tumbler of the amber fire water and took a hefty slug. The burning liquid shook him physically and mentally. *This is what men do*, he said to himself. He wandered around the apartment in a daze, slowly putting on his shoes and coat; then, grabbing his newspaper, he left the building.

He walked unsteadily down the road, feeling self-conscious, as if everyone was looking at him. As an obsessed precaution he prepared his paper as a weapon. He had been taught that a rolled-up newspaper was as good as a truncheon for both defence and attack. There was nowhere else to go, for someone like him, but to the pub. He'd feel better there.

And so he walked into one of his haunts. Richard liked to call pubs his traps. He liked a very traditional pub and this one, The Spread Eagle, was all brass, deep stained wood and red-velvet type-homely. He always felt a man in a pub and he stood at the bar waiting to be served as if he owned the place, playing the part he loved most.

'Hello, gov,' he said, 'a pint of Best.'

'Nice to see you again, sir. Is it a straight or handle?' the jolly landlord said.

'Handle, please.'

'That's right.' As he pumped the pint the landlord continued. 'Been a while, sir, have you been keeping well?'

'Yes, fine thanks, just got back. And you, all well here?'

'Can't complain, can't complain.'

'Jolly good,' Richard said, as he handed over a note. And taking a huge draught of the pint of frothy bitter, he waited for his change. He had quaffed half of it in one hit. 'That's better,' he said, taking the coins. 'Nothing better than getting back to a good ol' pint of ale.'

'Quite, sir, the taste of home.'

Richard held court at the bar for another hour and a half, shovelling pints like they were going out of fashion. He wanted to chat to everyone that came in, offering to buy drinks for some, interrupting others, and rapidly becoming more than a bit of a nuisance to the genteel crowd that used The Spread Eagle, Hans Crescent, Fitzrovia, London SW1. At one point he even began loudly telling rude, inappropriate jokes. 'How do you know whether your girlfriend or your dog loves you the most?' he shouted across the bar. 'Lock 'em both up in the boot of your car for twenty-four hours and see who's happiest to see you when you open up!' Eventually he got the message; the only person he was amusing was himself, and he left.

He decided he'd get himself a decent steak. The nearby Broughton's was not quite a Private Members club, but it was an exclusive gentlemen's eatery. With a cigar lounge it hosted a lot of jazz and had an incredible selection of rare malts and cognacs. It was all low lighting, booths (green velvet this time), more polished brass and waiters in creased black trousers and starched white shirts. It was that sort of a place. Okay, it was Friday lunchtime and there were quite a few businessmen on the razzle in the restaurant, celebrating deals or whatever, but Richard was on his own and plastered. A standout mess.

He was professionally steered into a booth by the maître d', who feigned knowing him better than he did. Richard proceeded to order a ridiculously gargantuan meal:

a Chateaubriand piece of meat meant for two people, and a stupidly expensive bottle of claret, from Saint-Estephe.

'I want to sit by the window,' he barked to a passing waiter.

'Of course, sir, I'll move you straight away,' the nervous young man replied.

Richard was now on public display, much to the annoyance of the maître d', who fluffed about in the background, sensing trouble.

Richard's choicest cut of beef arrived on a big wooden board, and his rare wine was corked in front of him, sniffed in approval and decanted. He guzzled, and hardly ate. To the shock and amazement of fellow diners Richard threw the steak out of an open window in front of him, right onto the street. 'Let the foxes eat it!' he declared loudly to all in earshot. He began to mutter and babble out loud to himself. Words like, 'That fucking kid,' or, 'you little prick.'

Eventually, and as swiftly as possible, the staff offered him his bill.

'Call me a cab,' he ordered, 'and while I'm waiting I'll have a Lagavulin, as old as you've got.'

Not long after Richard Reed was ushered out of Broughton's and helped into a waiting black London taxi. It was three p.m.

CHAPTER 27

Clippings...

God, I can't tell you how that last day at Rooksdown dragged. After breakfast Hal and I had both packed our bags that, from then on, sat on our beds in silent anticipation. We ourselves paced around from bench to TV room to smoking room, and back to our cubicles. And then we would start the circuit all over again. On one leg of our tour around Hal stopped a nurse. 'Oh nurse,' he asked, 'please can you go into the dormitory and let Kat know I really want to see her before I go?'

'She doesn't want to see you,' said the nurse when he returned a few minutes later.

'Oh, right. Okay, thanks.'

Hal turned to me and, for the first time that day, shrugged his shoulders and raised his eyebrows as if to say, 'What can you do!' Then he said out loud, 'Jonathan, do you want to come up to the shop with me? They sell cards there. I'll write her a note.'

'Only if you really want me to.'

'I do,' he said, and then turned back. 'Oh, nurse!' he called out. 'Would it be alright to go to the shop?'

'Yes, that's fine. Come straight back though. I'll be waiting.'

Off we went, one last time, up to the main asylum and through the depressing passageways and gantries of the old Victorian monstrosity. The same withered old inmates, both male and female, dressed in their grubby pyjamas and nightwear, clung to the corridor walls as we passed. There were only two looks on these patients' faces: utterly vacant, or haunted. Their withered limbs shook involuntarily, and from the bottom of the main internal thoroughfare, as we looked upwards, the ranks of these old patients resembled a mass of laundry flapping in the wind, hung out to dry. The sounds of doors banging and the odd wail echoed eerily through the corridors like a submariner's sonar.

Hal walked with his head up, wishing everyone that looked at us a good morning. Not one person responded in words; maybe there was an occasional groan, squeal or stifled giggle. Here we were on the cusp of leaving after a comparatively fleeting time and there they were, still incarcerated after what seemed like an eternity. They had been there for decades and would no doubt end their days there. Rehabilitation for them seemed impossibly remote after such a long time. I felt sorry for the staff too. There were no good-news stories. Talk about becoming institutionalised. I felt I was, in under two months. I walked sheepishly behind Hal. It was still all a bit too close to the bone for me to be convincingly objective.

When we reached the shop, which was more like a big cupboard with sparsely filled shelves selling discount teabags, cans of soft drinks and a range of cheap branded tins, Hal flipped through a cardboard box of tacky, dated cards.

'Christ, this'll have to do,' he said, picking up a juvenile teddy bear one, a Get-Well card.

He paid. We retraced our footsteps back through the all-pervading disinfected corridors, whooshing past the mass of Miss Havershams and Ebenezer Scrooges, and then we both breathed deeply, as we always did, when we got back outside. As if we'd been holding our breath.

'Phew,' Hal said, heaving deeply. 'Thank God we're not going to have to do that walk again. Remind yourself, Jonathan, seriously, about that if ever you are feeling wobbly. I will. Hold yourself together. Ending up like that feels like a fate worse than death.'

So, that's what he wanted me to come up here for. 'Yeah, right. Completely,' I said. 'This part of the hospital scares the hell out of me. Picturing myself there. Though I can't understand why they don't come outside into the fresh air, at least. Surely they'd feel better.'

'Frankly, I can't believe this sort of place still exists at all,' he said, as we walked.

'I know. It just crossed my mind that they were all probably admitted for the same reasons as us, generations ago, and they just got stuck here.'

'Yes, scary,' he said, shuddering. 'Hold that thought, and feel lucky. Come on, let's get out of here.'

It started to rain. Having clocked back in with the nurse, we went into the smoking room for Hal to write his card. They still had them in those days, smoking rooms. Hard to imagine now.

Liam and Frank were sitting side by side on their high-backed chairs facing the radio, poised like contestants on a quiz show. With their backs to us they eagerly awaited the next song to come on the airwaves.

'Madonna, *Like a Virgin*,' one would shout out. 'Got ya!'

And so it went on. They were surprisingly good at it. Somewhere in their minds were razor-sharp similar memories. One of them could generally nail the song within the first ten seconds. Their violent encounter had truly bonded them; they now had mutual respect. I thought it incredible that this could be the result of a fight.

Hal wrote his note to Kat, though I don't know what he wrote. I stood around awkwardly in this gallery of eccentrics.

'Lunch, everyone,' a nurse called out through the door.

And so we broke up and filtered out in dribs and drabs towards the dining room.

'Oh, nurse?' Hal asked on the way out. 'When you've got a moment, could you give this to Kat, please?'

Friday was always a good lunch, fish and chips, with peas that flipped off everyone's forks to be mushed into the carpet. The tradition of eating fish on a Friday was still institutional. With lunch over, and a break in the clouds, we stood under the relative protection of the old pines so Hal could smoke. He preferred to smoke outside.

'We're going to Drama Workshop,' a couple of fellow inmates called out to us in their peculiar fashion. 'Come on, guys. It will be fun.'

'Na, I'm not going,' Hal replied. 'Send my regards to the tutor though.'

'Yeah, sure, Hal,' they called back, as they plodded off. 'See you 'round.'

This particular therapy session had gained in popularity due to our little group's engagement in it. Word had got around that the performing of our play had been therapeutic and that had made acting something fashionable to do for others in the ward. Acting had become trendy. Everyone wanted to be doing it. *We'll have a bit of that*, they must have thought.

If one person in a group can rise above themselves and do something special like getting better, it impels others to do the same. Seeing others get well and leave had an effect on everyone else in the ward. *If he can do it, then so can I*, was the attitude that was now pervading Rooksdown. Seeing Matt leave last week, and now me and Hal, probably made everyone ask themselves: *Why not me? How do I do it? What's the secret?*

Although home was generally where our problems had originated, deep down we all longed for our own beds, our own space. Being normal and having a sensible routine. Like going anywhere for a few weeks, it is always good to get home, if only for a short time.

It was three o'clock.

'I'm going to have a lie down, chill out and read my book,' Hal said. 'Unless you want to do anything, Jonathan? I've only got an hour to kill before my mum arrives and we have this meeting.'

'Na, not really.'

'The only thing I've got to do is see Kat before I go, I don't know what to do,' he said, as we walked back in.

'Why don't you try and knock on her window? I know which one it is.'

'Yeah, why not? I've got to give it a go.'

And so we went around the back of the building to the reflection of our dormitory and as we crouched like guerrilla soldiers on an assault mission, I pointed and whispered, 'That one there.'

'Okay, you wait here,' Hal mouthed, and crept forward. I could hear him knock on the pane I had pointed to and faintly heard him call out, 'It's me, Kat, it's Hal. Kat, Kat?'

And then I saw him recoil as Kat's muffled but as clear as a loudhailer voice roared through the glass, 'Fuck off and die, will you, I never want to see you again. Just go away.'

She really was ranting, possessed even. It sounded horrible. Poor Hal just stood back in obvious shock, staring like a rabbit in the headlights of abuse. Kat continued to rant and rave on the other side of the window.

'Okay, okay, calm down, Kat, please. It's okay,' I could hear him plead, holding his arms out, palms face forward in submission. 'I'm sorry.'

Then I could just make out a curtain closing; the light on his face had changed, and Hal came back to me, numbed. 'Jesus Christ, man,' he said weakly. 'Did you hear that?'

'Yeah, I did.'

'I've really got to lie down now.'

'Me too,' I echoed.

And that is what we did, both silently taking our suitcases off our beds and closing the curtains in unison.

'See you in a bit,' he whispered.

I lay down and fell asleep immediately.

When I woke up I looked up and saw Hal's cubicle was empty. I jumped up and ran to the nurses' station. Not a soul was around. I dashed outside and was so relieved to see Hal's mum's car there. I went back in and took up my sentry position in the corridor. Like the elder inmates up in the main body of the asylum, I too seemed to be spending too much time clinging to walls, shuffling around. But I was waiting for something, for someone. I had more of a purpose.

And then the consultant's door opened and out filed Hal, followed by his mother and finally Dr Feltz.

'Thank you doctor, for all you've done,' Mrs Reed was saying.

As Mrs Reed reached out to shake the doctor's hand I heard the main entrance door bang rudely open to my left and, behind them, coming up the corridor, was a dishevelled older man.

'There you are, you little fucker,' he ranted, pointing, and continuing upwards.

The little group turned towards the commotion.

'Richard!' Hal's mum exclaimed.

'Dad,' Hal echoed in shock.

Richard continued his lurch forward towards them.

'I'm gonna kill you, you little bastard,' he roared.

'Get in the office, now, everyone,' Dr Feltz ordered, responding professionally and immediately. She called out, 'Nurses, get out here, all of you.'

Hal's father continued, staggering forward. 'You think you're clever, do you? Fucking me around. You know three people died because of your antics. Do you hear me?' His voice crescendo'd to a shout as he repeated, 'Three people died.'

He began banging on the closed-to-him office door.

For a brief time it was only me and him in the corridor. I stared at him as he beat the wooden frame with his fists. 'Three people died,' he repeated again.

Soon a crowd of inmates mustered at the top of the corridor between me and Mr Reed. *Oh shit*, I quaked to myself, *my hack really has worked*. The snippet of the play and my piece to camera *had* gone through. I gawped dumbly at Mr Reed rapping furiously on the door.

'Get out here,' he barked.

A nurse who had been in the main body of the ward rushed past me and approached Mr Reed.

'Sir, sir, please stop that,' she urged assertively.

'No, I will not. Get that son of mine out here now. He's caused enough trouble. I'll sort him out,' he slurred.

'No, you won't,' I said.

At that, he looked around towards the nurse, and glimpsed me behind her. His cold, sea-glass eyes honed on me and, although they were fully frosted, they froze me. Like laser beams, his inflamed reddened eyes honed in and burnt into me. He had stared at me for a second too long. His glare had locked onto me. I had fused. *He must have recognised my voice on the video*, I thought. But due to his inebriation perhaps he couldn't quite place me. I'd been stunned.

I was suddenly brought back to reality by the flickering of blue flashing lights flooding the corridor, then came the screeching of brakes outside, and two police officers appeared, rushing up and apprehending Mr Reed. *Saved by the boys in blue*, phew.

'Get your hands off me,' he demanded, as the handcuffs clicked tight. 'Don't you know who I am?'

When he was secured Dr Feltz appeared nervously from the office and closed the door behind her, leaving Hal and his mum within. As Mr Reed was frogmarched down to the panda car, I could hear one of the officers saying, 'Well, doctor, we'll take him down to the station, find out more about him, assess him, and go from there. He's obviously drunk. But he might well be back up here in no time.'

'Yes, of course, officer, many thanks for such a swift response. We appreciate it,' she said.

Dr Feltz raised her eyebrows and they exchanged a knowing look as the officers disappeared as quickly as they had appeared. This was a common enough routine here, I guessed. A well-oiled machine.

Hal and his mum came out of the office visibly shaken as the flashing lights receded. I was quivering in shock too.

'Are you okay to drive, Mum?' I heard Hal saying, as he put an arm around her shoulder.

'Yes, I'm fine, let's just get home now,' she answered.

They walked slowly towards the door where they met Dr Feltz coming in, followed by a taxi driver.

'What about my fare?' the cockney was demanding. 'It's well over a hundred nicker! I brought that rantin' nutter all the way dan from Londin.'

'All I can do is take your name and address and tell the police. I'm sure it'll get sorted out,' Dr Feltz replied in a matronly way. 'Give me a minute, please, I'll just see my patient off.'

'It blinkin' well better be,' he muttered.

And so she left me in the corridor with the fuming cabbie, to go and see Hal and his mother off the premises. I made one last effort and dashed after them. As I stumbled past the taxi driver I could hear him continue to blabber, 'That was the worst ride of my life, what a day!'

I could see Hal helping his mother into her seat and he closed the door for her as I came out.

'Bye, Hal,' I managed to call out feebly.

'Oh, see ya Jonathan, take care of yourself,' he responded warmly, though clearly still shaken, as he went around to get into the car himself. As he did so, he held out twisted upturned palms and raised his shoulders for the second time that day, which I interpreted to mean, *What the hell went on there?*. He got in, wound his window down and waved, calling out, 'Thank you, thank you,' to Dr Feltz, and me, as we in turn waved back at him. *Thank you, sir*, I mumbled to myself.

CHAPTER 28

Mulch…

Dr Feltz spoke, turning towards me. 'Let me know when your mother arrives, Jonathan…' And then she stopped. 'Are you feeling alright? You don't look well, my dear. Here, let me give you a hand.'

The diminutive doctor assisted me, a gangly six-footer, into the ward. When we reached her office, I said I was feeling fine and that I'd just go for a little lie down. But as I walked - well, wobbled - towards my bed, I felt absolutely shattered. My legs had turned to jelly. All life had gushed out of them. My current reality was too much for me to absorb; Hal, my rock, had left, gone, and there was no doubt now that my interference, my hack into the CIA and MI6's security system, had worked.

Three men dead, what on earth did he mean? I buckled to the ground on that thought as I neared my cubicle and was forced to grope my way forward and onto the bed. I physically couldn't move any further, my body had given up on me, yet my brain reeled in the final spasms of a meltdown. If I could have got up I would have, and run, and run, and run. That is what I needed to do, to escape my thoughts. To run away from my mind. But I couldn't, no one can – only in sleep and death and perhaps deep meditation can thoughts be quelled. I lay twitching in a catatonic state like a fettered prisoner with locked-in syndrome. I became fevered, and then… I passed out.

Sleep is the most marvellous restorative. Go to sleep with a problem on your mind, and you invariably wake up with the answer. It may take days of sleep but somehow sleeping, and particularly dreaming, pigeonholes and files thought content. Like a shuffled pack of cards, sleeping puts the houses back in order - most of the time. What I had done though, my grand hack, clearly wasn't a straightforward case of hearts and diamonds, it was obviously going to be a brutal inquest into clubs and spades. What the hell had happened?

'Jonathan, Jonathan, can you hear me, darling?' I faintly heard my mother saying, as if through ether.

'Ungh, ungh,' was the only response I could muster.

She must have gone off to fetch a nurse.

'Nurse, what's happened to him?' I heard her exclaim on her return.

'I really don't know, Mrs Runcorn. I'd better get a doctor.'

My mother began to roughly mop my boiling brow. My eyelids began to flutter.

I vaguely heard a distant Dr Feltz. 'I saw him about half an hour ago, Mrs Runcorn. We had an issue with one of the patients. He seemed shaken by it,' she said. 'We've got a general practitioner coming over now. I suggest we take his clothes off and get him into bed.'

Even hearing that bombshell - my mother and the doctor stripping me - couldn't revive me. I just grunted as they propped me up and yanked my trousers off. They kept my pants on, thank God, and the two women manhandled me under the covers.

'My God, he's wet through,' my mother declared. 'I can't take him home like this, can I, doctor?' *Good girl*, I thought, *always thinking about yourself.*

And that was the last thought I remembered having for three days and three nights. I really don't know what had snapped so dramatically to make me collapse into catatonia like that. Perhaps it was a combination of me going home, which I wasn't really fully prepared for, or it was Hal leaving or… Mr Reed arriving in such a state. That was it, he was the thunderbolt who had struck me down. Surely to God, that piercing look he gave me was the bullet in my brain. *Three men dead because of my hack*? It all came quivering back. *How could that have happened*? He must have been lying, thoroughly confused through being shit-faced drunk. *How could my innocuous, silly little message have killed three people*? It was an impossibility, a ridiculous, preposterous notion.

When, the following Monday, I could finally sit up in bed and recover, I realised for sure that the killer-look Mr Reed gave me when he had turned to face me must have been the knock-out punch that felled me for three days. I had felt suddenly caught, thunderstruck, in his glare. It was a look that permeated my core and exposed the truth. That brief haunting moment, when his crazed eyes suddenly closed in on me, was like sea ice. It was the most penetrating look I have ever had in my life. It stripped me bare, and it crushes me still. But, the reality was, I had cracked him.

I realised that the only person in the whole world who knew, or had an inkling that I was a top-secret hacker, was Mr Reed. In a way I felt a strange sort of release that at last someone knew of my undercover activity. *When the fog of his breakdown cleared, would he remember seeing me and put two and two together*? I now had an affinity with him. We had a bond. He knew my innermost secret that nobody else on the planet did, and therefore I felt a deep connection with him, and therefore Hal. I was part of their family whether they liked it or knew it, or not. I was the catalyst that had created the biggest upheaval going on in their lives. I clicked that Richard Reed had to keep the secret if he loved his son. If he exposed me, his son, his flesh and blood, would be arrested too. He had to keep quiet. *Deep down, surely, family comes first*?

It was too early to feel any pity for Richard Reed; that emotion didn't come into the equation quite yet. It had been a pathetic sight, him raging like that, and no doubt his outburst would be a huge embarrassment for him down the line, but that was the whole point of it in the first place. I had achieved what I'd set-out to do.

It had worked. *Yee-ha*. My one-man show had dramatically and perfectly played itself out and I was the only member of the audience. I was the monkey and the organ grinder combined. Perhaps that's what had made me collapse: the fact that what I had done had been so sublimely enacted.

It had all just played out right in front of me. It was magic. It was like blink and you'll miss it. There was no cavalry of men in macs or blacked-out vans, it was just one drunk, ranting MI6 operative who came to a mental home to inform me I'd achieved my mission.

Fate would have to see if, somewhere down the crazy river of life, Hal and his father would become closer. That is what I'd been really aiming for: for father and son to be reconciled. The goal of my master plan was some way off in the distance, though, by the look of things, and one in which I would probably never know whether it had truly worked out or not - whether Hal and his father would ever have a proper relationship.

But for now I rejoiced. My glorious opus, my coding masterpiece, had actually worked. It was official. No more ifs and buts: the hack was a success, and I was safe and sound in the protective confines of the hospital. I couldn't be touched, and here I still was, over a week after the event, with no signs of me being traced. Out there in the upper echelons of system design, the security-coding professionals were holding me up in highest esteem. No doubt about that. There were probably hundreds of boffins out there who, although kicking themselves with embarrassment - and no doubt a few of them were getting sacked – were considering the person who had broken their codes, me, to be a hero.

The three days of fevered sleep, caused by Richard Reed's blinding glare, had allowed my brain to filter, sort and absorb what I had done. The break from thinking, the deep rest, all combined to make me feel thoroughly refreshed and comfortable. I felt rearranged and put back in order. I lay in my hospital bed, basking in my private glory, being waited on hand and foot; I felt very much the victor, a right Iron Duke!

On the second day of my recovery, Tuesday, the sun was out in full force so I put on my dressing gown and slippers and walked out to the bench to let nature appreciate its creation. I was unsteady and weak physically but otherwise felt absolutely fine. I sat alone, feeling the strong solar rays penetrate deeply. Closing my eyes and facing up to the burning star of all life, I felt a worthy recipient of its beneficence, a classy creation. I felt truly empowered for the second time in my life. I had arrived to myself, thanks to Hal. And I was now extremely happy to be left in my own skin.

I was brought back to life with a shuddering crack, though. I opened my eyes to find myself in someone else's shadow.

'John-a-than? Jonathan,' a voice burbled excitedly.

'Yes, what is it, Liam?' I said, annoyed.

'Did you hear about Kat?' he said, and then giggled weirdly. 'She's killed herself.'

'What!'

'Yes, she did, she did. She cut her wrists in the bath with a tin.'

'Oh, my God, oh dear. Are you sure? Is she really dead?'

'Yeah, I'm sure. I don't know. I just wanted to tell you, that's all.'

'Alright, thanks,' I said. He stood there staring at me gormlessly. 'Thank you, Liam,' I was forced to repeat.

'Oh, right then,' he said, getting the message somewhat dejectedly. 'See you round.'

The horrific news took the wind out of my sails instantly. There I was in full flow, riding the crest of a wave, in the zone, and then suddenly, bumph, I was immediately deflated. Becalmed. When he, the bearer of bad news, had gone, I stood up. I was weak and unsteady again; there was no one around. I remember managing to put one foot in front of the other and move as if I was a stiff clockwork soldier. The sun, the heat, the terrible news, the sweat. I was stumbling inside towards bed like an automaton and then, thud, I went down like a sack of potatoes. I went to step into the ward, tripped, and careered forward, my left foot buckling awkwardly under my weight.

'Nurse, nurse,' I yelled from the deck and then more loudly, 'NURSE!'

I kept calling and then just shouted out feeble nothings, in pain. Help arrived and I was assisted to my bed. I yelped as I lay back, watching my foot swell up before my eyes. My whole consciousness homed in and wasn't allowed to focus on anything but my throbbing foot, which was rapidly in the process of changing shape and colour and going clubbed, *like that flipping idiot Liam's*! The medicine trolley was wheeled in, tinkle-tinkling like a toy fire engine, and pain killers were administered from it.

'Just keep calm, Jonathan,' a nurse prescribed. 'Keep your foot up on this pillow. A doctor will be down soon. I don't think it's broken.'

I'm not good with pain and whimpered accordingly as spasms shot up my leg. A doctor arrived. 'It's not broken, Mr Runcorn,' she said. 'You've torn the ligaments, that's all. There is nothing that can be done except rest. Keep your foot raised. And in a day or two do some light exercise. I will get some crutches sent down for you and I'll come back in two or three days and see how you are. In the meantime, do nothing.'

'Thank you doctor,' I said dreamily, in my opiated state. 'Are you by any chance the doctor who saw Kat, my friend, who I heard…' and I couldn't say the words *committed suicide*. But she knew what I meant.

'Yes, I am.'

'Is she…?'

'No, she is not, she is fine. She is up in the main hospital. She's lost a lot of blood but she is alive and well.'

'Phew, that's amazing. Thank God for that,' I said, utterly relieved at the thought of Hal not having to suffer catastrophically if he had to hear the news that she had killed herself.

You are sent to a mental home because your brain can't cope and then while there you encounter horrible incidents, which really should make you sink further into your mire. Like going into a normal hospital, ill and weak, and you end up catching another illness, compounding the original problem. But it doesn't work like that. Somehow, a survival instinct can kick in and you galvanise yourself to overcome. And you rise above to become stronger.

Part of this vast hospital complex housed a General Hospital with an A & E department and all normal wards for physical conditions, not just mental ones. The mental home was part of a larger medical multiplex. The general hospital was situated about a quarter of a mile away on the other side of the Victorian asylum. You couldn't even hear the ambulance sirens to'ing and fro'ing from our ward.

And so I sat up in bed for the next couple of days. My foot was elephantine and bruised; my toes resembled swollen tropical caterpillars, wriggling, about to burst and fly away.

The nurses, being sick of bringing me my meals and drinks, forced me up. I obviously had to go to the loo occasionally. To begin with I would hop along, aided, but over the following few days I began to use my crutches and would go for my meals with everyone else. There were a few new inmates but I ignored them and kept to the privacy of my cubicle. I avoided all unnecessary human contact. I had had enough of the ups and downs of transient friendships and was happy to be on my own. My fall and subsequent forced incarceration had humbled me.

'Jonathan, I want you to go for some physiotherapy on your foot,' the doctor suggested, when she returned as promised a few days later. 'One of the team will massage your foot. It will speed up the recovery and make you feel much more comfortable.'

CHAPTER 29

Cultivation…

That week and the next trundled by at a snail's pace. I welcomed it. As I had said I was utterly exhausted by all the shenanigans that had gone on and the solid break from computing stopped the rot. For that whole week and longer I sat in bed with my foot up on three pillows and only got up to go to the loo or to eat meals. It was just what I had wanted and I milked it. I behaved like a sick child, bed-bound for months with some old-fashioned illness. I even took to doing up the top button of my pyjamas, for crying out loud. God knows why! I just felt better if I looked the part.

I remember really enjoying doing stupidly long strides on my crutches when no one was looking. I would take my full body weight on my arms, holding my lame foot up and stretching the crutches out as far forward as I could possibly place them. Then I would swoosh my good leg past the raised, unusable one in as long a stride as I could possibly reach. Both feet off the ground. It was mathematical, an equation. Off I'd go, getting into a really good rhythm. When the coast was clear I'd hare up and down the long top corridor at a helluva lick. Click, click, clickety-clacking, I'd cover the ground in no time.

I thought this was so much more of an efficient means of transport than on foot. The conclusion I came up with was that in the future we would all be bionic. In generations to come we will do away with our bodies completely and have the body of our choice. Interchangeable ones if we want. Carbon fibre probably. Light and rust-free. I also thought that this will well and truly be the answer to feeding our world's population; there will be no need for crops as such. All we really are are our brains, anyway. I am sure our unique characters lie within the head too. If not, wherever our personalities are housed, wherever the soul may be, our future descendants can incorporate them into our future robotic casings too. No more medical problems and we can do away with the NHS. Being the third largest human institution on the planet, it will save a fortune.

Going home was off the cards that week as a result of my fall but, all being well, I was going to be released two weeks later than originally planned: two weeks after Hal leaving and the appearance of his father.

On that first Friday afternoon I went, or was taken up in a minibus, to the main hospital for this bit of physiotherapy. And who should I see as I swung and clicked into Reception but the black nurse, Josephine, the object of my sexual fantasy, coming towards me, also on crutches. *Shit*, I thought. But there was nowhere to go, nowhere to hide. She spotted me and hobbled forward, smiling.

'Am I happy to see you, Jonathan,' she said out loud. 'Very happy.'

'Yeah, right,' I mumbled. 'Instant karma, eh?'

'Yes, exactly.' A big wide smile exposed her brilliant teeth.

'I'm really sorry, nurse. About your work placement and all that,' I muttered. Then, clearing my throat, I asked, 'How is your ankle?'

'Call me Josephine, please. It's okay, thank you. It was a clean break. They've just done an x-ray. And what happened to you, my dear?'

'I just tripped going into the ward. It's only torn ligaments.'

She laughed and shook her head. 'I was very sorry to hear about Katherine,' she continued, more serious now.

'Katherine?' I questioned. 'Oh, Kat, yes, yes. She is in here somewhere, I believe.'

'Yes, she is. She's upstairs. She is doing well and will be going home next week some time, I believe.'

'That's great, thanks for letting me know, I appreciate it.'

'I have to go now, Jonathan. I see my car waiting outside, but I will come to the ward and say hello to you.'

'Oh great, when?' I enthused.

'Sometime soon,' she said with a twinkle in her eye. 'Very soon.'

And off she went, leaving me awkwardly twisting around to watch her handsome frame, supported on the crutches and the other fine ankle, swing majestically through the electric doors. As she got into the waiting taxi, swinging her bum around onto the rear seat, she saw me still gawping and she waved – well, jangled her fingers - towards me and smiled. I erected my free crutch in acknowledgement.

That weekend my mother visited me and said she had found a residential, pure mathematics, course up in Oxford that summer which she thought I should enrol in. I could come back home for a month and then go up there, and she'd even do the paperwork for me if I wanted. 'Go for it,' I said. At last we had a definite plan. I had a future.

And so I felt better again, and I was going to stay in that state, in that better place, for as long as I could possibly manage it. Being in that frame of mind placed me in a brighter, more positive space. Interacting with other people was all very well, but more often than not, they become a drain. People rarely give like Hal, and want nothing back. They are generally too demanding, too needy. I was happy to be on my own; in my world, with no one to rock my boat but me.

Although the sports-type massage I had in physio had really helped, I didn't want to move out of my sacred space – my bed. I really didn't want to interact with anyone else in the ward and get embroiled in yet more problems: other people's issues. When you are mentally unwell you are like a vacuous sponge, open to the universe, and you absorb every bit of cosmic debris radiating around you. You are a defenceless black hole sucking everything in and spitting shit back out. I just couldn't cope with spinning about, out of control, haywire, absorbing other people's problems anymore. I'd leave that to the professionals.

I remember reading Stephen Hawking's *A Brief History of Time* during my convalescence and thinking what a load of rubbish it was. He was making wild presumptions, totally unsubstantiated by facts. There was only about one sentence in the whole book I could agree with. It was as if he was concentrating on something so far-fetched that no one could contradict what he was saying. It was all totally unverifiable. Anyway.

In the second week I began to venture outside three times a day, in all weathers, keeping to Hal's routine, and sit on either the front or rear bench after meals: breakfast, lunch and supper. I did miss Hal, and Matt, and yes, I missed Kat, too – well, looking at her anyway, even though my personal interest lay with a darker beauty.

I was super-pleased just to be on my own, with my own thoughts, remembering the nightmares I had been through over the past two months; rewinding, re-calibrating and coming up to date and saying goodbye to this place and hacking in a calm, controlled manner.

Computing aside, I was determined not to stay on the medical, mental victim rollercoaster. I was going to get off it. I knew I had not just wallowed in a world of self-pity before Hal arrived but I had perversely enjoyed it. Playing the poor-me card. Receiving half-baked attention. He had made me see the light. I had been like a person who fell into a job, and before they knew it, their whole lives were completely dictated by the new role they played. I had had a breakdown and before I knew it I'd been transplanted into a world of pills, psychiatrists, benefits, daft coffee mornings and feebleness, and it had become harder and harder than I'd ever imagined to get off that band-wagon, back to reality, and to find myself.

The birds had exhausted their vocal chords after the joys of getting through winter, mating, nesting and child-rearing. As spring had progressed into summer being outside was now a much more peaceful place to be.

And then she arrived at my bedside, quite unexpectedly, poking her head around the closed screen. I lazily looked up from my book, caught in a thought, off-guard.

'Hello Jon-atan,' Josephine said, her warm tones wafting around my cubicle and making my toes curl. 'Can I come in?'

'Josephine, it's you,' I mumbled. 'Come in? Yes, yes, why of course you can come in.'

And so she negotiated her fulsome, ripe frame, all plums and grapes, into my humble abode. I moved my feet across and she plopped onto the end of the bed. My feet bounced up under the covers.

'Phew, that's betta,' she said, leaning her crutches on the ground. 'These 't'ings are hard work.'

When she leant forward her cleavage, these two huge throbbing aubergines, were revealed to me in all their glory. I put my book on the bedside table; I had some new material to work with.

'So, how are you, my darlin'?' she continued, now sitting back upright.

We talked. It is so nice to be alone with the one you love. It must be one of the best feelings in the world. I could just look at her, and her alone. And everything she said was for my ears only. Josephine told me that she believed any foot problem, when you have a fall and are forced to stop abruptly, is nature's way of telling you to slow down. 'When you are going too fast,' she said, 'but you can't stop yourself, life has to step in and help you. And that help is a fall, a crash.'

'Oh,' I said. 'If that's the case then what does a mental meltdown mean? That I think too much?'

'Yes Jonatan, it probably does, my dear,' she purred. 'You should get out more.'

Coincidentally she was lodging not too far from my home so before she left I got her address and said I'd come over the following week and take her out for a drink.

'That would be lovely,' she said. *Get in* - what a result!

It was just the impetus I needed to force the issue about me going home to Dr Feltz and my mum. So I virtually got it set in stone that I would leave after my physiotherapy session that coming Friday.

The only thing I remember doing that week, and it was the only thing of any importance, was to make surreptitious yet thorough notes about the coding and access routes I had taken to achieve my hack. I even wrote comprehensive paragraphs on how they should improve their security and build firewalls. How to stop this happening again. When I had written the document by hand, and re-worked it over a few days, I asked to borrow the same word processor Hal had used to script his play so I could type it out properly. I didn't realise just how therapeutic it was to get the hacking out of my mind. And not just out of my mind in a higgledy-piggeldy, flibberty-gibberty fashion, but in cohesive logic. I produced a proper document, a thorough report, printed out and looking pukka. I obviously deleted all traces of the document on the actual machine but I did print out a spare copy. This was going to be my way of saying sorry to the system. If I did get caught it would surely knock a few years off my sentence, and, as I was starting to feel slightly sorry for Hal's dad, I thought this might help him in some way.

'Hey, Liam, do me a favour, would you?' I asked the mutant giant after breakfast one day. 'Can you write?'

'Of course I can fuckin' write, man!' he grunted. 'What d'you think I am, an idiot or something?'

'Don't be stupid, Liam, of course I don't,' I replied.

And I got him to write the address out. Mr Richard Reed c/o MI6 Vauxhall Cross London SW8.

'M – what?' he had said.

'Yes, Liam – capital M, then next to it a capital I and then next to that the numeral six.'

'Is that right, Jonathan?' he said, passing me the infantile scrawl.

'Brilliant,' I said. 'I really appreciate it. Many thanks.'

'That's cool, man, no worries.'

I tucked it away as I had a plan for where to send it from.

At last Friday arrived. My day had come. I was up early and had my bags packed, and just like two weeks previously, they sat up on my bed in anticipation. I didn't really need the crutches so much now, but as it was quite a long walk up to the main hospital for my final physiotherapy session, I thought I would use them.

As I swung – well, hobbled - across the forecourt I saw a beautiful azure-blue, chauffeur-driven Bentley outside.

I went straight in and had my half-hour massage and as I came back out through Reception who should I see pushing a wheelchair but Hal.

'Hal,' I called out, and went forward.

'Hey, Jonathan. Great to see you!' He turned to meet me and laughed, seeing me on crutches. 'Been in the wars?'

'Something like that. Na, not really, just had a fall.'

'Look who I've got here?'

I peered around and down into the wheelchair and there was Kat.

'Hello, Jonathan,' she said, ever so meekly.

She looked incredibly fragile, like an angel dressed in swaddling clothes.

'Where are you going?' Hal asked, as we walked outside.

'Oh, just back to the ward,' I said. 'I'm going home later today though, for good.'

'Hey, that's great news - at last! What happened then?' he said, as we came alongside the roller.

'Oh, because of the fall everyone thought it would be better for me to stay a while. But I am going home today, for definite.'

'Here, jump in, let me give you a lift.'

'What, in this?' I exclaimed.

'Yeah,' he said, laughing. 'I've hired it for the day. I'm taking Kat home in it, to her house. I thought I'd throw the boat out.'

And so he helped her into the back seat with the help of the suited chauffeur. She seemed to have lost so much weight in the past two weeks, it was quite shocking. She was sweet though.

'Thank you, darling,' she said softly as he made her comfortable.

And so we wafted around to Rooksdown Lodge. Kat's skin had gone translucent due to the loss of blood from her suicide attempt. She resembled a fallen Hollywood starlet sitting in the cream leather plushness. Magisterial, removed, impassive. She made no sound but held her hand forward as I went to get out awkwardly, with the wretched crutches. Hal came around to help me. I instinctively took her soft, cold limp hand and kissed it. We looked at each other and our eyes smiled; it was a beautiful moment, very gentle yet very powerful.

'Bye, Jonathan, good luck,' Hal said as he gave me a hug.

'Thanks for the ride,' I managed to reply.

And he was gone. The three of us waved to one another as the car pulled off and floated away into the distance.

I ordered my terrier, Houdini, to heel as I stood outside the ward. I was in exactly the same spot where I had stood twenty years previously, when I had waved Hal goodbye in that Bentley for the last time. I have never seen or heard from him since.

I pulled up the collar on my overcoat, as it had started to rain, and walked back to my car to catch the ferry to France. To hell with the cost, I thought; I'd give my wife a call in Africa and let her know where I was. I got my mobile out as I walked across the playground and dialled.

'Darling, Josephine, it's me, sweetheart,' I said into the device.

'Jon-atan, are you okay, my angel?' Her dulcet tone purred back into my ear.

'Yes, yes, fine, my love. You'll never guess where I am?'

THE END

Lightning Source UK Ltd.
Milton Keynes UK
UKHW01f0616300518
323444UK00001B/250/P